Mercy's Crown

A Novel

By

Matt Walker

3 Suns Press

ISBN: 979-8-9937108-3-9 (Paperback)

ISBN: 979-8-9937108-4-6 (eBook)

First Edition: December 2025

Printed in the United States of America

For those who know the cold is more than weather.

Table of Contents

Frozen Maze

The flame in Rowan's lantern shivers as they move, a small, uncertain sun cradled in glass. It throws long, bending shapes along the stone, turning the carved walls into ribs, into fingers, into the inside of something that has spent centuries learning how not to breathe.

Their breath clouds the air in front of them, pale strands that hang for a moment before dissolving into the stillness. The cold down here isn't the sharp kind that bites the skin; it sinks in quietly, settling into joints and behind the eyes, a damp chill that makes every blink feel slower than it should be.

They listen for their footsteps.

The sound doesn't travel right. The soles of their boots meet the packed earth and stone with soft, solid contact, but the echo comes back thin and delayed, as if the corridor is thinking about whether it wants to repeat them. Sometimes it doesn't. Sometimes it just swallows the sound whole.

The corridor narrows, then widens, then narrows again. It's familiar in the way a dark room is familiar once you've lived in it long enough: not because you can see, but because muscle memory has a catalog. Seven steps to the bend. Three to the low beam. Four to the little chip in the wall where the plaster never quite matched.

There should be a little chip, right...

Rowan lifts the lantern slightly, squinting at the stone to their left. Smooth. Damp. Faintly worn by the brush of coats and shoulders. No chip. They pause, fingers moving along the surface until nails catch on nothing.

"Okay," they murmur, because it's better than letting silence think it's won. Their voice sounds small against the walls, not quite an echo, more like a private note that chooses not to carry.

They turn in a slow circle. The lantern's light circles with them, brushing over the low ceiling, the floor, the place where the corridor folds back on itself in a gentle curve. They've walked this stretch of the catacombs hundreds of times. Thousands, if they count the errands and the patrols and the nights they took the long way just to avoid going home. The bones behind these walls, the names on the plaques above, the little offerings tucked into niches—they all live in the back of their mind like quiet neighbors.

But right now, the corridor behind them does not look like the corridor behind them.

Rowan takes three steps back the way they came, then stops again, heart ticking up a notch. Not racing. Just... noticing itself. The floor is correct: the faint rut where the maintenance carts roll, the slight rise near what should be the support pillar. But when they lift the lantern to find that familiar load-bearing column of stone, all they see is a blank wall.

No pillar. No seam. No sign the passage ever continued past this point.

The distant dripping starts as they're staring at the smooth stone. At first it's a steady beat—tap... tap... tap—that might as well be a clock if clocks bled. Then, slowly, the rhythm stumbles. Tap... tap...

tap-tap… tap… as if whatever's leaking somewhere in the warren has forgotten the pattern it learned.

Rowan licks their lips, tasting dust and the ghost of old incense. The smell down here is layered: cold stone, damp earth, a hint of iron from rusting fixtures and older things that have settled into history. It is not a frightening smell. It's the smell of their work, their routine, their day-to-day. They've crossed these halls at dawn and midnight, during funerals and after storms, with candles and with flashlights and with nothing but the glow of emergency lights humming like tired bees.

They know this place.

They should know this place.

The lantern shifts in their hand as they test the wall with their free fingers, pressing lightly, then harder. Stone presses back. No give. No trick.

It's possible they took a wrong turn. Possible they miscounted a step. Possible that fatigue has finally rubbed away one of the small, private landmarks they've always relied on. Possible.

Doesn't feel like it.

Rowan steps back, the lantern dipping with them, their breath fogging again as they exhale. The air's stillness feels heavier now, like the corridor is holding its lungs full and refusing to let anything move.

"Not this way," they say, almost conversationally, as if narrating a puzzle to themselves.

The sound of their voice steadies something inside their chest.

They turn away from the blocked passage and study the fork ahead. The left-hand corridor yawns a little wider, the darkness more open, as though it might lead back toward the older crypts and the main shafts that run beneath the chapel. The right-hand path is narrower. The stone there seems to lean in, the overhead arch dropping just a little lower, the walls damp with a faint sheen that catches the lanternlight in dull, matte streaks.

Both are wrong.

Left should lead to the engraved arch with the angel whose face has worn away. Right should turn quickly and drop three shallow steps. Neither looks like that. Rowan's mind supplies the expected shapes anyway, overlaying memory on the space in front of them.

For a moment, they consider closing their eyes and walking forward until their palms meet stone, just to see which version of reality their body believes.

Instead, they shift their weight and stand still.

Panic would make sense. Getting loudly, pointlessly angry would also make sense. But they don't do either. They've been misplaced before. They've been overlooked in crowded rooms, forgotten on invite lists, left waiting while everyone assumed someone else had already spoken to them. Being lost doesn't feel like a disaster. It feels like a familiar mislabeling.

Rowan lifts the lantern toward the left-hand corridor, watching the way the light behaves. The flame leans slightly with the movement and then steadies, gilding damp stone in a thin skin of warmth. Shadows stretch long and straight. The far edge of the light pool looks clean.

Then they turn the lantern toward the right.

4

There, the glow pulls strange. It spreads thinner, forced to fight for space along the close walls. The pale edge of the flame's halo brushes moisture that gleams not gold but a muted, icy blue, hinting at a colder depth waiting just beyond the fragile circle of light.

The drip sounds again. Closer this time. Still wrong.

"Of course," Rowan says quietly. They don't sound surprised.

They roll their shoulders beneath their coat, working out a little knot that's formed at the base of their neck. Their fingers tap once against the lantern's handle, a small, habitual rhythm. Think. Breathe. Choose.

They could sit and wait. Someone will come eventually—morning staff, the groundskeeper, the priest who always forgets his keys. When they realize Rowan hasn't checked in, when the shift log shows a blank return, someone will remember. Someone will notice.

They picture the empty space in the log, the line where their name should sit. The way the page might be turned too quickly, eyes sliding past. Not out of cruelty. Just… velocity. Other priorities. Noise.

Waiting has never done them many favors.

They adjust the lantern again and step toward the fork, letting the flame drag itself from left to right one more time. The wider corridor looks easier. The more narrow one looks honest about its intentions.

"Problem first," they whisper, choosing.

They angle their shoulder just slightly and move into the right-hand passage.

The walls accept them with quiet reluctance. The ceiling dips low enough they feel it pressing down on their awareness even if it doesn't quite force them to duck. The floor is subtly uneven, an old settling of earth and stone that never made it onto the maintenance list because no one walks this way often enough to complain.

The lanternlight compresses, the circle of visible ground shrinking until it's barely wider than Rowan's stride. Beyond that halo, the dark seems to absorb color and shape, becoming an absence rather than a substance. What the eye can't find, it starts to imagine. Corners. Hollows. Something turning just out of sight.

Rowan keeps their gaze low, tracking their boots, the shallow depressions, the little flecks of darker stone that might be fossil or flaw. They let the routine part of their brain— the one that inventories conditions, hazards, repairs—run in the background. Cracked mortar there. Water leak somewhere above. Old patchwork that never set right. The kind of cataloguing that usually ends with a note in a log and a follow-up request for supplies that never quite make it to the top of the list.

Their free hand brushes the wall now and then, fingertips gliding over the carved limestone. It's cool and faintly slick. No marks. No names. No alcoves for urns or bones. This is a passage meant more for access than ritual, a hallway between the rooms that matter. Backstage.

The dripping grows clearer the deeper they go. It doesn't sound like water from a pipe or a crack in the ceiling. Those have a weight, a splash that carries a certain pitch. This is thinner, sharper, with too much space between impacts. Drip... drip... drip-drip... drip.

Rowan slows, more to listen than from any sense of fear. They tilt their head, counting the beats. There's just enough irregularity to keep time from forming a pattern. That annoys them more than it unnerves them.

"Pick a rhythm," they mutter, not entirely to the leak.

The lantern flickers.

A small draft brushes past their face, cold and brief, the way a hand might move if someone thought about reaching for their cheek and then changed their mind. The flame bends sideways, thins, then rebounds, swelling again in a quick gasp of light. For an instant, the edges of its circle take on that same pale-blue bloom, as if the heat is remembering what it is to be cold.

They stop again.

The passage extends ahead, curving in a way that suggests it's leading back toward the heart of the catacombs, where the older burials rest in ordered rows behind stone and iron gates. If their internal map is still to be trusted, they're walking against the grain of the usual paths, moving in the negative space between them.

Rowan turns once more to look behind.

The narrowing they passed through a moment ago now looks exactly the same as the space ahead. The curve is identical. The walls mirror each other. There is no visual difference between the direction they came from and the direction they're heading.

They could mark the wall.

It's the obvious choice. Take the small knife from their pocket, carve a line at shoulder height, make some kind of human interruption in the stone so when they inevitably loop, they'll know. They picture

7

the blade scraping, the faint shriek it would pull from the rock. Another mark in a place full of marks that mean more.

For some reason, the thought sits wrong in their chest.

They take the knife out anyway. The handle is familiar, worn to the curve of their fingers. It's one of those objects that belongs more to habit than necessity—a tool meant for cutting twine, trimming old offerings, prying wax out of candleholders. Steel glints briefly in lanternlight as they test its edge with their thumb.

They put it back.

Not because they're afraid to scratch the wall. Not because they think the act itself is dangerous. It just doesn't feel… respectful. The bones behind these corridors shuffled into their permanent addresses long before Rowan ever came to brush dust from their ledges. Some of them have names no one visits anymore. Some of them have names that make the priest's voice soften when he reads the records.

Rowan is a guest. A servant, at best.

Guests don't carve directions into the furniture just because they got turned around.

A dry chuckle huffs out of them—more air than sound. "Fine," they say. "We'll do it the hard way."

They close their eyes for a heartbeat and map the distance traveled so far. Fifteen, twenty steps since the fork? No slope they can feel, no draft sustained, no change in smell. The drip is closer, but not much louder. That suggests a side chamber, a lower alcove, or a tight stairwell rather than a wide-open space.

Information. Not comfort, not danger. Just a layout slowly revealing itself.

Rowan opens their eyes again and moves forward.

The corridor tightens another inch around their shoulders. The lantern bumps against their chest as the handle shifts, a little thud that echoes too loudly in the narrow space. Their shadow stretches ahead of them, warped by the angle, head elongated, shoulders sloped, spine bowed a little more than they're actually stooping. It looks, for a moment, like there's someone else walking just in front of them, just out of reach.

They don't speed up to catch it. They've seen worse tricks of light.

The drip—which they've now decided is not a leak but something collected and persistent—hits again. Closer. The sound is just on the edge of the lantern's reach, somewhere along the curve they haven't yet rounded.

Rowan's hand tightens a little around the handle. Not fear. Readiness.

They breathe in once, slow, letting the cold settle in their lungs. Breathe out slower. The fog from their exhale blooms in front of them, suspended briefly, then drifts upward as if pulled toward some invisible seam in the ceiling.

"Stay steady," they tell themselves, voice low and even. "It's just stone."

Just stone that has rearranged itself overnight, maybe. Just hallways that aren't where they're supposed to be. Just a job that turned into a problem after dark.

They've seen worse. They've lived through worse.

They take the last few steps toward the curve.

The lantern's light crawls ahead of them, licking the bend, revealing the slow, tight sweep of the wall as it curls inward. No alcoves. No branching path. The floor is bare, the faint rut of old footsteps running right along the middle like a rule someone forgot to break. As Rowan reaches the apex of the curve, the drip finally reveals itself: a small, steady stream falling from a hairline crack in the ceiling into a shallow depression in the floor.

The water has pooled there, dark and still, a dimple in the stone filled with something that looks thicker than it should be. The lanternlight hits the surface and doesn't shimmer; it dulls, swallowed into a color that isn't quite red and isn't quite brown, something that suggests it once meant more than it does now.

The rhythm that had been so off resolves itself in front of them. The miss between drops wasn't the water's fault at all. It was the echo, the sound bouncing around corners and coming back in the wrong order.

Up close, the drip is as regular as a heartbeat.

Rowan watches it fall for a slow count of ten, then steps carefully around the pooled depression, giving it the same small, unconscious respect they would give a fresh grave. They don't touch it. They don't test the depth with their boot or fingers. Some things don't need verifying.

Beyond the little basin, the passage tapers further. The lantern's circle shrinks again, the edges fuzzing where pale blue creeps in at the rim, turning stone into something colder than it was a few steps ago.

The air feels heavier and thinner at once, pressing against their chest and leaving their lungs too aware of the work they're doing.

Rowan squares their shoulders.

No one is coming down here for them tonight. That realization lands not as a shock but as a mild confirmation of something they already knew. If the surface world notices their absence at all, it will be on paper first, in ink, as numbers failing to sum up right. A box unchecked on a schedule. A line without a signature at the end of a shift.
They have never been the kind of missing that raises alarms.

That's fine. It just means the task, like most things, is theirs to solve or surrender.

They don't surrender.

Their grip on the lantern relaxes; they'd been holding it too tightly without meaning to. Fingers uncurl. Their shoulders drop a fraction as they let breath in, let it out. The stone doesn't care whether they're calm or not. The cold doesn't either. But their body does, and it tends to behave better when their mind behaves first.

Another drip lands in the little basin behind them, muffled, almost apologetic.

Rowan doesn't look back.

They face the narrowing passage, study the way the dark thickens just beyond the lanternlight, and choose to enter it anyway. Not because it's inviting. Not because it promises anything good. Because it's there, and they are too, and staying still has never made the world turn toward them before.

They lift the lantern a little higher, angling it so its shrinking glow covers as much ground as it can.

Then they step forward, into the thinner throat of the corridor, into the press of cold that makes the flame's edge flare that faint, uncanny blue as if remembering that light is just organized fire trying not to go out.

The off-beat drip echoes one last time, closer now, like the sound has leaned in to listen.

Rowan keeps walking.

Invisible One

The corridor stretches out ahead of Rowan like a copied sentence—familiar in its structure, unsettling in its repetition. They pause beneath a low arch where the lantern flickers against the stone, casting a warm honey glow that clings reluctantly to the walls. For a moment, the flame lags behind the tilt of Rowan's hand, as if the light itself resists being moved forward.

The stone pattern to their right—an uneven swirl of limestone and a faint mineral stain like a teardrop—repeats itself ten paces later. Same depth, same angle, same smudge. Rowan slows, brushing fingers across the shape. Dust gathers onto their fingertips, but the pattern underneath feels too precise to be coincidence.

They release a quiet breath into the cold, watching it drift upward like smoke.

"Right," they murmur to the air, not expecting it to care.

Rowan keeps walking.

The catacombs had always been a maze, but a cooperative one. A map written in stone centuries before Rowan tended it, a map they knew intimately—by step counts, by the tilt of the ceiling, by the aging marks left by caretakers long dead. But what stretched ahead was an echo of the familiar rather than the familiar itself.

The lanternlight drags again, halo thinning before gathering itself, the flame stuttering as if clearing its throat. The cold remains steady— not biting, not sharp—but present in the way a closed hand is present: withholding warmth, not taking it.

Rowan rounds a small bend, boots whispering across the stone floor. The only sound beyond their steps was the faintest brush of cloth, like someone shifting their weight just out of sight.

Rowan stops.

The sound stops too.

Nothing moved behind them. Nothing breathed. Nothing cast a shadow that didn't belong to Rowan.

They angle the lantern back the way they came. The corridor stretched empty and still. No dust stirred. No motes danced. No footprints—not even their own—broke the smooth stretch of stone.

Rowan tilted their head, listening.

Silence, heavy and waiting.

They turn forward again and resume walking. The floor gently slopes downward, almost imperceptibly, the incline just enough to set a quiet pull beneath their feet. They follow it without hurry.

Behind them, the sound returned—one soft shuffle, like a heel brushing stone.

They didn't turn this time.

After a few more paces, Rowan reaches for the nearby wall and presses their thumb lightly into a patch of dust, trying to smear a line, a signal in case they looped back. The dust lifted obediently onto their skin—but the stone beneath remained smooth and immaculate, unmarked.

Rowan slid their thumb again, harder. Dust scattered onto the floor. The stone refused to take even the faintest trace of their touch.

They wiped their thumb against their trouser leg.

"Not helpful," they said softly.

It wasn't frustration. It was acknowledgment—another small refusal in a life filled with them. The maze didn't want their mark any more than a cashier wanted their name or a stranger wanted their apology.

Rowan wiped a fleck of dust from their palm and kept walking.

Their breath trailed behind them, dissolving slow in the stillness. The lantern flame stretched tall for a moment, reacting to a draft Rowan couldn't feel. The blue edge returned—thin, icy, an outline of light that made the shadows look deeper.

The shuffle behind them issued again.

Rowan pauses, listening. The shuffle stops.

A pulse of cold rolled across their shoulders. Subtle. Brief. Almost curious.

"You can follow," they murmured, "just don't pretend you aren't."

The quiet afterward didn't confirm or deny anything.

15

Rowan continues down the corridor, now noticing details that don't belong. The corridor narrowed, then widened, not organically but deliberately, as if the catacombs had edited themselves. The ceiling above rose higher, exposing old beams Rowan had never once seen during their years tending funerary rites and deep maintenance.

A faint scribing, old and shallow, snaked along part of the ceiling—symbols long eroded but undeniably deliberate. Rowan slows beneath them, lantern raised.

Not Latin. Not runes. Not markings from any caretaker's ledger or previous expansion. They looked more like shallow scratches made by fingernails.

Rowan didn't linger on them. There were enough oddities down here that if they paused for all of them, they'd never reach dawn.

Their boots brushed against the floor at a steady rhythm, and the shuffle behind them matched it a breath later, like an over-eager echo trying to keep up. Rowan didn't bother to check again.

Being followed wasn't new.

Being followed by something that didn't want to be seen—that, too, was familiar in a different shape.

At the next curve, Rowan slows, running their hand along the left side wall. The stone was smooth, worn by centuries, but the texture was wrong—too warm for the air around it, like the remnant of a body having just leaned there.

Rowan withdrew their hand quickly and shook their fingers out once, more from instinct than fear.

The corridor narrows again. The lantern stretched its glow thin across the stone until it felt like Rowan was walking inside the flickering edge of their own shadow. They blinked slowly, recalibrating to the new tightness of the space.

Not claustrophobic. Just close.

The shuffle behind them faded for a moment and returned, lighter this time.

Rowan inhaled deeply and let the air settle in their chest. The cold helped sharpen their thoughts. They stopped thinking about being lost—not helpful, not honest, not useful—and instead traced the potential layout of the tunnels based on where the slope had begun, where the drafts had shifted, where the stone temperature changed.

There would be a chamber nearby. A large one, if the air was any indication. Chambers held cold differently, like bowls holding water.

They lifted the lantern and walked with a steadier pace now, focusing on the way the flame flickered ahead of them, how the edges of its light brushed the walls before catching up. They thought about the way people brushed past them in crowded walkways above—eyes fixed on the floor or phones or companions, never on Rowan. The world moved around them, not through them. Not by malice. Not by cruelty. Just… absence.

Being seen had never felt like something they earned or lost. It simply wasn't part of the equation.

The shuffle behind them synced again with their thoughts, soft and unhurried, like something that had learned their pattern and found comfort in matching it.

17

"I'm not worth sneaking up on," Rowan says quietly. "If you need something, you can ask."

Only silence answered.

They nodded once, accepting the quiet as they always do.

Eventually the corridor widens until Rowan steps into a stone archway carved with old floral motifs—winter vines, bare branches, and the faint hint of holly leaves worn nearly smooth. The lanternlight caught on the carvings, making the shallow winter vines glisten like frost.

The cold deepened instantly.

Rowan steps forward into the widening dark and finds themselves standing inside a circular chamber with a high vaulted ceiling. The ceiling arched like the inside of an upturned bowl or a frozen sky held in stone. A single stone platform rose at the center of the chamber—knee-high, wide, and unadorned.

The air inside the chamber felt colder, sharper, almost metallic. Rowan's breath hit the air and didn't drift upward this time; it hung there, suspended, like breath exhaled into a winter too heavy to move.

The lanternlight dragged behind Rowan when they stepped inside, then snapped forward a heartbeat later, illuminating the chamber in a dim amber wash. Shadows clung stubbornly to the far edges of the circular room, refusing to recede.

Rowan took three steps toward the platform and halted when the cold brushed the side of their jaw, gentle and deliberate. It didn't feel like a warning. It felt like someone leaning close enough to breathe on their skin.

Their fingers tightened slightly around the lantern handle.

"Alright," they murmured. "I'm here."

Their voice traveled farther than expected, ricocheting softly around the chamber's round walls. No echo returned clearly—just the faintest impression of their voice returning: thinner, more fragile, as if the chamber considered the words before giving pieces of them back.

The shuffle sound behind Rowan didn't enter the chamber. It paused just outside the arch.

Rowan turned their head slightly, listening. Stillness. But the kind of stillness that contains intent.

The stone platform at the center of the chamber seemed untouched—no dust patterns, no disturbed edges, no scratches on its surface. It might as well have been carved yesterday. Rowan walked closer and inspected the edges, running their free hand along the cool slab. The stone was smooth, almost too smooth—like something had polished it repeatedly.

They circled it once, taking quiet inventory of the way the ceiling funneled cold downward. The chamber felt like a throat swallowing light and sound. Their lantern felt too small, too warm, too human.

Rowan exhaled and placed one hand flat on the platform, grounding themselves for a moment.

Then they let their hand fall away.

They didn't climb onto the platform. They didn't sit. They didn't kneel. They simply stood there and let the cold wrap around the front of their coat, pressing the fabric lightly against their ribs like unseen fingers mapping their breath.

Something was waiting.

19

Not hostile.

Not urgent.

Just waiting.

Rowan reached into their pocket and pulled out an old brass key—one they always carried when making rounds. A meaningless trinket down here now. But the weight of it in their hand reminded them of the world above, where locks made sense and doors stayed put and walls didn't rearrange themselves when no one was looking.

They turned the key over between their fingers before slipping it back into their coat.

The cold settled deeper. Rowan shifted their stance, listening again to the quiet.

"Whatever you are," they whispered, "you're better at silence than the rest of us."

A faint, almost imperceptible breath of air pressed against the back of their neck—the closest thing yet to a response.

Rowan didn't flinch.

They simply looked up toward the vaulted ceiling where the lanternlight failed to reach, and for a fleeting moment, it felt as if something unseen shifted in the dark beyond the light's edge.

Not threatening.

Not reaching.

20

Just present.

Rowan lowered their gaze and took one step closer to the platform, leaving the archway behind.

Whatever followed them remained in the corridor, just outside the threshold, watching them cross into the chamber alone.

The lantern flickered once, blue at its rim.

Rowan stood there, waiting for the room—or whatever listened inside it—to breathe next.

A Light in the Dark

The cold in the chamber held its shape around Rowan, a still, waiting thing. They stood near the center, lantern cupped close, watching the flame flirt with that faint blue rim at its edge. The light shivered more than it should, as if it too felt the weight of the stone pressing in from all sides.

The platform beside them remained blank and patient. The vaulted ceiling above lost itself in shadow, the darkness thick enough that even imagination had to work to give it edges.

For a moment, the only movement was Rowan's breath drifting out into the air, hanging there like something reluctant to dissipate.

Then a small warmth brushed their cheek.

It was light as a fingertip, a soft patch of air against the skin just in front of their ear. Not enough to be a breeze, not enough to be a draft—just a brief stroke of warmth in a room that had only grown colder with every step they'd taken.

The hairs along the back of Rowan's neck rose.

They turned.

The follower from the corridor should have been standing in the archway, all shuffles and half-seen shadows. Or there should have been nothing at all, the explanation only a fraying of nerves and long corridors playing tricks.

Instead, someone sat on the edge of the stone platform, watching them with a careful, almost apologetic smile.

He looked as if he'd been there the entire time.

He wasn't dressed like anyone who should belong in the catacombs. His coat was a soft charcoal wool, dustless and out of place against the roughness of the stone. Underneath, a pale sweater peeked at his collar, the knit pattern simple and worn-thin in a way that suggested years, not neglect. Dark trousers, boots scuffed but well-kept. He had the kind of face people trusted by instinct—open and symmetrical, with a quiet earnestness softened by the hint of permanent laugh lines around his mouth.

His hair curled slightly where it fell over his forehead, the color somewhere between brown and copper depending on how the lantern caught it. His eyes were the striking part, not because they were an unnatural color, but because they held too much—light and worry and humor all layered at once, a grey that the lantern turned almost silver at the edges.

He looked… warm. That was the simplest word for him.

The air around him felt a few degrees softer, enough that Rowan's skin noticed.

They stepped back on reflex, boots scuffing lightly against the stone.

The man lifted both hands a little, palms outward, a gentle surrender.

"Sorry," he said. His voice carried easily in the round chamber, filling it without forcing anything. "I didn't mean to startle you. It's... hard to make a normal entrance down here."

Rowan stared at him. The lantern quivered in their grip.

"You weren't there," they said. Their voice sounded smaller than his, but steady. "A moment ago."

"Yeah," he admitted, wince-soft. "That happens."

He glanced past Rowan to the archway they'd come through, as if checking something just out of sight, then back to them. He didn't seem afraid. He didn't seem particularly impressed with himself either. If anything, he looked like someone who walked into rooms at the wrong time more often than he'd prefer.

"You're not supposed to be in here," Rowan said. It came out more like observation than accusation. "This section's closed. Has been for a while."

He huffed a short, amused breath. "So have I, technically."

They didn't laugh, but something in their shoulders loosened by a thread.

He shifted on the platform, swinging one leg slightly as if testing its edge. "Are you alright?" he asked. "You look like you've been walking a while."

"Fine." Rowan's answer was immediate, reflexive. They adjusted their hold on the lantern. "I was making rounds. Took the wrong turn."

His gaze tracked the lantern for a moment, then came back to their face. He watched them in a way other people usually didn't: not searching for something specific, not trying to categorize, just... present.

"Is that what you think happened?" he asked gently.

Rowan frowned, the expression small. "What else would it be?"

The man tilted his head, considering the chamber, the platform beneath him, the unseen ceiling above.

"Well," he said, "either you took the wrong turn... or the place did."

That was not the answer most people would offer.

Rowan studied him more closely, cataloguing details. No ID badge. No flashlight. No keys. His boots were clean of dust that should have clung to them if he'd walked the same corridors they had. His clothes had no smell of outside cold on them—no trace of fresh winter air, no wet wool or faint tang of city. If he'd come down here, he hadn't used any of the routes Rowan knew.

"You're lost," they decided quietly. "More than I am."

He smiled at that. Not broadly. Just enough for the right side of his mouth to lift a little higher than the left, as if one side of his face trusted the expression more than the other. Light behaved differently around him – softening, bending, almost warming as though it remembered him.

"Maybe," he said. "Though I've been here longer than it looks."

He said it the way people talk about long nights, or bad years.

26

Rowan's fingers tightened around the lantern handle. The flame inside flickered in response, a nervous heartbeat.

"You shouldn't be down here," they said again. "It's not... it's not a place people just come to."

"I don't just come to places," he said. "I get pulled to them."

He let the words sit between them, not grand, not mystical, just factual.

Rowan didn't move. The air in the chamber cooled a degree away from him and warmed a degree around him, creating a small, almost imperceptible gradient that their skin picked up on.

"Pulled?" they asked.

He nodded.

"By whom?"

"Not who," he said. "More... what." He scratched at the inside of his wrist absently, as if the explanation itched. "It's hard to explain without sounding like I'm trying too hard to sound mysterious. I promise I'm not. It's just... the way it is."

Rowan's frown deepened. The lantern flame jumped.

"You don't look like staff," they said.

"Thank you," he said. "I've never pulled off the uniformed look."

He smiled again, softer now. "My name is Trevor," he added, as if realizing belatedly that introductions were a thing. "Just Trevor is fine."

Rowan didn't give theirs in return. Old instinct.

He didn't seem offended. "I can work without that," he said. "Names are nice, but not required. I'm more interested in whether you can feel your fingers."

Rowan glanced down, as if reminded they had hands. They flexed their fingers around the lantern's handle. Their knuckles were pale but still cooperative.

"I've had worse nights," they said.

"Sure," Trevor replied easily. "But that doesn't mean this has to be another one of them."

They watched him, wary but curious. Most people responded to their presence with a kind of distracted politeness, the minimal effort required to move the conversation along. Trevor seemed committed to being exactly where he was, with them, in this moment. No glances at a watch, no flicks toward a phone. The only thing he checked was their face.

"Are you stuck?" he asked. "Or just seeing how far down you can get before someone notices?"

Rowan's silence stretched.

"The latter would be a choice," he added. "The first is more my department."

"Your… department," Rowan repeated.

Trevor rubbed the back of his neck, laughing quietly at himself. "I'm not doing a great job explaining, am I?"

"You haven't explained anything," Rowan said, not unkindly.

"Right," he admitted. "Fair point."

He slid off the edge of the platform and stood. He was taller than Rowan by a head, but he held himself carefully, as if he'd learned long ago to make his height less about taking up space and more about giving distance.

The warmth around him expanded when he moved closer, a gentle shift that didn't push against Rowan so much as invite the cold to step back.

"I get... pulled," he said again, searching for a better phrase. "To people who are lost. Not just geographically. Though that seems to be part of it tonight."

"I'm not lost," Rowan said.

Trevor tipped his head. "No. You're not," he agreed. "The building is. Or wants to be. Hard to say."

He looked around the chamber again, the way someone might examine a painting they've seen a dozen times and only just noticed a new brushstroke.

"But you are," he continued, turning his attention back to them, "here. Alone. In a place that's decided to be more of a maze than it's supposed to be. That's usually enough to light up a flare, so to speak."

Rowan let the words settle somewhere between skepticism and recognition.

"Light up a flare where?" they asked.

29

Trevor touched two fingers lightly to his chest. "Here," he said simply. "And I get... redirected."

"Like a searchlight," Rowan said.

He thought about that, then nodded once. "Something like that. I'm not the one turning it on, though. I'm just the poor guy who has to follow where it points."

There was no pride in the way he said it. No claim of power. More like someone describing a part-time job they could never quite quit.

The lantern's flame steadied as he spoke, its nervous quiver smoothing into a slow, steady burn. Rowan noticed. They always noticed.

They lifted the lantern slightly, examining the glass. The light inside looked cleaner, clearer, less harried by drafts that shouldn't exist.

Trevor followed their gaze and gave a small, almost sheepish shrug.

"Yeah," he said. "That tends to happen, too."

"What does?" Rowan asked.

He gestured loosely toward the lantern. "Things settle. Lights behave." His mouth quirked. "I'm good with... warmth, I guess. And not much else."

That wasn't entirely true.

As he spoke, something changed in the flame.

It began slowly, almost shy. The gold at its center deepened, gathering hints of color like oil on water. A soft sheen rolled across it—green at one angle, pink at another, faint blue ghosting at the edges. The light turned opalescent, the usual harsh contrast of flame and shadow replaced by a layered, pearly glow that made the stone around them look softer, almost luminous.

Rowan's breath caught, the reaction internal, invisible from the outside.

The opal light washed over Trevor's face, catching in his eyes and turning them briefly into something not quite human, a swirl of reflected colors that looked like they contained more than one moment at once.

He blinked hard, and his expression flashed through surprise into something like regret.

"Sorry," he said, voice low. "I… didn't mean for that to happen."

"You made it do that?" Rowan asked.

His brows pulled together. "No. I just—" He stopped, searching for a better way to phrase it. "It happens when I'm close. I never ask it to. I never tell it to. It just… reacts."

He sounded, Rowan thought, genuinely apologetic.

Most people, given a moment of obvious magic, would reach for ownership. For control. Trevor reached for apology.

Rowan angled the lantern, watching the opalescent flame bend and shimmer without dimming. The light didn't hurt to look at. It felt like staring into a polished stone, depth and color layered inside.

"It's fine," Rowan said. Their voice had dropped softer without their permission. "It's... different."

He studied their face carefully, as if gauging whether different was acceptable.

"I know it looks like a trick," he said. "I promise it isn't. I'm not... doing anything to you."

People who intended harm rarely thought to say that.

"How do you know I'm lost," Rowan asked, "if you don't know me?"

Trevor hesitated.

"I don't know you," he said. "But I know how it feels in a room when someone doesn't realize how much weight they're carrying. The air... changes. It's like listening to a note that never quite resolves."

He shook his head, embarrassed by his own explanation. "Sorry. That sounded worse out loud than it did in here." He tapped his temple lightly.

Rowan considered him.

"You talk like someone who's been alone a lot," they said.

The comment surprised him. It showed in the brief widening of his eyes, the little lift of his brows. Then he smiled—soft, small, edged with an old sadness that didn't ask for pity.

32

"Maybe that's why I'm good at finding other people who are," he replied.

They let that sit between them. The opal flame sent out a warmer, gentler light than the lantern ever had, smoothing the hard lines of the stone into something almost welcoming.

Rowan realized, with a quiet, private start, that they could feel their fingers again.

He noticed the change in their posture, the way their shoulders had dropped a fraction, the way their grip had eased.

"Better?" he asked.

They didn't want to admit it. The word still came anyway.
"Yes," they said.

"Good." He exhaled as though relieved. "That part, at least, I don't mind."

Rowan narrowed their eyes slightly. "What part do you mind?"

Trevor looked past them for a heartbeat, toward the center of the chamber, the platform, the space above it where the darkness seemed thicker.

"The rest of the job," he said. "What comes after this bit." He rubbed his hands together once, not from cold but from restlessness. "I'm not just here to… warm up lanterns."

Rowan watched him, waiting.

"I help people see things," he continued. "Things they've forgotten. Things they didn't realize they were still carrying. I don't choose what. I don't choose when. I just—" He lifted one shoulder in a half-shrug. "I am a guide. That's the best word for it."

"A guide to what?" Rowan asked.

He gave them a look that mixed humor with sympathy. "To themselves," he said quietly. "Unfortunately."

The word sat heavy, not because he disliked it, but because he seemed to know what kind of strain that kind of word created.
"I don't need a guide," Rowan replied.

Trevor's smile didn't falter. "Most people who do say that," he said. "And some who don't need one say it too, just in case."

A faint pressure gathered at the base of Rowan's skull. It felt like the beginning of a headache, or the moment before a storm changes the air.

"Who sent you?" Rowan asked.

He considered that, then shook his head. "That's a bigger answer than we've got time for right now." He gestured vaguely around them. "The short version? I'm a sort of... seasonal complication. I show up when nights get long and cold, and people are closer to the edge than usual."

He winced again. "That still sounds worse out loud."

"Seasonal," Rowan repeated.

34

"Yeah." His gaze flicked toward the unseen sky above them. "This time of year is... loud. Lots of calls. Lots of flares." He looked back at them. "Yours was... very clear."

They didn't remember sending anything.

"I didn't ask for help," Rowan said.

"I know," Trevor replied. "You're not the asking type."

That surprised them more than anything else he'd said.

He held up his hands before they could respond. "Look, I'm not here to fix you," he said. "Or judge you. Or drag you into some moral inventory you didn't sign up for. Trust me, if it were up to me, I'd pick a quieter line of work. But I'm here now. You're here. And the place is... not behaving. So."

He spread his hands, as if laying options out on an invisible table. "We can ignore that and wait to see how bad it gets. Or you can let me help you not freeze down here, and maybe we both get out with fewer regrets."

"You talk a lot," Rowan observed.

"I get nervous," he admitted. "Which is ironic, considering my job description."

They didn't smile, exactly, but something softened at the corner of their mouth.

He changed tack with subtle ease. "Do you have somewhere you're supposed to be in the morning?" he asked. "Or is staying down here all night your idea of a holiday?"

"There are relief staff," Rowan said. "They'll come." They considered. "Eventually."

"How long is eventually?" he asked.

They didn't answer.

"Right," he said. "That's what I thought."

He took a small step closer, still leaving a respectful distance between them, palms visible at his sides.

"Let me make this simple," he said quietly. "You don't have to trust me. You don't have to tell me anything. You don't have to believe what I am, or how I got here, or what the lantern is doing. You only have to decide whether you'd rather be alone when this place decides what it wants from you."

Rowan's gaze flicked toward the archway, where the unseen follower still lingered. They couldn't see it. They could feel it—a quiet, patient attention waiting just outside.

They looked back at Trevor.

"You're… what, exactly?" they asked.

He hesitated a fraction of a second, then answered with startling honesty.

"I'm a kind of ghost," he said. "Not the rattling-chains sort. I don't… haunt. I don't belong to one place. I belong to this night. To this… season." He squinted as though the words themselves were too grand. "You'd be more comfortable calling me a ghost of Christmas than whatever the real term is. So. We can start there."

Rowan stared at him, waiting for the punchline.

He didn't offer one.

"You don't look dead," they said.

Trevor smiled, pained and fond all at once. "Thank you," he said again. "I try not to."

The opal light in the lantern brightened subtly, as if reacting to the name of what he was. The colors inside the flame seemed to stretch deeper, like layers of history stacked in glass.

Rowan realized they believed him long before they found a reason to say so.

"I'm not helpless," they said.

"I know," he replied. "If you were, I probably wouldn't be here. I get sent to the stubborn ones. The ones who think they can carry it all themselves."

"That sounds inefficient," Rowan said.

"It is," Trevor agreed. "I don't design the system."

The pressure at the base of Rowan's skull sharpened. The air along their arms prickled, not from cold now, but from something warmer pushing itself into the room. The chamber's shadows seemed to lean in, as though the past were crowding at the door.

Trevor's expression changed.

Every trace of humor slipped away, replaced by a familiarity Rowan hadn't seen before, a look that said he'd stood in this exact moment more times than he could count.

His shoulders dropped slightly in resignation.

"Here we go," he murmured.

The opal flame swelled inside the lantern, filling the glass with color. The stone around them glowed faintly with its reflection, as if the chamber itself had been waiting for this particular light.

Rowan's chest tightened. The sensation wasn't entirely physical. It felt like a hand had reached into them and closed gently around something they'd shoved deep a long time ago.

"What is that?" they asked.

Trevor shook his head once, slow. "The part I can't control," he said. "I'm sorry. I tried to buy us more time."

The air thickened, warm now, the cold peeled back in layers. The breath Rowan exhaled didn't hang heavy anymore; it seemed to be drawn toward the lantern, toward Trevor, toward whatever was opening on the other side of this moment.

"I didn't agree to anything," Rowan said.

"I know," Trevor replied. There was real sorrow in his voice. "Neither did I. Not really."

Their eyes met.

His held no triumph. No satisfaction. Only a kind of tired compassion that made Rowan want to step back and step closer at the same time.

"You should know," he said quietly, "that this—what's about to happen—it's not punishment. It's not a test you can pass or fail. It's... a showing. Of where you've been. Of how you got here. After that, what you do with it is yours. I never get to know that part."

The pressure in Rowan's skull became a pull, a gravity that didn't have a direction so much as an inevitability. For a heartbeat, the chamber blurred at the edges, the platform, the walls, the carved vines at the archway all softening as if seen through glass.

Trevor took a half-step closer, not reaching for them, just anchoring himself in their line of sight.

"I'm sorry," he said again, more quietly now. "Once it starts... I can't stop it."

The lantern's opal light flared and warmth rose around Rowan in a slow, unstoppable tide, carrying them backward, inward, toward a night they had never planned to see again.

Christmas Eve, Before

The opal light lifted the catacomb stone like a curtain rising at the end of a long, breathless silence. Rowan felt the cold loosen its grip on their ribs, felt the lantern lighten in their hand as if it suddenly remembered how to glow. The chamber blurred at the edges, warmth blooming beneath its surface, and then the whole room dissolved into a shimmer of soft, pearly color.

When the world steadied, Rowan stood in the middle of a small apartment.

It was dim except for a drooping string of warm Christmas lights hung crookedly across a window. Snow drifted down in slow, fat flakes, catching in the amber glow of a streetlamp outside. The air here was warm, soft, lived-in — nothing like the sterile cold of the tombs. Rowan breathed in and found the scent of cinnamon, dust, and something faintly sweet, like the tail end of holiday baking.

Trevor appeared beside them, quiet and reverent, as if he didn't want to disturb whatever memory they had stepped into.

On the counter, two mugs still sat by the sink. Steam didn't rise from them, but there was a sense they had once been warm. A casserole dish rested on the stove, a kitchen towel thrown over it to keep the heat in. A board game lay half-finished on the coffee table. Someone had left mid-play — a red token teetering between spaces, a tiny die frozen mid-roll.

This wasn't a place abandoned.

It was a place paused.

Trevor's eyes softened. He didn't say anything. He didn't need to.

A small patter of socked feet scurried down the hallway, and Rowan turned just as a child rounded the corner.

Rowan felt something in their chest loosen — or twist.

It was hard to tell which.

Child Rowan couldn't have been older than seven or eight. Their face was rounder, softer, cheeks flushed pink in a way Rowan hadn't seen in decades. They wore a Christmas sweater that had clearly been pulled from a store bin years earlier — the kind of thing bought not for holiday spirit, but because it had been on sale and warm enough.

But the child was humming.

Quietly.

A little off-key.

A small, hopeful tune, like a secret offered to no one in particular.

They held a crayon drawing — a tree, if Rowan remembered correctly, though the proportions were wrong in the way only children can make charming. A star sat on top, or maybe it was a sun. A gift or two sat at the tree's base. The lines wobbled. The green crayon had been pressed too hard.

The child crossed to the small tabletop Christmas tree sitting on a side table and flicked the switch. The tiny bulbs blinked weakly to life — green, red, gold, and one that flickered stubbornly between blue and purple.

The child knelt, folded the drawing carefully in half, then placed it under the tree with a kind of ceremonial gentleness.

Trevor whispered, "This was yours?"

Rowan didn't answer.

They couldn't.

The child sat back on their heels and whispered something to the drawing — too quiet to catch, but soft, affectionate, and full of belief. Then they looked toward the hallway as if expecting someone to return. Their small face stayed neutral, but Rowan recognized something in the eyes — a kind of quiet certainty that no one would appear.

Trevor watched with the sort of sorrow reserved for things that don't need fixing — only understanding. For a heartbeat, Trevor looked at her like he'd almost named the sadness they carried. Almost.

The child stood, drifting through the apartment with a practiced sort of independence. They climbed onto a chair in the kitchen to poke experimentally at the casserole dish. Their nose scrunched up — it was too hot. They didn't move it. They didn't eat. They simply checked, as though confirming for themselves that dinner had existed at all.

Rowan's throat felt tight. The air held a strange echo, memory overlapping reality. Everything in the apartment whispered the same contradiction:

Someone had been here.
Someone would be back.
Someone had prepared something.

43

Someone had loved enough to leave warmth behind.

But child Rowan didn't see it.

They moved through the room with the careful quiet of someone who didn't want to disturb anyone — but also didn't expect to be disturbed.

Trevor walked slowly to the couch, eyes taking in each detail.

The board game.

The towels.

The coat missing from the hook.

A pair of adult boots near the door.

A folded blanket.

A greeting card tucked half-open on the counter.

He looked at Rowan, expression full of something soft and devastating.

"You weren't invisible," he said quietly.

Rowan didn't respond.

They were watching the child — the small figure who climbed onto the couch, wrapped themselves tightly in a blanket, and clicked on a tiny battery-operated candle on the coffee table.

The candle flickered with a warm orange glow. It wasn't enough to light the room.

It was enough to make the child smile.

Trevor knelt beside the couch, though the child could not see him.

"You were waiting," he said softly.

"Just waiting."

Child Rowan hugged the pillow tighter, watching the blinking Christmas lights above the window. The lights blinked a little unevenly; one bulb flickered out, then returned, then glowed brighter for a moment.

Rowan remembered thinking, as a child, that the lights meant something — that the pattern was a message, or a sign, or a signal that someone was on their way.

Present Rowan saw only electrical aging.

Yet the memory held its sweetness.

"What time is it?" Trevor asked gently.

Rowan looked at the clock on the wall.

The red digital numbers glowed: 6:18 PM.

Early evening.
Not abandonment.
Not even late.
Rowan swallowed.

Child Rowan slid off the couch and wandered to the window. They pressed their small hand to the cold glass, watching the snow fall

45

in thick clusters. Street sounds were muffled, distant — a passing car, the faint laugh of someone outside.

The child whispered to the empty room, voice hopeful, unbroken:

"Maybe they're bringing something back."

Trevor's breath hitched faintly — the smallest break in his composure.

"You weren't unloved," he murmured, looking at the child as though speaking to them directly.

"You were just… early."

Rowan's jaw tightened. Their hand flexed at their side, as if resisting the urge to reach out and correct the memory. But the truth of it — the soft, painful truth — was settling like dust on an untouched shelf.

Child Rowan moved back to the tree, checking on the drawing as if it might have changed in their brief absence. They sat cross-legged, whispering a story to the paper — a story about what they hoped Christmas would be tomorrow, or maybe next year, or maybe someday.

It wasn't sad.
It wasn't desperate.
It wasn't tragic.
It was gentle.
It was hopeful.
It was lonely in a completely human way.
Trevor watched all of it.
Quiet.

Still.
Present.

His kindness filled the room with a warmth that did not disturb the memory but softened its edges.

"You thought you were alone," he said softly to Rowan.

"All your life you've believed that."

Rowan kept their eyes on the child. "I was."

Trevor's voice dropped.

"You weren't."

The Christmas lights flickered.

A few bulbs glowed softly opal, blending memory-light with magic-light until the entire room shimmered at the edges.

Rowan looked down as the child glanced at the door — not with dread, not with disappointment, but with a soft, expectant hope.

That tiny gesture hit Rowan harder than all the emptiness they remembered.

The lights flickered again — once, twice — then stretched into a smear of warm color.

Trevor whispered, "There's more," just as the memory dissolved into opalescent light, lifting the apartment away in a quiet breath until Rowan stood once more in shimmering, shifting brightness.

And the Past reached for them again.

Between Echoes

The opal shimmer receded with the softness of a sigh. Rowan felt it loosen its hold before the world reasserted itself, stone walls growing back into focus like something sketching itself into being. The catacombs settled around them — dim, cold, ancient — their silence suddenly louder after the memory's warmth.

The lantern swung gently in Rowan's hand, its flame still tinted with faint opal at the edges. That wasn't normal, Rowan knew, but Trevor didn't comment on it. Maybe he didn't notice. Maybe he assumed it meant nothing.

Rowan braced a palm against the nearest wall, pretending the gesture was about balance rather than needing a moment. The stone was cold enough to sting.

Trevor stepped beside them but kept a careful inch of space.

He always respected space.

"You alright?" he asked softly.

Rowan didn't look at him. "I'm fine."

It was a flimsy lie. It evaporated in the cold air before it reached the ground.

Trevor studied their profile — not with suspicion, never with suspicion. With concern that held no weight, no pressure. Concern that was offered, not pushed.

"You don't have to be fine," he said. "Not with me."

Rowan's throat tightened. They kept their eyes on the lantern flame, pretending interest in nothing. The opal edge pulsed faintly, then receded, then pulsed again. Rowan moved the light away as though shifting its weight.

"I wasn't expecting that memory," Rowan said, voice thin. "It was... old."

Trevor nodded. "Past doesn't have a timeline. It just shows where the ache sits."

Rowan stiffened. Trevor didn't notice the reason for it — didn't even realize how perceptive he'd been.

"Come on," he said gently. "Let's rest a minute."

They moved a few steps down the tunnel and stopped beneath an arch carved with years of erosion. Trevor reached up and hooked the lantern onto a protruding stone so it hung at eye level. The opal tint softened into its usual gold, though faint threads of color still clung to the curve of the glass.

Trevor leaned his shoulder against the opposite wall, crossing his arms loosely. Rowan stayed standing, hands in pockets, posture tight.

The quiet stretched.

Trevor broke it with the kind of voice you use with frightened animals — soft, steady.

50

"You were very small in that memory," he said. "But you handled the quiet well."

"It wasn't quiet to me," Rowan replied. "It was just... Christmas."

Trevor tilted his head. "And Christmas wasn't happy?"

Rowan hesitated. The truth rose before they could stop it — how the apartment had felt too big, how the lights had seemed too dim, how the silence had nestled into their ribs like it belonged there.

Instead they said, "It was just normal."

Trevor nodded slowly.

Normal could hurt more than pain.

"The first Christmas I ever helped someone," he said, "they were a widower. He made two cups of cocoa every year. One for him. One for the wife he'd lost decades before."

Rowan's jaw tightened. "Why would he do that?"

"Because hope doesn't always make sense," Trevor said. "Sometimes it's the ritual that keeps you warm, not the meaning."

Rowan swallowed.

Their eyes lowered.

Trevor watched them a moment longer.

"You've carried a lot of quiet with you, haven't you?" he asked.

51

Rowan didn't answer — didn't need to.

He wasn't accusing.

Only seeing.

They hated that he could see.

Trevor stepped forward slightly. "Rowan… I know I can't undo whatever made you feel overlooked. But I'm here now. Tonight, you're not—"

"Don't," Rowan said quietly.

Trevor stopped.

Rowan took a slow breath.

Adjusted their coat.

Looked away.

"I don't want pity," they said.

Trevor's expression softened with something like hurt. "That wasn't pity."

Rowan looked at him then — really looked — and saw sincerity, simple and unadorned. Not pity. Not obligation. Not guilt.

Just… care.

That made it worse.

Trevor tried a different approach, voice gentler:
"What do you want Christmas to feel like? If you could choose."

The question hit Rowan like cold water.

Their mouth opened before their mind could stop it.

"I want…"
The truth hovered.
I want warmth.
I want to belong.
I want someone to choose me.
I want to be seen without fear.

But those desires were too open.

Too dangerous.

Rowan's breath stuttered. They caught themselves, redirecting sharply.

"I want it to feel… quieter," they said.

Trevor watched their face carefully.

He heard the lie.

But he thought it was a lie of pain, not deflection.

"I think you deserve warmth," he said softly.

Rowan looked away, jaw tight enough to ache.

The lantern flickered — not with wind, not with breath. With something else. A faint pulse of opal light shimmered across the glass, blooming outward for a second before fading to gold again.

Trevor didn't notice.

Rowan did.

Their pulse quickened.

Memory and magic shouldn't bleed.

Not unless something else was stirring.

"What was that?" Rowan asked.

Trevor looked up.

"What?"

"The light." Rowan gestured. "It flickered."

Trevor smiled. "Draft, maybe."

His tone was warm. Unconcerned.

Rowan didn't correct him.

A quiet shiver rolled down the tunnel — too soft to be anything more than stone settling, but Rowan felt something beneath it, a tremor of memory brushing against present time.

"I think we should keep moving," Rowan said.

Trevor nodded. "Alright."

He took the lantern down carefully.

Rowan started forward first, shoulders straightened, eyes forward.

Trevor walked at their side, humming softly — a tune that wasn't quite the one from the apartment but carried the same warmth.

As they stepped deeper into the catacombs, Rowan felt their shadow linger behind them a fraction too long, as though the opal glow didn't want to let go.

They didn't look back.

The Christmas Party

The opal shimmer folded inward like a curtain being drawn tight. Rowan felt a brief tug in their chest, a soft rush of warmth, and then the catacombs evaporated into light.

When the scene settled, Rowan stood at the threshold of a small office suite hastily transformed into a Christmas party.

Fluorescent lights had been dimmed, replaced by tangled strings of multicolored bulbs that blinked at erratic intervals. Cheap tinsel drooped from filing cabinets. A Bluetooth speaker perched on a stack of old invoices blasted a Christmas playlist just loud enough to warp the high bells into static.

Plastic cups clinked.

People laughed in overlapping bursts.

The air smelled faintly of sweet punch, cinnamon cookies, and too many bodies in one warm room.

Young Rowan stood a few steps ahead — nineteen, maybe twenty — clutching a red plastic cup with both hands. Their shoulders were drawn up a little too tightly, as though bracing for a blow that would never come. Their holiday sweater was plain green, sleeves pushed up, a small run near the hem they'd failed to notice.

Trevor appeared beside present Rowan, his presence smoothing the noise in a quiet, impossible way.

"They look… young," he murmured.

Rowan said nothing.

The younger version of them drifted toward the wall, settling into the safe perimeter of the party — close enough to be included if someone tried, far enough that no one would accidentally bump into them. Their expression was neutral, but Rowan recognized the flicker in their eyes: the early, unarticulated shape of a belief that would one day harden into a worldview.

No one sees me.

A cluster of coworkers laughed near the makeshift snack table, clinking cups. Another group swapped half-serious holiday stories about bad gifts. A woman with reindeer antlers waved in Rowan's direction — or at least, that's how Trevor saw it.

Younger Rowan blinked, looked behind themselves, saw no one, then gave a stiff, uncertain nod before retreating another step into the shadow of a cubicle partition.

Trevor's brow furrowed. "That wave was for you."

"It didn't feel like it," Rowan said.

"That doesn't make it untrue." His outline shimmered for a moment, barely, like a breath on glass. Rowan had noticed this when she looked directly at him, the shift in his taken space.

Younger Rowan took a sip from their cup — plain soda — and drifted toward the doorway before stopping, reconsidering, stepping

58

back. Their eyes stayed low, flicking up only when someone brushed past them.

A man in an ugly sweater turned, grin wide.

"Rowan! You made it!"

He paused as the music spiked with static. The grin faltered, not from disappointment, but because Rowan didn't respond quickly enough. By the time younger Rowan produced a thin, awkward smile, the moment had passed and the man had been absorbed into the next conversation.

"He tried," Trevor whispered.

Rowan's jaw tightened.

Someone else approached the snacks, glancing at Rowan with a friendly if distracted smile.

"You should try the cookies," she said, offering the tin. "They're not bad this year."

Younger Rowan's spine stiffened. They shook their head too quickly, too sharply, muttering something polite before retreating. The woman blinked, startled, then shrugged and moved on.

"She wasn't pitying you," Trevor said gently. "She was just... being kind."

"It didn't feel like kindness."

"I know."

The party churned around them, messy and earnest. People exchanged Secret Santa gifts — mugs, scarves, novelty pens. Someone teased their manager about being "too cheap" for holiday bonuses, and he laughed louder than necessary, cheeks flushed from spiked punch.

The lights flickered overhead, casting the room in uneven bursts of red and gold. For a moment, Rowan thought they saw the bulbs shift toward opal, but it was just reflection from the punch bowl.

Younger Rowan lingered near a potted plant, fingers tapping the cup nervously against their palm. They hovered at the edge of every conversation, close enough to hear pieces but never the whole.

"Were you lonely then?" Trevor asked softly.

Rowan exhaled through their nose. "I was used to it."

"That's not what I asked."

Rowan didn't answer.

Someone turned the music down for a moment.

A coworker cleared their throat loudly.

"Uh, okay, everyone! Time for the silly awards!"

People groaned and laughed.

Younger Rowan shifted back against the wall, half-expecting to be mocked.

But the awards were harmless — "Most Likely to Double-Check the Printer," "Best Doodler During Meetings," "Most Patient with

Customers." A few people clapped, a few joked, a few rolled their eyes.

Then someone called out, "Where's Rowan?"

Younger Rowan froze.

"I made this one for them!" the woman with the antlers said, holding up a small paper crown labeled Quietest Competent Human Alive.

A few people laughed — lightly, not unkindly. It wasn't a joke at Rowan's expense. It was affectionate. The kind of teasing reserved for someone people liked but didn't know how to engage with fully.

Younger Rowan hesitated too long. Someone stepped forward and claimed the crown "on their behalf," earning a wave of laughter. The moment dissolved.

Trevor let out a breath that trembled faintly.

"You were part of this," he whispered.

"You didn't believe you were, so you… weren't."

Rowan swallowed hard.

Then came the moment Trevor had been waiting for.

A young colleague — timid, probably newer than Rowan — stepped out from the back room holding a small, unevenly wrapped gift. They approached younger Rowan slowly, almost nervously.

"I, um… I made this for you," they said, voice barely above the music. "Because you always help me when the system breaks."

61

The gift was wrapped in crinkled red paper with too much tape.

Younger Rowan looked stunned.

"I... thank you," they said stiffly.

The colleague brightened, relieved. "I hoped you'd like it."

Before Rowan could respond further, someone shouted for a group photo, and the colleague hurried away, leaving younger Rowan holding the small package as though unsure what to do with it.

Trevor crouched slightly to look at the younger Rowan's face.

"You had a place," he murmured.

"You just didn't know how to step into it."

Rowan looked away.

The music picked up again.

A group formed a loose dance circle near the desk area. Someone gestured Rowan over—one hand sweeping in an enthusiastic "come on!" Younger Rowan glanced at them, startled, then immediately assumed the gesture meant the person next to them. Rowan sidestepped, and the circle closed without them.

A small, nearly invisible moment.

But it lived in Rowan's memory like rejection.

Trevor let out a soft sigh.

"You weren't invisible," he said.

"You were afraid."

Rowan's hands clenched into fists.

The lights began to flicker again, and this time Rowan could see the opal shimmer growing at the edges. The laughter blurred. Conversations slowed. Music stretched into a distant echo.

Younger Rowan looked down at the small gift again — hesitant fingers brushing the messy wrapping — right as the entire scene began to dissolve into pale, pearly light.

Trevor's voice filtered through the fading party, warm and certain:
"There's still one more."

And the Christmas party melted into opalescent shimmer, pulling Rowan forward as the next memory opened its hand.

The Bridge

The opal shimmer didn't break neatly into a memory this time.

It loosened, unfurling in slow, deliberate threads, like silk being tugged apart by invisible hands. The air itself grew thinner, quieter. Rowan felt the shift before they understood it — the way the light seemed to breathe, not in a pulse but a long exhale, as if the world were bracing.

The catacombs were gone.

Trevor was there beside them.

Not close enough to touch.

Close enough to feel.

The in-between space was pale and pearly, like standing inside the softest part of dawn. Light pooled around Rowan's boots, soft waves rippling outward with each slow breath. There was no ceiling. No walls. No floor beyond the faint suggestion of one.

Just stillness.

A held moment.

A small mercy before the next reveal.

Trevor remained quiet for several seconds, studying Rowan with a kind of tenderness he usually hid behind humor or hope. His expression here was unfiltered, stripped of performance.

"You don't have to be afraid," he said softly.

The sentence landed with a warmth that clung to Rowan's ribs.

"I'm not," Rowan said.

The words were steady. But the faint tremble in their hands said otherwise, and the void around them reflected it — light shifting in small, sympathetic ripples.

Trevor didn't call attention to it.

He never did.

The opal glow deepened.

It gathered weight.

It thickened into something with gravity.

Rowan felt the pull along their spine as the shimmer condensed, collapsing inward in slow, reverent folds. It moved like memory remembering itself. Like time choosing its shape.

Then it opened.

Cold hit first — sharp, crisp, real.

The kind that steals breath and makes lungs tighten.

A winter bridge formed beneath their feet, stone slick with frost. Snow fell in heavy flakes, each one illuminated by the orange glow of streetlights dotting the walkway. The river moved below in sluggish swells, dark water catching fragments of light and carrying them downstream like drifting embers.

Wind curled around Rowan's ankles, threading through the loose edges of their coat. Somewhere in the distance, a muffled car horn bled into the night. The city was there — alive and unwatched — but here, on the bridge, the world was hushed.

Present Rowan's breath fogged the air.

Trevor's did not.

He stared at the scene with a look Rowan couldn't decipher — part wonder, part ache, part something older and deeper. Something that recognized a moment he had never actually remembered.

"Oh," he whispered. "Here."

Rowan swallowed.

They didn't answer.

Young adult Rowan stood at the railing a little ways ahead — maybe twenty, maybe still carrying the softness of adolescence in their features. Snow clung to their eyelashes. Their coat was thin, not inadequate but worn, the kind of item someone keeps because it still functions even after the comfort has faded.

Their posture was a blueprint of quiet:
shoulders slightly hunched from holding themselves together,
hands in pockets not for warmth but for stillness,

gaze fixed on the river as if the water held an answer they hadn't yet learned how to ask for.

It wasn't despair.

It wasn't collapse.

It was isolation worn thin.

A muted ache disguised as contemplation.

A familiar kind of human loneliness.

Trevor's voice lowered. "It was Christmas Eve."

Rowan didn't respond.

Their throat tightened.

The snowfall hushed the world. Each flake caught the light as it fell, drifting sideways, sticking to the railing in soft, temporary ridges. Distant apartment windows glowed faintly across the river, tiny squares of warmth Rowan didn't notice back then.

Footsteps sounded on the walkway.

Soft.

Measured.

Steady.

Past Trevor emerged through the snowfall — not glowing, not spectral, not magical. Just a man. A warm, human presence wrapped

68

in a coat, scarf tucked just slightly askew. Snowflakes caught in his hair as though choosing to rest there.

He hummed quietly, breath clouding the air in a gentle rhythm. A tune Rowan couldn't place, probably something simple, something comforting.

Young Rowan didn't turn.

Trevor slowed when he reached them, adjusting his distance with care. He leaned one hip lightly against the railing. Not invading space. Not demanding attention. Simply existing beside them.

"Cold night to be out," he said, voice soft enough to avoid echoing.

Young Rowan blinked, eyes shifting just slightly toward him — not startled, not threatened.

Just... noticing warmth.

"It's pretty, though," Trevor added. "When it falls slow like this, it feels like the world is taking its time."

The words settled like a blanket across the cold.

Young Rowan didn't smile, but their breath steadied.

Snow gathered on their sleeve.

Light haloed around them both through the drifting flakes.

"Christmas Eve is strange," Trevor continued. "Too loud in some places. Too empty in others."

Young Rowan's voice was barely audible.

"Empty fits."

Trevor glanced at them, really seeing them now — not in pity, not in assessment, but with the simple kindness of a person who doesn't want someone to feel alone, even for a moment.
"You waiting on someone?" he asked.

Young Rowan hesitated. Their lips parted, closed, opened again.

"I don't know," they said. "I just… walked."

Trevor's smile softened, warm without intruding.

"Walks help," he said. "Sometimes they're the only part of the day that belongs to you."

Young Rowan gave the faintest huff of breath, the beginning of what might one day become a laugh. Snow clung to the hem of Trevor's scarf. The river carried reflections downstream in long streaks of molten orange.

"Not sure that's a good thing," Rowan murmured.

"Depends what's rattling around in there," Trevor replied.

The wind swept across the bridge, swirling flakes between them.

Trevor didn't step closer.

He didn't push.

He didn't perform hope.

70

He simply was hope — quietly, unobtrusively, without asking for anything back.

Young Rowan finally turned their body a fraction toward him.

Not fully.

Not openly.

But enough to acknowledge the presence beside them.

"It's quiet," Rowan said.

Trevor nodded.

"Quiet can mean different things," he said. "Sometimes it's how you hear your own head."

A beat.

"Sometimes it's just... quiet."

They stood that way for another stretch — two strangers sharing a small sliver of night.

Then Trevor pushed lightly off the railing.

"Take care of yourself tonight," he said warmly. "It's easier when you do."

He walked on, boots crunching softly through snow. His scarf trailed slightly behind him, brushing the cold air.

Young Rowan watched him go.

Their shoulders loosened.

Their breathing deepened.

A small, subtle shift spread through them — not revelation, not rescue.

Just… recognition.

Rowan, watching, felt their chest tighten, though they couldn't name the feeling.

Present Trevor's voice was almost reverent.

"That was it," he said. "That was the moment."

Rowan stared, unable to breathe.

"You didn't even know me," they whispered.

Trevor shook his head slowly.

"I didn't know anyone. Not really." His eyes softened.

"I just followed your sound. You needed a friend, you needed warmth. I was happy to oblige."

The snowfall thinned.

The river blurred.

The night collapsed into opal light.

Past Trevor faded first, his human warmth dissolving into shimmer. Young Rowan followed, dissolving into light like mist evaporating.

Present Trevor whispered:
"I found you that night."

Rowan didn't tell him the truth, that he hadn't found them at all.

He had simply existed beside them.

And somehow, that had been enough to change the entire shape of Rowan's world.

The opal glow surged, pulling them back toward the catacombs, swallowing the bridge in a final wash of color.

Rowan's pulse carried one thing back with them: the memory of being seen.

The Space Between

The world came back in pieces this time.

First, the sound of their own breathing — harsh, too loud, like it didn't belong to them.

Then the cold — seeping in around the edges of sensation, a creeping weight that started in Rowan's fingertips and folded inward until it found bone.

Then the stone.

Rowan hit the wall with enough force to send a dull crack along their shoulder. The impact rang through the corridor, slow and hollow, rolling away into the dark until it was just another sound swallowed by the catacombs.

They stayed there a second longer than they needed to, cheek pressed to chilled stone, eyes closed. The roughness of the wall anchored them more than the lantern's glow did.

"Rowan?" Trevor's voice came from just to their right, low and careful. "You with me?"

They exhaled slowly, then pulled back. The stone left a faint imprint of grit on their skin.

"Yeah," they said. Their voice came out steady. "I'm here."

Trevor's hand hovered near their arm, fingers trembling slightly from the cold or the trip between times — Rowan couldn't tell. He didn't touch them. He never assumed that right.

"That one dropped us a little harder," he said. "You took the brunt of it. I'm sorry."

"It's not your fault." Rowan pushed away from the wall fully, rolling their shoulder once to make sure nothing was seriously damaged. A dull ache bloomed, deep and manageable. "Gravity exists. Who knew."

The joke landed softer than they meant it to. Trevor smiled anyway. He always did.

The lantern in his other hand burned with that deep, steady violet-gold now — the color it always returned to when they were back in the here and now. The opal sheen from the bridge memory had bled out of it in a slow exhale, like light remembering where it belonged.

The corridor around them looked familiar enough to pass: narrow stone walls sweating faint beads of condensation, the floor packed down from decades of caretakers' boots, faint alcoves cut in where old plaques and flowers had once lived and long since rotted away. The air smelled of dust, old air, the faint metallic bite of cold.

But something in the way it all sat felt... heavier.

Maybe it was just the temperature. The further they moved from the main descents, the more the cold sank its teeth in and refused to let go. Rowan flexed their fingers once, twice, then tucked them back into their sleeves.

"Give me a sec," they said.

"Take two," Trevor replied. "We're not on anyone's schedule but dawn."

Dawn. Right.

Rowan glanced toward where the ceiling was just a little lower, counting the invisible distance between them and the upper levels. Somewhere above all of this, snow was falling in a world that still had sky. Somewhere above, people were sleeping in warm beds and would wake to coffee and daylight and the casual assumption of safety.

Down here, it was all stone, breath, and time.

"How long do we have?" Trevor asked, reading something of the calculation on Rowan's face.

Rowan checked the thin watch on their wrist, the metal so cold it had gone numb against their skin. "About… five hours until the relief shift," they said. "Give or take."

"Plenty of time to get bored of my company, then." Trevor attempted a lightness that snagged on its own weight.

Rowan didn't take the bait. Their gaze moved to the side of the corridor instead, tracing the line where the mortar between stones had cracked in a familiar pattern. They had passed this way dozens of times in the past year. They knew the feel of this path under their boots.

Or they thought they did.

"We should move," they said. "Standing still just makes the cold happy."

Trevor sobered, nodding. "Lead the way."

He handed the lantern over without needing to be asked; Rowan took it easily. The metal handle bit into their fingers. The light threw their shadows long against the wall, Trevor's stretching wide, Rowan's clinging thinly at their heels.

They set off down the corridor, Rowan in front, Trevor half a step behind.

For a few minutes, the only sound was their footsteps. The packed earth and stone underfoot made a muted, muffled rhythm — not the sharp click of shoes on tile or pavement, but a dull, almost respectful tread. As if even sound agreed to keep its voice down in a place meant for quiet.

"Rowan?" Trevor said eventually.

They didn't look back. "Mm?"

"Where does this part lead again?" His tone wasn't nervous, just curious. Trusting.

Rowan let the lantern play over the nearest wall. Their light skimmed over old chisel marks, a faded number etched into the stone — 19C — and a deep groove where a casket trolley had bumped the same spot over and over.

"Outer ring," Rowan said. "It curves around, then drops in near the older niches. If we ride it right, we'll cut back toward the main path without having to double back."

They didn't mention the other reason they liked this route: fewer side chambers. Fewer open doorways where cold could creep. Fewer places to see shapes that weren't there.

"Outer ring," Trevor repeated. "Got it."

He said it like a student repeating notes. It made something almost like affection stir at the back of Rowan's thoughts. They pushed it down.

The cold moved with them. Not dramatically — no sudden gusts, no overly theatrical chills — just a persistent, creeping presence. It gathered around their shins and wrists, crept beneath the hem of Rowan's coat, threaded its way into the edges where wool and skin didn't quite seal.

Their breath fogged the air. Trevor's did too, in slow puffs that drifted and then broke apart against the lantern's glow.

He cleared his throat gently. "Can I ask you something?"

"Depends," Rowan said.

"Fair." A pause. "That bridge... the one we just saw. Was that the first time we met?"

There it was. The chandelier, creaking almost imperceptibly above them.

Rowan didn't slow, but their focus sharpened. The number carved into the wall ahead — 20A — came into view. Good. They were still where they thought they were.

"You tell me," they said. "Your memory. Your magic."

Trevor winced slightly. "Right. But it felt… I don't know. Familiar. Like walking into a room you haven't been in for a long time but could still find the light switch blindfolded."

Rowan gave the faintest huff through their nose. "That's specific."

"I've had practice."

Another few steps of quiet.

Rowan could feel Trevor looking at their back, weighing his next words. He was gentle even with his curiosity. That should have made this easier. It didn't.

"I just…" Trevor tried again. "You looked so alone that night. I didn't know it mattered. I thought I was just another person on the bridge, you know? Another passerby saying something awkward and going home. But seeing it now—"

"Trevor," Rowan said.

It wasn't sharp. It wasn't cold.

It was… precise. A line drawn in the air.

He stopped mid-sentence. "Yeah?"

Rowan let a heartbeat pass. Two. They kept their eyes on the path ahead, watching the way the lantern carved just enough light into the dark to make a narrow tunnel of visibility.

"I don't live there anymore," they said. "On that bridge. It was a long time ago."

"I know," he said quickly. "I just meant—"

"And I appreciate what you said," Rowan went on, calm, almost conversational. "Then. And now. But that's... mine. That night. It doesn't feel good to keep pressing on it."

Silence folded in around them for a moment. Not heavy. Just present.

Trevor's footsteps slowed half a fraction, then matched their pace again. "Okay," he said softly. "Thank you for telling me that. I won't bring it up again."

There was no wounded edge in his voice. No offended hurt. Just acceptance.

Rowan's shoulders dropped a fraction they hadn't realized they were holding.

"Alright," they said. "Good."

They turned the next corner, the lantern grazing the ceiling where it dipped just a little lower. Condensation had thickened here, beads of moisture clinging to the stone like a veil. Rowan traced the pattern with their eyes out of old habit, following the way it gathered more on one side than the other.

"Vent here," they murmured.

Trevor blinked. "What?"

Rowan nodded toward the wall. "Condensation's thicker on the right. Air's coming from that side. Means the next main junction's not far."

"You can tell that just from the... sweat?"

"It's not sweat." Rowan made a face. "Stone doesn't sweat. It's condensation. Temperature meets air flow. You look long enough, you see patterns." They paused. "It's my job, remember?"

"Hard to forget," Trevor said. "You wear it like a second coat."

That drew an actual smile from Rowan, quick and small. "That sounds heavier than the real one."

"Could be why you're so tired," he offered, tone light again.

"I'm tired because I've been hauling your Christmas tour through my workplace all night," Rowan said. "And because it's below freezing. And because I haven't eaten since... a while."

"That too."

He fell quiet for another stretch, letting their steps fill the space. The corridor widened slightly as they approached the next junction, the ceiling lifting just enough for the air to feel less compressive.

Rowan slowed near the intersection, letting the lantern sweep across both paths. The left fork sloped downward, darker, narrower, the smell of stale air thicker. The right held a faint hint of fresher cold and the ghost of old incense — chapel direction.

"Right," Rowan said. "We stay on the ring."

"No dive into the abyss yet?" Trevor asked.

"We're not sightseeing," Rowan replied.

82

They turned right. The sound of their footsteps changed subtly, picking up a softer echo now that the space had broadened a little. Somewhere ahead, water was dripping in a slow, irregular rhythm, like someone tapping a fingernail against the world.

Trevor exhaled carefully, letting his breath fog out in front of him.

"If you ever do want to talk about it," he said after a moment. "The bridge, or any of it. I'll listen. You don't owe me anything. I just want you to know the door's there."

Rowan let that settle. It sat neatly between them, not a weight, not a demand. Just an offered thing.

"Noted," they said. "For future use. Or non-use."

"Either way," Trevor said. "Still there."

There was something about the steadiness of that that unsettled Rowan more than any flickering light could've. Not because it hurt. Not because it threatened to crack them open.

Because it was durable.

Hope that didn't bargain.

They weren't sure what to do with that.

"You're very persistent," they said.

Trevor huffed softly. "Occupational hazard."

"Ghost of Christmas Boundaries," Rowan said dryly. "Terrifying."

"I prefer Ghost of Christmas Reasonable Expectations," he replied. "Good with kids. Terrible branding."

The banter smoothed some of the edges off the air. The weight loosened its grip a fraction, still hanging, still present, but less oppressive.

Rowan adjusted their grip on the lantern, fingers flexing around the handle. Heat from the metal had leached away long ago; it was just cold wrapped in cold now.

"Arm okay?" Trevor asked.

"Fine."

"Knee?"

"It exists. It's doing its best."

"Heart?"

Rowan shot him a look over their shoulder. "Don't get poetic on me."

He held his hands up, lantern throwing strange shapes of finger bones across the stone. "Just taking inventory."

"You're not the one who has to fill out the incident reports if we fall down a shaft," Rowan said. "Focus on your ankles."

"Yes, ma'am."

They moved on.

The cold deepened as they passed another set of sealed niches. Faded numbers were carved in above the blocked recesses, the chisel marks softer with age. Rowan's eyes flicked over them automatically — 24B, 24C, 24D — filing their presence away.

Rowan's lantern light wavered for a moment, catching the edge of one niche just right. For a split second, it seemed like something darker sat inside, a shadow within a shadow.

Rowan shifted the lantern back, revealing nothing but blocked stone and old plaster.

Trevor's breath hitched once. "Thought I saw…"

"Trick of the light," Rowan said immediately. "These alcoves mess with depth perception. Brains like patterns. We fill in gaps with whatever's waiting behind the eyes."

"Comforting," Trevor muttered.

"It should be," Rowan said. "Means your brain's still trying to help."

"Feels more like it's auditioning horror films."

"That too."

Their shoulders brushed once when the corridor narrowed unexpectedly. Trevor pulled back fractionally, giving Rowan the full path. Rowan pretended not to notice the way his warmth briefly ghosted across their arm.

They walked like that for another few minutes, the rhythm of their steps syncing up again without either of them consciously deciding to match pace.

The drip of water grew louder, then faded as they passed the source — a thin line running down the wall from a hairline crack near the ceiling. Rowan touched it with the back of their hand.

"Still cold," they murmured. "Good."

"Good because it's not... what? Melting?" Trevor asked.

"Good because it means the upper levels haven't thawed enough to send a flood down here," Rowan said. "Last thing we need is to start wading."

Trevor grimaced. "You do this cheery forecasting every day?"

"Most days I just count flowers and knock ice off stairs," Rowan said. "You're getting the extended cut."

"Lucky me."

They reached another junction — a T-shaped break in the corridor. To the left, the passage narrowed sharply, roof slanting downward, the air from that direction heavier and more still. To the right, the passage kept its size but the darkness felt thicker, like a curtain hanging heavier in that direction.

Rowan paused, listening.

Nothing obvious: no voices, no shifting stone, no mechanical hum from the distant heaters on the main levels. Just the drip, their breath, the faint hiss of distant air moving through a vent they couldn't see.

"We keep right," Rowan said. "Left drops toward the sealed sections. No point."

Trevor nodded easily. "I trust you."

Rowan didn't reply. They turned right.

For a stretch, nothing changed.

Then, gradually, the silence grew a different kind of quiet.

It wasn't louder. Just... denser. The way a room feels when a conversation has ended but the air hasn't accepted it yet.

Trevor must have felt it too, because his next words came almost in a whisper.

"Does it ever... get to you?" he asked. "All this?"

Rowan kept their eyes forward. "Define 'get to.'"

"The being down here," he said. "Alone most nights. With all the... non-living neighbors."

Rowan considered that.

"It's work," they said. "Like any other."

"Most people don't spend their nights in catacombs," he pointed out.

"Most people overestimate their comfort with being seen," Rowan replied. "Up there, people look at you. Or worse, around you. Down here, I know where I stand."

"And where is that?" Trevor asked gently.

Rowan let the lantern skim over another number — 25A — checking their internal map.

"Between," they said. "Not in anybody's way. Not a spectacle. Just… necessary infrastructure."

Trevor was quiet for a beat.

"That sounds lonely," he said finally.

"It's accurate," Rowan replied.

He let that go. He was good at that — hearing something that could have been pulled apart, interrogated, dissected, and choosing instead to lay it down gently and leave it intact.

They walked on.

The cold shifted once, brushing against Rowan's neck like the memory of wind. Not a gust. Not a breath. Just a faint, unplaceable caress.

They shivered, more from nerves than temperature. Trevor must have noticed the movement.

"Warmer up top," he said, trying for something like brightness. "We'll get you cocoa or coffee or whatever your poison is when we're done being trapped in your workplace."

Rowan huffed softly. "You're assuming I'm letting you into my cocoa habits."

"I've seen your death-spiral staircase and your basement full of bones," Trevor pointed out. "I feel like beverage preferences are a reasonable next step."

"Mm." Rowan adjusted the lantern, letting his shadow stretch long ahead of them against the wall. "We'll see if you survive the tour first."

"Motivating," he said. "Thank you."

"You're welcome."

They rounded one more bend.

Up ahead, the corridor continued on in a straight, slightly downward slope. The air smelled faintly different — a hint of old incense and stone polish.

Rowan recognized it instantly. "We're getting closer to the chapel access," they said. "Once we hit that branch, we can decide whether to go up and try the east stairs or stay on the ring."

"Which do you recommend?" Trevor asked.

"Depends what the doors look like when we get there," Rowan said. "And how generous the ice has been feeling."

"So not generous, then?"

"Usually not."

They kept moving, their steps echoing in overlapping patterns — Rowan's stride precise and measured, Trevor's looser but careful. The silence between their words didn't feel hostile. It just felt full, like something waiting to see which way it would tip.

Rowan could feel the bridge memory dogging their steps. Not the image of it — they'd walked over that moment so many times in their mind it had worn a groove — but Trevor's new context for it. The fact that he'd seen —

Her.

Not as a blurred silhouette. Not as a nameless figure on a winter night. As a girl at a railing, alone, speaking to a stranger. As someone who had been reachable once.

She hated that.

Not because it hurt.

Because it made everything feel precarious in a way she hadn't planned for. Hope made the ground uneven.

She shifted the lantern to her other hand, shoulder aching now in a low, steady throb. Trevor noticed.

"Do you want me to carry it for a while?" he asked.

Rowan shook her head. "It's fine. My arm knows what to do with it. Yours swings too much. You'd paint the walls."

"That's a very kind way of calling me clumsy," he said.

"If I wanted to call you clumsy, I'd use the word 'clumsy,'" Rowan replied. "I like my job. I'm not letting you dent it."

Trevor smiled, small and real. "Fair enough."

They walked on.

The cold didn't recede, but it stopped pressing in quite as firmly, settling instead into a constant presence. The stone around them felt less like a tunnel and more like a throat — not actively swallowing, not yet, just holding.

Trevor hummed under his breath — nothing distinct, just a low, tuneless sound to keep silence from hardening.

Rowan let the sound ride beside her thoughts. It didn't make them feel safer. It didn't make them feel warmer.

But it did make the catacombs feel a fraction less empty.

That felt... dangerous, somehow.

She tightened her grip on the lantern and kept walking, deeper into the space between where they had been and where they were going.

The chandelier above them — that invisible, unspoken thing — stayed hanging.

Silent. Steady. Waiting.

The First Wrong Thing

They walked for a while without talking.

The corridor ahead narrowed and widened in quiet rhythms, the stone bulging where the earth had chosen to push back over the years. The lantern threw its cautious circle of light in front of them, retreating and regrouping with each step. Behind that circle, there was only dark, and behind the dark, the sense of more stone, more tunnels, more emptiness.

Rowan counted niche markers under her breath as they passed them.

"Twenty-six A… twenty-six B… twenty-six C…"

It was habit more than need. She already knew where she was. The counting just gave the air a shape.

Trevor walked half a step behind, close enough that Rowan could hear the soft scuff of his boots but far enough that their coat sleeves didn't bump. That small, respectful distance again. He'd given it back to her after the bridge and the conversation that wasn't one.

Rowan didn't look back at him. She kept her gaze on the next stretch of stone, the next curve. One thing at a time. Forward.

At first, she almost missed it.

The change was tiny, like someone had tuned the air half a step tighter. Rowan's lungs noticed before her mind did: a slight resistance when she inhaled, as if the space didn't want more breath in it.

Behind her, Trevor slowed.

His footsteps went out of rhythm with Rowan's for two beats, then stopped completely.

Rowan took two more steps before she realized she was alone in motion. The light dragged forward with her, pulling shadows tight, then snapped backward when she turned around.

Trevor stood where she'd left him, shoulders drawn in, head tilted slightly like he was listening for something that hadn't spoken yet. The lantern hung just shy of his knee, the flame smaller than it had been seconds before.

"Trevor?" Rowan said.

He didn't answer right away. His eyes were aimed past her, down the corridor, not at anything she could see—just into the space itself. His pupils had gone narrow again, the way they did when the light in his head was doing… whatever it did.

"Hold on," he murmured.

Rowan's heart gave a single hard knock against her ribs. "What's wrong?"

Trevor took and raised the lantern a few inches. The glass cupped the light like a trembling hand. For a moment, the flame flicked sideways, as if something had breathed on it from a direction that didn't exist.

"I don't know," he said. His voice was too quiet. "Something's... catching."

"Catching," Rowan repeated. The word felt wrong in her mouth.

Trevor pressed his free hand to the center of his chest, right over his sternum. "It's not a pull. Usually I get pulled—like there's a person at the end of a line tugging." He shook his head once, slow. "This is more like... stepping on fishing wire. You weren't looking for it, but now it's around your ankle and you can't shake it off."

Rowan glanced down the corridor. Stone. Curving away. The usual damp dark. Nothing waiting for them that they could see.

"What does that mean?" she asked.

"It means something's here," Trevor said. "But it's... wrong. Like someone tried to reach out and froze halfway through."

His fingers twitched where they rested against his chest. His face pinched, the way it always did before for him, more often than he'd care to admit. Except those times, there had been a living body attached to the feeling. A person he could walk toward.

Rowan felt her palms begin to sweat, despite the cold. "Are you in pain?" She saw the pain across his face.

"A little." He grimaced. "Like a migraine trying to fit through a keyhole." He blinked hard and forced his shoulders to roll, as if adjusting the fit of his own skin. "It's fine. I've had worse. I just... I've never felt it like this."

"Like what?" Rowan asked.

He finally looked at her then, and for a second, she wished he hadn't. There was something unsettled in his eyes, something that made him look younger.

"Like I'm late," he said.

The words dropped between them with a weight that caught Rowan off guard. She swallowed against the dryness in her throat.

"We didn't know we were coming down here tonight," she said. "You couldn't be late. You weren't expected."

"That's the problem." He drew in a slow breath through his nose, let it out through his mouth. "It's not about clocks. It's... there's usually still a choice. Some slack in the line. If I get there a little later than ideal, there's something left to salvage. This?" He shook his head again, more firmly now. "This feels like the choice is gone. Like whatever I was supposed to do already failed, and I'm just being dragged to the scene out of habit."

The headlamp-like focus in his eyes snapped back toward the corridor behind Rowan.

"Trevor." Rowan stepped closer without meaning to. "You don't have to go toward it."

The look he gave her then was almost apologetic. "You know that's not true."

The lantern brightened—not by much, just a subtle tightening at the core of the flame, a white-hot pinprick at the center that made the glass look briefly deeper than it should, amethyst trying to seep in around the edges.

Rowan's stomach dropped.

96

She tried again anyway. "There could be other ways out. We don't have to follow whatever this is. We can take another loop, go back toward the chapel, wait nearer the stairs—"

He moved past her before she could finish.

There was nothing hurried or reckless in it. No heroic bravado. Just the quiet inevitability of someone walking toward a sound they couldn't ignore.

"Stay close," he said softly. "If it's nothing, we'll just turn around and laugh about me being dramatic."

"You're not dramatic," Rowan said, following because the alternative was letting him go alone. "You're exhausting."

"See?" His voice flickered toward a smile. "Drama."

They walked.

Rowan shortened her stride to match his, whether he noticed or not. The stone underfoot felt the same as it had a minute ago, but the air didn't. It had that texture she recognized from the moments just before a storm: charged, but without obvious source. Her ears strained for new sound and found none, which only made the silence ring harder.

After a dozen paces, a smell hit her.

Faint. Metallic. Old.

Her brain supplied the word before she let herself consider it.

Blood.

97

She swallowed and told herself it could be anything. Rust. Old pipes. A nosebleed from days ago tracked on someone's shoe. Cemeteries were full of the echoes of blood. It didn't have to be—

The passage veered slightly right, and a narrow side corridor opened up on their left. Rowan had walked past it a hundred times. It led toward a dead-end maintenance pocket and a string of older niches.

Tonight, it didn't feel like a dead end.

The lantern tugged toward it.

Trevor's body followed.

Rowan's hand shot out and caught his sleeve.

"Don't," she said. The word came out thinner than she meant it to.

He glanced at her hand on his arm, then at her face. Her fingers were white where they clenched the fabric.

"You feel it now too," he said quietly.

Rowan didn't answer. She didn't have to.

The smell was stronger here. Not fresh. Not the sharp penny-sting of new blood, but something older, dried and cold. Like a copper coin that had spent a night in snow before someone picked it up.

Trevor dipped the lantern toward the narrow passage. The flame flinched, guttered, then steadied again, the gold paling at its edges as if some other color were trying to bleed through.

98

"Stay behind me," he said, gently this time, not in the protective bark of before but like he was asking her not to add herself to whatever waited ahead.

"Trevor—" Rowan tried. Her voice fractured in the middle. "We don't know what's—"

"It's already happened," he said. "Whatever it is. I can feel that much. There's no changing it now. That doesn't mean we get to look away."

He stepped into the side corridor.

The temperature dropped at least five degrees.

Rowan followed because her body refused to do anything else. The walls here were closer together, the ceiling lower, the air thick enough it felt like it had weight. Moisture clung heavily to the stone, beads of condensation fat and unbroken like the corridor had been sweating and no one had wiped it down.

Trevor walked three more steps and then stopped again.

The lantern's light reached farther than Rowan wanted it to.

The man was propped in a half-sitting, half-slumped position against the right-hand wall, near a sealed niche. His back rested against stone, legs sprawled crookedly, as if they'd buckled and twisted beneath him when he went down. His head lolled to one side, chin on his chest, hair plastered to his temple by something that had dried there and stiffened.

His name rose into Rowan's throat before she could stop it.

"Hal," she breathed.

Trevor went still.

He was wearing his winter work jacket. The same faded navy with the stitched-on patch over the breast: Greenlark Memorial – Grounds. The jacket was zipped halfway up, crooked, as if he'd tried to tug it closed against the cold and hadn't finished. One of his boots was missing; the other was still on, but the laces had snapped, leaving the tongue partly loose. His sock, visible on the bare foot, was dark, saturated to the ankle with something that had soaked and frozen in layers.

There was blood on the floor. Not in a dramatic pool, but in the slow, ugly way real blood moved once it had time. It had run out from under him in thin rivulets, following the shallow grooves and imperfections of the stone, then hardened there, a dark map of his last minutes. Some of it had climbed partway up the wall where his shoulder rested, leaving tide lines of brown-black that looked almost like smeared ink.

His right hand was raised, bent at the elbow, fingers hooked in toward his palm. They'd frozen that way. Two fingernails were broken down to the quick. Something pale and ragged was still under them— stone dust or scraped skin, Rowan couldn't tell and didn't want to.

His throat—

Rowan's body registered it before her mind did. A horizontal wound, too low to be from a botched hanging, too deep and too clean to be from a fall. The edges had opened and then collapsed again as the cold tightened everything, turning the skin around it waxy and tight. The dark line of it was almost black now, a sharp slash against the gray of his neck.

Rowan's vision tunneled.

Her knees hit the ground.

It wasn't graceful. Her left knee cracked against stone, pain jolting up her thigh. Her hand flew out to catch herself and landed in a patch of moisture she didn't look at too closely. The lantern's light swung wildly, throwing Hal's shadow up the wall in a jagged, reaching smear.

"Rowan—!" Trevor grabbed for her, but she was already folding.

Her breath came in a torn, ugly sound. Not the soft cinematic hitch of shock, but the broken inhale of someone whose body had decided to panic before they could decide not to.

"I know him," she heard herself say. Her voice sounded far away, too thin. "Trevor, I—I know him."

Trevor sank to one knee beside her, one hand hovering uncertainly at her back, the other clenching the lantern handle. "Rowan, hey, look at me—"

She didn't. She couldn't.

"He brings the wreaths," she said, the words spilling without permission. "Every December, he brings the wreaths for the front gates. He… he complains about the cold and then stays out in it anyways because 'the dead shouldn't look unattended on Christmas'." Her mouth twisted around the memory. "He has—had—had a dog named Pepper who keeps chewing his gloves, and he always smells like coffee and chain grease and…"

The next breath broke completely. She slapped a hand over her mouth, shoulders heaving once, twice. Her eyes burned hot, tears blurring the edges of Hal's shape into something softer and worse.

Trevor's hand landed on her shoulder, firm and steady. "You don't have to—"

"Why would you show me this?" she demanded suddenly.

The question wrenched out of her with too much volume for the narrow corridor. It cracked off the stone and came back smaller, distorted. For just a heartbeat, it had the feel of a line meant for an audience.

Trevor flinched at the force of it.

Then the façade shattered, or maybe it had never been façade at all. Rowan's voice dropped, dragged down by something heavier.

"He wasn't—he wasn't mine," she said, quieter. "He's not…" Her gaze skittered over Hal's face, the slackness of his mouth, the frozen stutter of his last attempt to speak. "This isn't how it's supposed to work, right? You said you see people because they're connected. Because they need you."

Trevor swallowed, his own face going a shade paler.

"I do," he said. "I'm supposed to. They're supposed to be alive when I see them. Or close." He forced himself to look directly at Hal's body, at the throat, the hand, the bootless foot. "He's not. He's… gone. I can feel it. Whatever line there was, it's cut."

The lantern flickered as if agreeing. For a moment, the flame guttered, revealing a seam of violet deeper inside it, then steadied again into its usual gold.

Trevor lowered it a little, letting the light pool more gently across Hal's form. The details softened, but didn't disappear.

"How long?" Rowan asked. She hated the way her voice sounded. Fragile. Small. Like she didn't spend her life down here among the quiet. "How long has he been like this?"

Trevor shook his head. "I don't... know in that sense. Time isn't stamped on it for me." He hesitated. "But the echo is faint. It's not... recent."

Rowan's stomach twisted. She'd walked this ring two days ago. Yesterday. Had she come this far? Had she passed this corridor and chosen not to look down it? Had he been slumped here while she made her rounds and counted numbers and knocked ice off railings?

She couldn't remember. That bothered her more than anything.

She pushed herself upright, legs shaky, and took a step closer to the wall. Her boots crunched faintly over a patch of something brittle—ice, she told herself, only ice. From this angle, she could see more of Hal's face. His eyes were open just enough to show the glassy slice of dark beneath his lashes. Something like dried tears had crusted at the corner of one.

Her breath fogged over him and dissipated.

"Rowan," Trevor said, "you don't need to—"

"I do." The words came out low, hoarse. "He worked for me."

That wasn't technically true. They both worked for the cemetery. No one belonged to anyone. But he'd been on her winter crew rotation. He'd answered her emails. She'd signed off on his overtime. She'd told him to go home early once when his back was hurting.

She stared at the broken nails, the blood. The missing boot.

"How does this happen down here without anyone noticing?" she whispered. "How long was he—" Her throat closed around the rest of the sentence.

Trevor let a slow breath out through his nose. "It didn't happen without anyone noticing," he said. "We're noticing it now."

"That's not what I meant," she snapped, then winced at herself. "Sorry. I just... we have protocols. Schedules. I saw his initials on today's sheet when I came in. I saw his name."

Something hot and messy prickled behind her eyes. She blinked hard, but one tear escaped anyway. It ran down, hot against chilled skin, and dropped off her jaw.

It hit the stone with a tiny, almost imperceptible sound.

Trevor watched her for a moment, the way someone watches a roomful of wobbling shelves, waiting to see which one is going to fall first.

"This isn't how it's supposed to work for me either," he admitted. "I've never been pulled to someone already gone. I'm not... I'm not an archivist. I don't get reruns."

"Then why?" Rowan demanded again, quieter but with the same desperate edge. "Why him? Why here? Why now? What does this do for anyone except hurt?"

Trevor didn't answer right away.

He set the lantern down gently on the floor between them, careful to avoid the dark rivulets, and lowered himself into a crouch beside Hal. For a moment, he just breathed, letting his face soften, letting whatever part of him did this work settle into whatever shape it needed.

Rowan watched his hand. It hovered above Hal's arm, fingers splayed, not quite touching.

"I'm not supposed to tighten knots," Trevor said finally. "I'm supposed to ease them. I don't force anything. If a moment is gone, it's gone. I can't reopen it. Can't rewind it." He exhaled slowly. "But sometimes there's residue. Not of the person—of the hurt. The world doesn't always know what to do with that, so it... sticks."

Rowan swallowed. "You mean..."

"I mean I don't think I'm here for Hal," Trevor said. His eyes flicked away from the body, landing somewhere around Rowan's boots. "I think I'm here for someone who has to live with this."

Rowan's skin went cold under her clothes.

"That doesn't make any sense either," she insisted. "You've only seen me one night before tonight. I'm not—" She gestured around at the walls, at Hal's crumpled form. "I work here. Death is literally on the job description. I don't get tuned up over it."

"Except you are," Trevor said quietly.

For a second, she hated him for that.

Not because it wasn't true.

Because it was.

"I knew him," she said again, helplessly. "And I didn't know he was missing."

105

The confession landed between them like a dropped tool.

Trevor didn't try to fix it. That, somehow, made it worse.

He shifted his attention back to Hal, studying the angles of how he'd fallen, the way his legs were arranged, the direction the blood had taken.

"There was a struggle," he said. "Here, and there." He pointed mildly with his chin toward a section of wall a few feet away where the stone was scuffed and a faint smudge of darker residue clung. If Rowan looked too long, she could see the shape of a handprint where someone had tried to brace themselves.

Her heart lurched up into her throat.

She remembered the phone call two nights ago. A muffled voice saying they were a little shorthanded, someone had gone home early. She hadn't asked who. She'd been halfway through her dinner and an email and thinking about the snow and—

Her knees wanted to give again.

"You should sit," Trevor said softly. "You're pale."

"No." She straightened aggressively, like that could hold her up by itself. "No, I'm fine. I'm not—" She cut herself off. Fine was the wrong word. "I'm... here."

The theatrics slipped back in on that last word. Just a shade. A tiny extra weight.

Trevor's brow furrowed, not in suspicion but in sympathy. He misheard performance as someone trying very hard not to fully break.

He picked up the lantern again, rose, and stepped just close enough to her that their shoulders brushed.

"I'm sorry," he said. "You shouldn't have had to see this."

Rowan let out a noise that might have been a laugh if it had any room to be. "You dragged me down here," she said. "In my workplace. During my shift. I think 'shouldn't' left the building a while ago."

"Fair," he said. "Then I'm sorry it had to be him."

That landed somewhere slightly left of her heart.

They stood there for another thirty seconds that felt like three hours. The cold pressed in, patient. Hal did what the dead did best and waited without complaint.

Finally, Trevor inhaled slowly through his nose. "We can't stay here," he said. "Not for long. Whatever this was, it's... static now. I can't untie it. I can't change it. But we can't pretend we didn't see it either."

Rowan wiped at her cheek with the heel of her hand. The tears had slowed, but hadn't fully stopped.

"What do we do, then?" she asked.

"You tell whoever you tell when something goes wrong down here," Trevor said. "Tomorrow. After dawn. When you can get back to the surface. And I..." He trailed off, looking faintly lost for the first time since she'd met him. "I stay with you. Because for some reason, that's where the knot is now."

Rowan hated that answer for how much sense it made.

She took one more step toward Hal, forcing herself to really look at his face. To see the man she'd said goodnight to outside the service door three nights ago. The one who'd laughed about his dog dragging his scarf through the snow and said he wouldn't be caught dead in festive socks.

"Hal," she whispered. "I'm sorry."

The words felt insufficient and stupid and late, but they were all she had.

She turned away before they could drag anything else out of her.

Trevor lifted the lantern higher, letting the light sweep one last time across the scene. As he turned, shadows swung back over Hal, folding him into them. The wound at his throat flashed once, reminded them it existed, then disappeared into the dark.

They stepped back into the main corridor like divers breaking the surface of a cold lake.

The air out here didn't feel warmer.

Rowan leaned a hand briefly on the nearest wall. The stone was damp, rough, blessedly solid.

Trevor stayed close enough to catch her if she slipped, far enough not to loom.

"We're not alone down here," he said quietly.

Rowan closed her eyes.

When she opened them again, her voice was steady.

"We never were," she said.

He nodded once, like that confirmed something he'd already suspected, and they started walking again, leaving the first wrong thing behind them in the dark.

The Wrong Turn

The silence followed them for a long stretch— not the gentle quiet of reverence, but a thick, pulsing stillness that clung to their clothes like frost. Rowan's boots echoed too loudly. Or maybe it was only that everything else had stopped making sound.

Trevor stayed close, a few feet behind her, letting her lead. He didn't speak, didn't try to make sense of what they had just seen. Even his light footsteps felt wrong in the dim, as though the catacombs themselves wanted them to tiptoe.

Rowan rubbed her thumb across the seam of her glove. Back and forth. Back and forth. The rhythm was the only thing holding her breath steady. She could still see Hal's frozen eyes if she blinked too slowly. She could hear her own voice—too loud, too panicked—still hanging somewhere back in that hallway, refusing to settle.

She hated how Trevor had looked at her then.
Like she was breakable.
Like she was grieving.
Like she was normal.

The echo of that look rattled inside her chest in a way she hadn't expected.

The corridor ahead opened wider before narrowing again into a long strip of stone. The lantern light stretched long shadows before snapping them short as Rowan passed beneath an arch. She reached her left hand out and dragged her fingertips along the cold wall. The stone was damp. Condensation beading. Too much moisture for this deep. Too cold.

Trevor cleared his throat softly.

She didn't turn.

They walked several more yards before he tried again. "...Rowan?"

She forced her hand to drop from the wall and kept walking. "What?"

"Do you—want to stop for a minute?"

"No." Too quick. Too sharp. She softened it immediately. "No. I'm fine. Just—processing."

Processing.
Trevor let the word sit between them. It didn't feel quite true, but he accepted it anyway.

Rowan felt the lie sit poorly in her throat. She slowed just a little, pretending to study the archway they were approaching. She knew it well—recognized the chipped corner, the faint green discoloration from a long-dried water leak. She'd repaired it once. She'd bled on it once.

So why did the sight of it make her stomach tighten?

She stepped under it—and stopped.

Trevor nearly collided with her. "Rowan?"

She didn't speak at first. She stared ahead, into a short corridor she knew should not have existed. Or... no. That wasn't exactly right. The corridor was real—had always been real. But the way it bent, the angle it took, the small alcove on the right-hand side—

Wrong.

It was wrong.

Slightly. Only slightly. But she knew these passages as intimately as she knew her own hands. She knew where cold drafts formed in winter, where floor stones rose slightly from old earthshift, where the walls sweated more heavily after storms.

This?
This corner was new.
Or looked new.
Or felt new.

Trevor followed her stare. "Is that not the way through?"

"It... should be." Rowan's tongue felt heavy behind the words.

Trevor's brow creased. "Should be?"

"It's fine," she said quickly, stepping away from him, away from the wrongness of the angle. "Let's take the central ring instead."

He studied her for a moment, the subtle tremble in her fingers, the way she avoided looking at the new corridor again. "Are you sure?"

"Yes."

They turned left instead of right, Rowan leading them into the safer, older loop that cut around the heart of the catacombs. The familiar walls steadied her pulse. But not by much.

Trevor caught up to walk beside her. Not imposing. Just present. His presence was warm in a way Rowan wished it wasn't.

After several dozen quiet steps, he finally spoke again—not loudly, not prying—but with a gentleness she hated for its accuracy.

"Rowan… how long had it been since you last saw Hal?"

She kept walking.
She didn't look at him.
Her throat tightened around the memory that wasn't a memory.

"Last week," she answered. "Or—maybe the week before. Time's weird in winter."

That was true. Entirely true.

Trevor nodded slowly. But she could feel him thinking through it, placing her reaction alongside her answer, comparing the grief of recognizing someone you worked with to the horror of seeing how that person died.

"How long have you been working alone down here?" he asked.

Rowan felt it in her shoulders—a small, involuntary hitch of breath. Trevor noticed.

"A while," she said. "The night crew rotates. Sometimes it's me, sometimes someone else. Depends who calls out."

114

Trevor's tone remained soft. "And you're down here most nights?"

"Most," she admitted.

That part wasn't a lie either—just not the whole shape of the truth.

Trevor glanced at her hands, at the way she wiped her palms on her coat. Once. Twice. Then again. The tremor in her fingers was faint but unmistakable.

"You're shaking," he murmured.

She stiffened instantly and hid her hands behind her back. "Cold."

Trevor didn't believe that, not fully, but he respected the boundary. He looked forward again.

Their footsteps echoed differently now—like something in the acoustics had changed. Not supernatural. Just… off. The space ahead felt narrower than it should. Rowan felt it in her ribs.

They were approaching a cluster of old memorial niches when Trevor slowed. The lantern dimmed slightly, no color shift, no flare—just a soft dip in light, like a candle flickering from a draft.

He stopped walking, held the lantern up, and frowned.

"That's strange…"

Rowan turned, careful to keep her expression neutral. "What is?"

Trevor angled the lantern, watching the faint tremble in its glow. "The wick isn't loose. The oil's fine. It's just… hiccupping."

Rowan's stomach tightened.
She said nothing.

Trevor looked at her, a thread of unease crossing his face for the first time. Not fear of her. Fear of this place. Fear of the unpredictability. Fear of whatever was bending the rules tonight.

"You felt that too, right?" he asked.

Rowan swallowed. "Drafts get caught in the tunnels. Makes the flame behave oddly."

Trevor didn't argue. But he didn't agree either.

He lowered the lantern, breath steadying. "Let's keep moving. Slowly."

Rowan nodded.
He stepped ahead, and she fell into step beside him.

As they walked, the cold behind them didn't fade. It lingered— like something had paused in the dark to watch them go.

Rowan didn't look back.
Looking back felt dangerous.

Trevor held the lantern just a little closer to her now.

Neither of them said another word.

This One Wasn't Supposed to Be Here

The lantern jerks so hard it yanks Trevor forward.

Not a flicker.
Not a pull.
A violent, downward wrench — like someone beneath the earth has grabbed it by the base and tried to drag it into the stone.

Trevor's boots slip. He catches himself against the wall, the slap of his palm echoing in the narrow corridor. The lantern glass bites heat through his glove, the flame inside spasming against the metal like something trapped.

A cold gust sweeps through the passageway — a sudden inhale of the tunnels themselves.

Rowan reaches him before he can stand straight.

"Trevor—Trevor, look at me—are you hurt?"
Her breath fogs in front of her lips, trembling with every word.

Her hands clamp onto his arm—cold, claw-tight—before she realizes how hard she's gripping him. She pulls back abruptly, wiping her fingers on her coat as if shocked by her own desperation.

"I'm sorry—I shouldn't have grabbed you—I just—are you alright?"

117

Trevor steadies the lantern. Its opal glow is faint now, a heartbeat-light pulsing weakly inside the glass.

"I'm fine," he says, though his pulse is pounding. "It wasn't me. Something pulled it."

Rowan's eyes fix on the lantern, the way you'd fix on a venomous thing. "Trevor... no more," she whispers. "Please. Whatever that was—please, not again."

Her voice carries a quiet, razor-edged dread.
Not fear of the lantern.
Fear of what the lantern is about to show.

Trevor mistakes it entirely.

"Easy," he murmurs. "Just stay close."

They move.

The corridor feels tighter than before — not narrower, but heavier, as though the air has thickened. The lantern strobes jittery light across the stone, revealing ridges, cracks, and old tool marks in brief flashes before swallowing them again.

Rowan's footsteps sound uneven beside him.
Trevor's echo once again seems delayed — as if the darkness is chewing on it before giving it back.

Then the smell hits.

Iron.
Thick enough that Trevor tastes it before he breathes it.

118

And beneath it — an antiseptic sting, chemical and wrong in an ancient place like this.

It clings to the roof of his mouth.
It burns faintly behind his eyes.

Trevor stops.
Rowan stiffens.

"Do you smell that?" he whispers.

"No," Rowan says too sharply. Too fast.
"Trevor, let's go. We shouldn't be in this hallway."

He watches her as the lantern's frail glow ripples across her face. There's terror there—real terror—but layered over something else. Something like bracing. Recognition. A flinch that isn't just fear of what they might see... but fear of what she already knows.

"Something's up ahead," Trevor murmurs.

Rowan swallows hard, throat tight.

They walk into a narrower passage, where the walls glisten with condensation. The moisture blurs the lantern's reflection, making the stone appear to breathe. A faint drip echoes somewhere far off — a single droplet puncturing the silence in long, uneven intervals.

Trevor rounds the corner.

And the lantern catches her.

The young woman sits slumped against the stone, back half-supported by the wall as if she'd been placed there gently. A rime of cold clings to her hair, darkening the strands. Her blouse is stiff with dried blood, the fabric warped and puckered around the wound.

Her throat is cut in a clean, unwavering line — too clean.
The sort of cut that knows anatomy.
Knows precision.
Knows intent.

Her arms rest neatly at her sides, palms upward. Her fingers curl delicately, like a doll's hand posed by someone both careful and unhurried.

Pinned to her shirt is a small, blank white card.
The lantern light reflects off its surface with a sterile gleam.

Trevor inhales sharply—cold rushing into his lungs so fast it burns.

"Oh… Rowan…"

Rowan steps forward like her body is being pulled by an unseen wire. Her eyes widen as the scene registers — the blood, the precision, the card — and the breath leaves her in one fractured sound.

At first she's silent.
Just staring.
Her face hollowing out in a moment that feels too long, too suspended.

Then something inside her gives.

"She… she didn't deserve to die like this…"
It comes out strangled, raw, as if dragged over broken glass.

She covers her mouth with both hands, shoulders folding inward. Tears slip down her cheeks faster than she can wipe them, dripping onto the stone at her feet.

Trevor reaches for her—instinctively, protectively.

She jerks away from him with a soft, wounded gasp.
Like touch might shatter her entirely.

"I can't—I can't look at her—I can't—Trevor, please—"

He steps between her and the body.
"Alright. Don't look. Don't look."

But Rowan is coming apart.

Her breaths come in sharp little bursts, her shoulders shaking as if she's trying to hold herself together by force. She presses her forehead to the wall, fingers trembling against the cold stone.

Trevor forces himself to look back at the young woman.
He doesn't touch her — even the thought feels intrusive — but he crouches near enough to see the details.

The cut is smooth as a blade through ice.
The blood spray on the wall is arched, controlled, not chaotic.
Her skin is pale and crisp with cold, suggesting she's been dead only hours.
Her legs are aligned perfectly, heels touching.
Her eyes are half-open — not wide in terror, but soft, unfocused.

"This isn't tied to you," Trevor murmurs.
"This isn't a memory. Or a Past. Or a Present. This isn't anything I've ever been shown."

121

Behind him, Rowan whimpers — a fragile, involuntary sound that echoes off the walls as if the catacombs are holding it gently.

Trevor rises.

The lantern flickers hard, shadows twitching sharply across the stone.

"Rowan…" he says softly. "I think something's wrong with the magic."

Her hands fall slowly away from her face.
Her eyes dart toward the body—just once—before she forces them elsewhere.

Trevor reaches out and rests a hand on her shoulder.
The cold beneath her coat feels deeper than the air.

She flinches.

Then, after a trembling breath, she leans into him — a small weight seeking warmth.

"Trevor…"
Her voice is barely a breath.
"Please. We need to go. Now."

Too urgent.
Too informed.
Too personal.

Trevor hears terror..

He nods. "Alright. Let's go."

They leave the body behind, Rowan keeping her gaze locked to the ground. Her steps jitter, uneven. Her breath fogs the air in short bursts as she fights to keep control.

Trevor lifts the lantern.
Its opal glow is now barely a pulse — a heartbeat under skin.

The darkness ahead feels denser.
Heavier.
As if the catacombs themselves are bracing for what comes next.

And somewhere deep inside Rowan Mercer, beneath the fear and grief and trembling panic—

a colder truth begins to stir.

This is only the beginning.

The Walls Are Too Close

The corridor changes the moment they leave the dead woman behind.

The cold sharpens into something brittle, slicing across Rowan's spine and making her shoulders curl forward as she pushes ahead of Trevor. Her boots scrape the stone in abrupt, jittering patterns. Her breaths come in thin, ragged bursts that bloom into fog and vanish as quickly as they appear.

Trevor keeps pace a few steps behind, the opal lantern trembling in his grip. Its flame sputters with an uneven pulse, throwing strips of broken light across the walls. The shadows respond by twitching and swallowing their footsteps before they can echo.

"Rowan," he murmurs. "Can you slow down a little?"

She doesn't.
Or can't.
It's hard to tell which.

Her posture is too tight, too held-together-by-threads. The catacombs absorb every sound she makes, muting the scrape of her boots and the stutter of her breath until the silence becomes something oppressive, heavy enough that Trevor's chest aches with it.

Rowan stops only when her hand strikes the wall—fingers splayed, palm flat, as if she needs the stone itself to keep her upright.

125

Trevor slows a few feet behind her, hesitant to close the distance without an invitation.

The wall seems to be the only thing holding her up.

Her voice slips out as a whisper, fragile as cracked glass.
"Why would someone do that to her? Why would they do this to... us?"

The last word falters, unintended, a slip of something deeper.

He steps a little closer, lifting the lantern to soften the light around her. "Rowan, none of this is your fault. You're overwhelmed. Anyone would be."

She pushes her hair back with a rough swipe of her hand—too forceful, almost angry at herself for feeling anything. "Sorry," she mutters, voice tight. "I just—sorry."

Trevor wants to help.
Rowan wants to disappear into the stone.

"We should keep moving," she whispers. "I can't... I can't be near that room."

Trevor nods gently. "We'll go together."

They move on.

The further they walk, the more the air changes.
The tunnels tighten, ceilings dipping low enough that Trevor instinctively ducks. Dust drifts down in a slow, shimmering fall,

catching in the weak lantern-light like ash suspended mid-drop. The walls begin to feel damp beneath Rowan's fingers, a thin cold moisture coating the stone like breath.

A faint mineral smell creeps in—iron, limestone, and something faintly earthy, like the first turn of soil in a grave.

Trevor's steps falter as dizziness slams into him. The corridor tilts, just for a heartbeat, and he stumbles sideways.

Rowan grabs him instantly, both hands gripping his arm with startling force, grounding him against the stone.
"Trevor?" Her voice cracks. "Talk to me—Trevor, please."

He blinks, vision stuttering with the lantern's flicker. "Yeah. I—yeah, I'm okay. The magic… the lantern… it's not behaving right."

Her expression goes taut—fear layered on fear—before she forces her face back into something neutral.

"Let's just go," she whispers.

He nods, and they press forward.

But the corridors twist in ways Rowan can't place.
A turn he doesn't remember.
A slope he doesn't recall descending.
A fork where there shouldn't be one.

Nothing supernatural—nothing that would betray the truth yet—but the kind of shifting that belongs to old, collapsing places where time and weight have pressed stone into new paths.

Their footsteps make no sound at all.

Rowan keeps brushing fingertips along the wall, grounding herself. Trevor watches her hand tremble—not just from cold, but something internal, something she's trying to cage.

When they reach the fork, she stops.

The lantern struggles to illuminate either path. The flame whistles faintly when it flickers, a thin sound like a held breath escaping.

Rowan's voice comes small, almost swallowed by the stone: "Trevor… there are things you don't know about me."

Trevor steps closer, careful, gentle. "You don't have to tell me anything you're not ready to."

She rubs her face with both hands—too hard, like she's trying to scrub something off her skin. Her breath shakes. "It's not that I'm scared. It's that I—"

The sentence fractures and dies.
Her jaw locks.
Her shoulders stiffen.
Her eyes dart to the shadowed tunnels like something there might spill the truth for her.

Trevor takes her hand.

This time she doesn't pull away.
She clings to him with a frantic, bone-deep grip.

"You're not alone," he says softly. "Whatever this place is doing to you—we'll get through it."

Rowan squeezes his hand harder—too hard, almost like she's drowning or punishing herself. The pulse in her wrist flutters rapidly, betraying everything her face tries to hide.

The lantern snaps violently, a burst of near-amethyst light that washes over their faces for a split-second—too bright, too sudden.

Rowan freezes.
The light collapses back into a weak, trembling opal glow. Rowan's features lock into place again, brittle and unreadable. Trevor lifts the lantern slowly, its flame wobbling like a heartbeat skipping beats.

They stand between the splitting corridors, suspended in the cold, breath turning to fog in the deadened air as the catacombs press close around them.

The Third Body

Trevor feels the temperature drop before the corridor narrows.

It's not the usual cold of these catacombs—the general, steady chill of stone and burial air—but something sharper, something that slices across the skin rather than settling into it. A thin, invisible blade glides along his jaw as the two of them walk deeper, the lantern's opal flame flickering with a faint, nervous pulse.

Rowan stiffens first.

She stops walking for a heartbeat, just enough to listen, to feel the space ahead of them. Trevor would miss the hesitation if he weren't watching her shoulders—how they rise, lock, fall, then fail to drop completely. She murmurs something under her breath, but the sound is swallowed by the stone.

Trevor lifts the lantern a little higher.

The corridor appears unchanged at first glance, but the shadows behave differently. They clump in corners, thicken along the ceiling, stretch strangely behind Rowan as though pulled by an unseen force. The air carries a faint, gritty dryness; every breath feels like inhaling powdered rock.

"Rowan?" Trevor's voice is soft. Concerned. "Talk to me."

She doesn't turn around. Her head tilts slightly, listening again. "Do you smell that?"

Trevor inhales—and nearly chokes.

The scent is unmistakable.
Copper. Fresh. Wet.
Wrong.

Not the faded metallic tang of old air or rusted hinges.
Not the stale, lingering scent from the previous two bodies.

This is sharp and new.
Vibrant.
Violent.

Trevor's stomach twists hard.

Rowan takes a step backward—then forward—then stops entirely. Her fingers lift to hover near her throat, trembling just slightly as if holding back a retch or a flood of memory.

Trevor moves up beside her. "Stay behind me."

She doesn't argue. She doesn't say a word.

He wishes she would—anything would be better than this silence.

They round the next shallow corner slowly, Trevor leading, lantern extended ahead like a fragile shield.

The shadows deepen, and for several steps, Trevor sees nothing. Only darkness and the thickening scent of fresh blood, so strong now it coats the back of his tongue.

Rowan's breath stutters beside him, shaky, rapid.

Then the lantern catches something on the stone floor.

A smear.

Long.
Wet.
Dark enough to drink the light.

Trevor crouches instinctively, lantern angled downward. "No, no, no…"

Rowan's breath breaks into a gasp that sounds half-sob, half-animal.

The smear runs along the left side of the corridor wall, dragged in a stuttering, uneven line. Fingertip streaks appear halfway through it—five distinct marks gouged upward like someone being hauled by the wrists, fighting against the floor with their hands.

Trevor stands.
His pulse hammering.

"Rowan," he whispers. "Stay behind me."

But Rowan edges closer anyway, drawn despite herself, her body bent slightly as though bracing for something she can feel before it is seen.

Trevor steps forward.

And the lantern reveals the third body.

The light hits the figure in pieces:

133

a shin, blood-soaked;
a hand, rigid and curled;
a shoulder at an unnatural angle.

Then the whole image snaps into focus.

A woman.

Late twenties, maybe early thirties.
Her clothes are torn at the shoulder and hip, soaked heavily on one side.
She has been propped sitting upright, back against the wall, but the angle is wrong—her head lolls just barely, chin dipped into the bloody collar of her shirt.

Her hair is dark. Very dark.
Close enough to Rowan's shade to be confusing in the half-light.

Her face—God, her face—
The exposed eye is half-open, staring upward, glassy and frozen in a moment of pure terror.
A deep, ragged slice runs across her jawline, trailing into a series of rapid, panicked defensive wounds along her arms.

Blood has pooled beneath her, still glistening wet.

Trevor inhales sharply.
His hand clamps around the lantern handle hard enough that the metal creaks.

Rowan doesn't scream.
She doesn't collapse.

She stops.

Everything inside her stops.

A sound escapes her—so quiet Trevor almost misses it. A small, choked whimper that shakes itself loose as if against her will. She presses one hand hard against her lips, the other curling into a fist by her chest as though she's trying to physically contain her reaction.

"Trevor…" Her voice cracks like a thin pane of glass. "Trevor, I— I know her."

Trevor's breath falters.

He turns to look at her fully now—and Rowan is pale in a way he hasn't seen before, eyes blown wide, body shivering so hard her hair trembles. She looks like she's unraveling from the inside, like the sight of this woman has hit her in some private, devastating place.

Trevor steps toward her, hands raised as if calming a wild, wounded animal.
"Rowan, don't look. Don't—"

But she is already crying.

Soft, broken tears falling down cheeks that had been stiff and quiet only moments ago.

She whispers, "Why would anyone do this? Why her? She—she didn't deserve—Trevor, this is wrong. This is so wrong."

Trevor swallows, throat tight.
"Rowan, hey—listen to me—look at me."

He gently grasps her shoulders.
She is ice cold.

135

"I'm right here," he tells her. "We need to move away from this. We don't know who did it or if they're still here. You are not safe."

The last words come out harsher than he intends—raw with fear.

Rowan's knees buckle.
Trevor catches her before she hits the ground, pulling her against him, her forehead pressed to his shoulder as she sobs into his coat.

"I don't want to die down here," she whispers. "Please, Trevor. Please don't let them hurt me."

Trevor's arms tighten around her instinctively, protectively.

"No one is going to hurt you," he says into her hair. "I swear to you—I won't let it happen."

Her fingers curl into the fabric at his back like she's holding on for her life.

When she pulls back slightly, Trevor cups her face in his hands.
Her tears catch in the lantern light.
She looks young suddenly.
And breakable.

He wipes her cheek with his thumb.
"Rowan… do you hear me? We're getting out. Together."

She nods, shaky.

Trevor guides her backward down the corridor—slow, cautious steps.
Rowan refuses to turn her back to the corpse, staring at it with a mixture of horror, grief, and a trembling disbelief Trevor misreads as trauma.

Her voice is a ghost when she finally speaks:
"I—I saw her last winter. We talked. She… she was kind to me."

Trevor's stomach flips.
Of course Rowan knew her.
Of course this is why the magic brought him here.

Someone is targeting Rowan.

His fear crystallizes into something sharp.

They reach a wide corner in the corridor and Trevor turns Rowan
away from the direction of the body, pressing the lantern against the
wall to cast more light around them.

"Sit," he tells her softly.

She obeys without argument.
Her legs fold underneath her, and she curls her arms around
herself. Trevor kneels in front of her, hands still shaking from
adrenaline, breath tight.

He brushes her hair gently behind her ear.
"You're okay," he repeats. "You're okay. You're okay."

Rowan looks up at him, her mouth trembling.
"Why is this happening to me?"

Trevor closes his eyes briefly, pained.
"I don't know.
But I'm not letting it take you too."

Her breath stutters.
She leans in, forehead touching his shoulder again.

Trevor holds her until her crying slows—though it never entirely stops.

As her breathing evens slightly, Trevor lifts the lantern again to check their surroundings.

That's when it happens.

The flame leaps.

Not just a flicker, not just a response to movement—but a violent, sudden surge of light that blasts across the corridor like a flare. Trevor jerks his hand back with a startled curse as the lantern fills with brilliant violet, the color deepening to rich amethyst for a full, pulsing heartbeat.

A rush of cold air sweeps past them.
Rowan gasps and grips Trevor's sleeve with both hands.

Then—

Just as fast as it came—

The light collapses.

The amethyst drains from the lantern in a rapid, shuddering breath, leaving only the weak, trembling opal glow behind.

Rowan's eyes are huge.

Trevor stares at the lantern with a sick realization tightening behind his ribs.

"That," he whispers, "is not supposed to happen."

Rowan swallows hard.
"What does it mean?"

Trevor forces a calming breath he doesn't feel.
"It means… the magic is shifting. It's reacting to something."

He doesn't finish the thought.

Rowan watches him carefully—her fear real, her trembling genuine, her grief like a black hole.

But somewhere behind her expression, buried deep,
something else waits.
Quiet.
Still.
Listening.
Learning.

Trevor doesn't see it.
Not yet.

All he sees is Rowan.

And all Rowan sees
is the lantern's weak opal shimmer reflected in Trevor's trusting eyes.

The tremor in her smile isn't sadness at all.

It's anticipation.

Lantern of Truth

Trevor can't stop shaking.

Not from cold—though the temperature has plummeted again—
but from the horrifying momentum of everything that's come before.
The third body's memory hangs over him like a suspended blade, and
Rowan sits curled in the corridor as though all her bones have
forgotten how to hold her upright.

She looks so small.

Trevor kneels a foot away, lantern cradled in both hands, the opal
flame trembling in a way it hasn't done before. It flickers in fits, as
though it's trying to gather enough breath to speak.

He watches Rowan's breath stutter in her chest.
She drags her sleeve across her cheek, smearing tears into the grit
on her skin. Her eyes are red, her lips parted, her palms resting
uselessly on her knees like she's forgotten what hands are for.

"Rowan," Trevor says softly. "Hey. Look at me."

She doesn't look. Not right away.

Her gaze stays fixed on the far corner of the floor—a dead,
unfocused stare. It's the stare of someone who's been pushed too far,

141

too fast, but something about the way her eyelids flutter seems strangely… deliberate.

Trevor leans closer, lowering his voice to a whisper meant only for her.

"You're not alone," he tells her. "Not anymore. I'm here."

Slowly—almost cautiously—Rowan lifts her head.

Her eyes find his.

Trevor's breath catches.
There's a hollowness in her expression he can't make sense of, like a candle whose flame has sunk into its own wax. She studies his face with an unreadable intensity, the muscles in her jaw tightening once, twice, as though she's deciding what shape her next thought should take.

"Talk to me," he murmurs. "Please."

She blinks—slow, heavy, sedated.

Then her eyes drift downward to the lantern.
To the quivering flame.
To the thinning opal glow that now looks more like a dying ember than a guiding light.

"Trevor…" she breathes.

He leans in before he even knows he's moving.

Her voice is a ghost of itself.

"This has always been for you…"

Trevor stills.

Her words slice through the silence with a delicate, unsettling precision.

Rowan's brow twitches.

Then she shakes her head—tiny, sharp, chillingly thoughtful.

"No. That's not right."

Trevor swallows, pulse thundering in his throat.

Her eyes rise slowly to meet his, something flickering behind them—not pain, not fear, not despair, but something else entirely. Something quiet and clean and dangerous.

"It was always for me."

Trevor's voice catches.
"Rowan... what are you saying?"

But she doesn't answer.

She doesn't breathe.
Doesn't blink.

She just watches him.

Something deep inside Trevor fractures, a soft crack like thin ice under too much weight.

The lantern jolts violently.

Rowan flinches.

Trevor clamps both hands around the handle, but the metal burns against his palms, vibrating like a live thing trapped in a cage.

The opal flame swells—bloats—whitens—

Then erupts into violent, blinding amethyst.

Trevor cries out, shielding his eyes.
The light floods the corridor, spilling into every crack, swallowing every shadow, devouring everything except Rowan's silhouette carved in stark relief against the wall.

Rowan gasps—not in surprise, but in something closer to recognition.

The amethyst light deepens, saturating the stone with unnatural brilliance.

Trevor feels the magic drag the air around him tight.

He knows what this is.

Not Past.
Not Future.

Present.

The truth.

Forced into being whether they're ready or not.

Whether Rowan wants it or not.

The flame hums, low and resonant and ancient, the sound of something very old waking from a long sleep.

And then—

The corridor splits.

The world blurs.

And the first vision bleeds into life.
The stone around them softens, going out of focus as if someone has breathed on glass. The corridor stays where it is, but another version of it overlays the first—offset by a fraction of a degree, like a reflection misaligned with its source.

Trevor's breath fogs in front of him.
Except—he realizes with a jolt—the air isn't that cold.

The fog belongs to someone else.

A woman stands a few paces ahead in the vision, superimposed over the empty stretch of tunnel. She's young. Wrapped in a thin coat that isn't meant for this kind of winter. Her hair is pulled into a loose knot at the back of her neck, frizz escaped and catching the phantom light.

She looks lost.

"Is that...?" Trevor's voice dies in his throat.

Rowan presses back against the wall, one hand gripping the stone at her side, the other hovering uselessly near her chest. Her eyes are huge, locked on the woman with a kind of horrified recognition.

"It's her," she whispers. "The second one. Trevor, that's—"

145

The name doesn't come. It breaks on her tongue, dissolving into a painful, strangled sound.

The woman in the vision shivers. She rubs her hands together, breath blowing out in quick, frightened bursts. She looks over her shoulder, into a darkness that doesn't exist in the corridor Trevor and Rowan are actually standing in.

Then, from just beyond the lantern's radius, another figure emerges.

The killer.

Trevor's pulse skips a beat.

He can't see the face. The vision's edges flicker and stutter just enough to blur those important details. But the shape—the outline—

Shorter than him.
Shoulders slightly rounded forward.
Head tilted in a familiar way when listening.

The coat sleeve flutters, the same length as Rowan's.
The hair falls to the same point on the neck.

Something cold and thin slides under Trevor's sternum.

"No," he breathes. "No, that could be anyone. It's just... it's coincidence."

The killer in the vision steps closer to the first woman.
Not rushing.
Not lunging.

Approaching.

Gently.

They say something Trevor can't quite hear. The sound is muffled, like voices through snow. But the tone—

Soft.
Reassuring.

The first woman's shoulders loosen a fraction, her posture shifting from defensive to hopeful.

Trevor's stomach rolls.

"Rowan," he says, trying to keep his voice steady. "Don't look. You don't have to see this."

But when he reaches back to shield her, his fingers graze only air.

She hasn't moved far, but she has slipped half a step out of the lantern's direct glow. The violet light hits her at an angle, leaving one side of her face in shadow.

Her eyes are glued to the vision.

Tears shine there—but her jaw is clenched, muscles working as though she's biting down on something hard.

The killer reaches for the woman in the vision.
And for an instant, the amethyst flicker clarifies just enough to expose the hands.

Not big.
Not rough.
Fine-boned, familiar.

Trevor looks down at Rowan's hands.

He tells himself it's not a match.

The lantern crackles.

The corridor stutters again, like a film jolting forward in the projector. The woman jerks, a flash of metal glinting in the corner of Trevor's eye—

—and then the vision snaps, blurs, smears into violet, and resets.

The first woman is gone.
The scent of blood—that sharp, metallic whisper—seems to seep in from somewhere Trevor can't locate.

Rowan's breath saws unevenly beside him.

"Why are you showing us this?" she whispers to the lantern. To him. To whatever force is behind all of this. "They're already dead. What's the point?"

Her voice shakes on the last word. It sounds like despair.

Trevor, aching for something to anchor to, believes it.

He wipes a hand down his face. The skin feels numb, like it belongs to someone else. "It's the Present," he says distantly. "It doesn't show what will happen. It shows what is. The truth of now." He swallows. "Sometimes… that truth is what we refused to see."

Rowan flinches at that. It's subtle, but the lantern catches the movement and makes it impossible to miss.

Before Trevor can parse it, the flame surges again.

The amethyst deepens, thickening into something almost physical.

The second vision hits.

In a different corridor now. One Trevor recognizes only by feel: the narrower section near the broken arch where they found the second body.

Except in the vision, the corridor is full.

There's a body on the floor. Alive at first, then not. The change is almost imperceptible; one moment she's breathing, the next moment she isn't. The magic doesn't linger on how it happened this time. It lingers on what came after.

The killer's hands slide under the victim's arms.
Lift.
Haul.

Boots squeal faintly on stone.
Flesh drags.

The head lolls, hair trailing.
Blood smears across the floor in jagged, broken lines—the same pattern Trevor knelt beside hours ago.

He feels sick.

"That's…" His throat closes around the words. "…that's not right. Rowan, this isn't—"

He stops.

149

Because as the killer strains, the coat pulls tight across the shoulders. The lantern makes the color bleed out, leaving little more than shapes and contrasts. But he can see the way the fabric hangs, the way the sleeves ride up when the wrists flex.

He's seen that coat. That exact coat.
He followed it through the snow the night they met.

The killer's boots slip. They catch themselves, plant their feet, continue dragging the corpse.

Trevor's gaze drops to the floor at his own feet, mapping where the real smear dried beneath the vision's ghost.

A dizzy wave passes through him.

"It could be anyone," he says again, except now it sounds like pleading. "We don't know. We're only seeing pieces. It could be someone you know, someone you—"

"Stop."

Rowan's voice isn't loud, but it cuts through his spiraling thought like a blade.

When he looks back at her, he finds her pressed flat to the wall, as though she's trying to fuse with the stone itself. Her chest rises and falls too fast. A tear has tracked a clean line through the grime along one cheek, but the rest of her face looks carved. Controlled.

Her eyes flick from him to the killer in the vision and back again.

"Please," she says. "Please don't make this about me."

150

Trevor's heart lurches.

"I'm not—I didn't mean—"

"I know what it feels like," she pushes out, words tumbling now, brittle and sharp, "to live in a world where everything terrible has to belong to you. Every bad thing is your fault, every hurt is your punishment. I am so tired of being the center of someone's tragedy."

Her voice breaks; a sob slips through, strangled and raw, and she covers her mouth with her hand as if ashamed of it.

Trevor is already moving, the lantern swinging wildly between them as he closes the space.

"Rowan, no," he says urgently. "That's not what I think. I don't— I would never—"

His chest aches with the need to fix this, to fix her, to fix something. He sets the lantern down between them, its glow pooling at their feet like liquid amethyst, and takes her gently by the shoulders.

"Listen to me," he says. "You are not a curse. Do you understand me? You're not a magnet for monsters. You're not a punishment. You're a person who got trapped in this place—like them. Like me. Whatever this… thing is showing us, it's not about blame. It's about truth."

"Truth," she echoes. It sounds like she's tasting the word for poison.

"Yes." His fingers tighten reflexively, trying to keep her from slipping away—emotionally, physically, he isn't sure. "If it wanted to hurt you, it would show you something else. It would show you your darkest memories, your worst choices. Instead it's— it's making you watch what was done to other people. That isn't punishment. That's…"

He searches for the word.

Mercy.

The thought brushes his mind like a cold feather.
He does not say it out loud.

Rowan swallows. Her throat works around something jagged.

Very quietly, she says, "You really believe that, don't you?"

He meets her eyes. "Yes."

There is nothing in him that doubts it. Even now, with the visions staining the corridor, with fear creeping up his spine, he clings to the version of Rowan he's come to know in these hours. Soft-voiced. Dry-witted. Startled by kindness. Braver than she thinks she is.

He would rather have his bones crushed by the truth later than drop her now.

Rowan's expression ripples.

For an instant, Trevor sees something like sorrow.
Not at what she's seen.
At him.

Then the lantern shrieks.

It's not a sound he hears with his ears, not entirely. It slices straight through his teeth, humming along the nerves in his skull. The amethyst flame elongates, spearing upward in a narrow column that nearly hits the glass.

The second vision shudders, then tears open wider.

The corridor in the overlay twists, and Trevor knows without knowing how that they've been yanked forward in time again.

The third body's corridor.

His hand flies back to the lantern, fingers closing around the handle as if he can stop what's coming by physically steadying it.

He can't.

The third victim appears in the vision exactly where her corpse sits in reality—half-propped against the wall, one leg folded beneath her, the other stretched uselessly forward. She's alive in this version. Shaky. Breathing in fast, hitching gulps.

Her hair is a dark, tangled curtain around her face.

Trevor doesn't want to recognize the pattern on her coat, but he does. He has seen it under harsh fluorescent lighting above a metal table. He has seen it on reports. He has seen it in the hollows of the eyes of people left behind.

Rowan's breath stops beside him.

The killer steps into view.

And this time the lantern does not blur.

The amethyst light sharpens, cutting around the figure with surgical precision. Every detail is rendered:

The fall of the hair.
The set of the shoulders.
The tilt of the head.

Rowan Mercer, as she truly is.

She kneels in front of the third woman. Carefully. Almost reverently.

Trevor's body goes cold.

"No," he says, but it's a cracked, paper-thin sound now. "No, that's—this isn't—"

Rowan reaches out in the vision.

Her hands are gentle.

She brushes the victim's hair away from her face, tucking it behind her ear. Her touch is soft, the way someone might touch a frightened child. Her lips move; this time the sound carries.

"There you are," she whispers to the woman. "I see you."

Trevor's heart stutters painfully at the familiar phrase.

How many times has she said something like that?
How many times has she savored it?

The woman in the vision sobs once. "Please… please, I don't want to die. I don't… please—"

"Shh." Rowan's voice is warm. Almost tender. She presses a hand to the woman's cheek, thumb stroking slowly back and forth. "I know.

I know it hurts. I know you're scared. No one ever came for you, did they? Not really. Not when it counted."

The woman's hands clutch at Rowan's wrists.

Trevor realizes his own hands are doing the same thing to the lantern's handle, knuckles bleached white.

Rowan leans closer, her forehead nearly touching the woman's.

"I'm here now," she says. "I'm listening. I see you. I see all of you."

Her smile is small and heartbreakingly sincere.

Trevor feels something inside him tear.

Rowan's hand leaves the woman's cheek and dips out of frame for a second.

When it returns, it's holding a blade.

The knife isn't enormous, isn't theatrical. It's plain, functional, already stained from other work. It looks almost embarrassed to be here.

Rowan's expression doesn't change.

"Please," the woman whispers. "Please, I'm not— I don't want—
"

"I know," Rowan murmurs. "You shouldn't have been left like this. You shouldn't have been forgotten." She cups the back of the woman's neck with her free hand. "No one will look away from you ever again. I promise."

Then, with the same calm tenderness she might use to cut a noose, she slides the knife between ribs.

The woman jolts.
Gasps.
Claws at Rowan's shoulders.

Rowan holds her, cradling her close, eyes never leaving the other woman's face.

"It's alright," she soothes, voice low and steady. "It's alright. You can stop now. I'm here. I'll carry it for you. I'll take it all."

The woman's body shudders, then slackens.

Rowan lowers her gently to the floor, arranging her limbs with an almost ceremonial care. She smooths the coat. Straightens the collar. Closes the woman's eyes with a brush of fingertips.

Then she sits back on her heels and exhales, a slow, satisfied breath.

A faint, peaceful smile touches her lips.

Trevor can't breathe.

Every part of him that used to know what mercy looked like recoils in horror.

The corridor around them wavers, struggling to contain both realities. The cold sinks into his bones; his knees feel numb, his chest squeezed, his lungs stubbornly refusing to pull air all the way in.

"No," he whispers again, but now the word is cracked open with something raw and terrified. "No, Rowan, no. You… you didn't… you wouldn't…"

In the vision, Rowan rises to her feet.

She reaches down, grabs the woman beneath the arms, and begins to drag her.

The scene aligns perfectly with what they saw earlier—the smear, the gouged fingerprints, the smudged trail toward where the body was ultimately staged.

Trevor watches his own footprints overlap with the ghostly ones in the vision.

"You told me you were alone," he hears himself say. He doesn't remember choosing the words. They fall out of him on reflex. "You told me you were just… stuck here, like them. Just like them."

Beside him, Rowan doesn't answer.

In the vision, her face is still soft. Not blank, not vicious. Soft. Serene. Radiant with the quiet joy of someone who believes, with their entire being, that they have righted a great wrong.

Trevor's throat closes.

She believed this was kindness.

The magic doesn't spare him a single moment of ambiguity. It doesn't jump away, doesn't blur, doesn't offer a convenient obstruction. It holds the image until the only thing left in his world is Rowan Mercer kneeling in fresh blood with a smile that looks horribly like love.

The lantern's humming drops an octave, turning into something like a groan.

Then the vision shatters.
The amethyst light implodes back into the glass, the corridor slamming into sharp focus around them. The real stone. The real damp. The real air.

The lantern dims to a small, trembling flame—still violet, still wrong.

Trevor realizes he's on his knees.

His hands are numb. His fingers ache where they've locked around the lantern handle. He loosens them slowly, blinking through the blur in his eyes.

There's moisture on his face. He doesn't remember crying.

"Rowan…" he whispers.

His voice barely exists.

He turns toward the wall where she'd pressed herself moments before—

—and finds empty stone.

"Rowan?" Louder now. Cracked. Frantic.

No answer.

Trevor staggers to his feet, the lantern swinging wildly, throwing warped shadows across the corridor. His legs don't seem to understand how to support him anymore; he lurches more than walks.

"Rowan!" The name tears out of him. The stone swallows it, offering no echo, no direction.

His heartbeat is a roar in his ears.

It can't be her.
The thought claws desperately at the inside of his skull.
It was her. He saw her. He heard her.

But it can't be her.

He stumbles forward, rounding the corner they'd used to retreat from the third body. The air feels thinner here, the cold slicing instead of numbing.

"Rowan, please!" he calls. Begs. "Just—just talk to me. Tell me it isn't what it looked like. Tell me something. Anything."

His voice fades into the dark ahead.

It feels like a long time before he hears his own footsteps change. The sound shifts as the corridor widens slightly, the ceiling lifting, the walls smoothing. Ahead, the stone seems almost polished, worn down by countless hands and backs and passing shoulders.

Trevor slows.

The lantern flickers once. Twice.

Then he sees her.

159

She stands at the far end of the widening tunnel, just before it spills into a larger chamber. She's facing away from him, her body outlined in clean silhouette against a wash of soft amethyst light pooling somewhere out of his sight.

Her posture is easy, balanced.
Not hunched.
Not broken.

You'd never guess she'd been crying.

You'd never guess she'd killed anyone.

Trevor's breath trembles out of him. "Rowan…"

She doesn't flinch.

The lantern's flame gutters in his hand, the glass chiming softly as it vibrates. For the first time since he can remember, he feels the magic recoil.

The light doesn't want to touch her.

That realization terrifies him more than the visions did.

He takes a step forward anyway.

"Rowan," he says again, louder this time. "Please. You don't have to run from me."

Her head tilts—barely. Just enough to show she's listening.

Trevor swallows.

"I saw you," he says. The confession hurts more than he expected. "I saw... I saw what you did."

The words are heavy, wrong-shaped, sticky in his mouth. Saying them feels like dragging his own ribs out through his throat.

For a long moment, she doesn't respond.

Then, slowly, Rowan turns.

The amethyst light from the unseen chamber behind her catches her profile first—nose, cheek, the sharp angle of her jaw. Then her full face comes into view, and Trevor's lungs forget how to work.

Her eyes gleam like polished stone, reflecting the violet light back at him. Beautiful. Inhuman.

There are still tear tracks on her cheeks.

"Trevor," she says softly.

His name sounds different now. Less like a lifeline, more like an observation.

He lifts the lantern a little higher.

It shudders violently, flame flaring, then shrinking, as though straining to retreat back into the fuel.

The magic is afraid of her.

The thought lands with a grim kind of finality.

His voice shakes. "Tell me it wasn't real."

Rowan studies him.

She doesn't look ashamed. She doesn't look proud. She looks…
curious. As though someone has handed her a mirror she's never seen
before, and she's not entirely sure what to make of the reflection.

"I don't lie to you, Trevor," she says quietly.

The words punch the air out of his chest.

He takes a faltering step back, the lantern scraping against his leg.

Rowan sees it. Something like hurt flickers across her face—
sharp, quick, genuine.

Then it's gone.

Her shoulders straighten. Her head lifts. She stands there in the
violet light—neither hiding nor advancing, neither apologizing nor
gloating.

Just existing.

Trevor feels the world tilt.

The Lost Soul he came to save is gone.

Or maybe she was never there at all.

Somewhere behind Rowan, deeper in the catacombs, a draft
brushes past, carrying with it the faintest whisper of all the voices that
have ever begged these walls for mercy.

This has always been for you, she'd said.

No. That's not right.
It was always for me.

Trevor's fingers tighten around the lantern until his knuckles ache.

"...Rowan?" he asks, one last time.

There's more in the word than a question. There's a plea in it. A history they barely had time to write. A future that just disintegrated under the weight of three bodies.

Rowan tilts her head the other way, regarding him with those strange, reflective eyes.

When she finally answers, her voice is almost gentle.

"You finally see me," she says.

The lantern's flame drops to a thin, shaking thread.

And Trevor understands—with a clarity that hurts—that whatever happens next, he is no longer standing beside a lost, frightened caretaker.

He is standing in the mouth of the trap she built.

The amethyst light behind Rowan flares once, briefly crowning her in violet.

The new shape of her shadow stretches toward him like a hand.

And Trevor ran.

The Hollow Corridor

Trevor doesn't move for a long time.

The corridor lies around him in the aftermath of the visions—quiet in a way that feels more like stunned disbelief than peace. The lantern's amethyst glow has dimmed to an unhealthy violet sputter, as though whatever power drove the visions drained it down to its marrow. The stone walls drink the light and offer nothing back. Shadows cling thickly to the corners, pulsing with the faint rhythm of something Trevor no longer trusts.

His fingers ache from how tightly he grips the lantern's handle, but loosening his hands feels impossible. If he lets go, he knows something inside him will split open, spill out, and never gather itself again.

He whispers Rowan's name.

It barely leaves his mouth.

"Rowan..."

His voice fractures around it, the sound trembling away as if the corridor itself wants nothing to do with it. The silence that follows presses into him with suffocating weight. His vision blurs. His knees give out. He slumps sideways against the cold stone wall, breath stuttering like a clock whose gears have slipped.

Tears gather without permission.

Not because he wants to cry.
Not because he's sad.
But because his body cannot understand what it's seen.

Rowan.
Warm-faced in the glow of Christmas lights.
Quiet.
Gentle.
Lonely.
Someone worth saving.

Rowan.
Standing over a dying woman.
Tender.
Serene.
Murdering like she was offering a blessing.

He squeezes his eyes shut, trying to steady the tremors running
through him.

"No… she—she didn't—" His voice shudders. "Please, no…"

The lantern flickers, casting its light unevenly across the corridor.
As it pulses, faint echoes of the past visions shimmer across Trevor's
eyes—Rowan's face haloed in warmth, Rowan's fingertips brushing
away a tear on her victim's cheek, Rowan whispering something he
can almost hear but cannot bear to decipher.

Trevor's chest tightens painfully.
He presses his forehead to the lantern's metal frame, breathing in
the warmth of it, the last vestige of something he once understood.

"Please," he whispers to no one, "don't let this be real."

But the lantern does not soften.
It does not comfort.
It does not deny.

It only flickers once—sympathetically, mournfully—and that hurts more than anything else.

Because the lantern never lies.

Trevor swallows hard, pushing himself up from the floor. His legs wobble, nearly folding under him. He forces himself upright anyway, because sitting still feels like surrender.

He wipes his eyes on his sleeve, though they immediately tear up again. He tries to breathe, but his breaths come short and uneven. He forces himself to move forward, step by step, drawn toward the spot where Rowan's silhouette had stood.

That horrible, quiet silhouette framed in amethyst.

Where she looked at him not as a friend.
Not as someone she trusted.
But as someone she was finally done pretending for.

Trevor stops when he reaches it.

The space is empty.
Hollow.
Silent.

He kneels, running trembling fingers across the stone floor. It's cold—colder than the rest of the corridor. Like she took whatever warmth she had left with her.

Trevor lifts the lantern higher, casting its violet shimmer across the walls. The corridor's shape seems different now. Not actually changed, but distorted by fear. Corners feel sharper. Shadows seem thicker. The air feels tighter in his lungs.

He takes a small, terrified step forward.

The quiet is broken by a sound—soft, delicate, almost polite.

A scrape.
Not far.
Not close.
Somewhere in between, like it came from the breath of the corridor itself.

Trevor's pulse leaps painfully.
He grips the lantern tighter.

"Rowan?" he calls out, though the name feels dangerous on his tongue now.
Not because she'll hurt him.
But because she might answer.

Only silence greets him.

He takes another step, lantern trembling.

The violet light stutters across the floor—and catches on something small lying near the edge of the corridor. Something soft and familiar.

Trevor kneels again, heart thudding against his ribs. He reaches out, fingers brushing fabric.

A glove.

Rowan's glove.

The one she wore on the bridge in the vision.
The one she clutched to her chest while crying in the cold.
The one Trevor had reached for before being pulled into the truth.

He lifts it carefully, as though it might crumble in his hands.

The fabric is stiff with cold but not frozen. The shape feels intentional—folded in on itself, left in the open like a breadcrumb. He closes his fist around it, pressing it to his chest, the sensation landing like a punch.

"Rowan..." he whispers into the glove, voice breaking, "why?"

The lantern spits a small, brittle spark—an involuntary sound that startles Trevor so violently he nearly drops both glove and lantern.

But he doesn't.
He can't.

He forces the glove into the pocket of his coat, his fingers lingering on it for a moment longer than necessary. Then—finally—he straightens.
The corridor behind him feels heavier now.

He turns slowly.

The shadows are thicker.
Darker.
Waiting.

His breath hitches.

He raises the lantern, light quivering over the stone.

"Rowan… we can fix this," he calls into the dark, voice splintering. "Please—we can fix—"

A sound cuts through him.
Soft.
Barely there.
Like someone letting out a long, slow breath.

Not words.

Just… presence.

Trevor's knees nearly buckle again.
He takes a single, terrified step forward anyway.

He feels her now. Not beside him. Not behind him.

But everywhere.

Watching.

Waiting.

And for the first time since he entered the catacombs, Trevor realizes something he should've felt sooner—

He is no longer the guide.
He is the guided.
He is the prey.
Trevor swallows against the dryness in his throat.

"Rowan?" he tries again, quieter this time. Not calling her back. Not anymore. Just testing the shape of her name in the air to see if it still belongs to the person he thought he knew.

There's no answer.

His boots scuff softly as he moves forward, lantern swinging in his grasp. The violet light throws uneasy arcs along the stone, catching on irregular textures and patches of damp. The catacombs feel different now—less like a maze and more like a throat.

He keeps one hand on the wall as he walks. Just to feel something solid. Just to prove to himself the world hasn't warped completely out of shape.

The glove in his pocket feels like it's burning. A heavy little ghost of fabric and memory.

Trevor tries to focus on practical things. The map of the tunnels in his head. The placement of the bodies. The route they took. The places Rowan hesitated versus the places she moved confidently.

He realizes, with a cold rush, that she was never trapped down here.

He was.

His steps slow.

He thinks of the first time he appeared to her. The way she'd looked at him on that bridge—like he was a miracle she'd never thought to ask for. The way she'd listened. The way she'd let him be warm for someone again.

Had she known then?

171

Had she known when she smiled at him afterward, whispering that line he'd clung to for years?

You showed me there's still something worth staying for.

Did she mean him?
Or just… the crown she had glimpsed through him?

The lantern's flame flickers erratically, a thin, anxious ribbon of violet hugging the wick.

"You brought me here for a reason," Trevor mutters under his breath, not sure if he's speaking to the magic, the stone, or himself. "You always do. You wouldn't show me that, and then just… leave me to it."

He doesn't know if he believes that anymore. But he needs to say it. Needs to pretend the rules still exist.

The corridor narrows, then widens again, spitting him into a low, broader section where the ceiling dips and the walls are crowded with old stone niches. The remnants of old plaques line the edges—names and dates half-erased by time.

The lantern's light runs over them like a reluctant hand.

Trevor slows, breath fogging faintly now as the temperature drops further. The silence here isn't empty; it's layered. Countless unspoken things pressed into stone.

"Rowan," he says, softer now. "You don't have to hide from me."

His words drift out, snag on the air, fall away.

He takes another step.

The prickle at the back of his neck intensifies, like a hundred invisible eyes just blinked at once.

He turns. Slowly. Carefully.

Raises the lantern.

The amethyst washes across the corridor behind him, but it doesn't push very far. It seems to curl back on itself, hesitant. The shadows near the far bend of the tunnel remain thick, stubbornly resistant to light.

Trevor's pulse jumps.

"I know you're there," he says.

He doesn't. Not for sure. But fear has a way of filling in blanks with certainty.

"I saw what you did," he continues, voice tremoring but holding. "But I also saw you. Before. On the bridge. In the past. You... you could've let go. You didn't. You stayed. You listened. You were kind. You can't tell me that wasn't real."

He waits.

A long, long beat.

Then—
A sound, faint, like the scrape of a foot on stone. Or a shoulder grazing the wall. Or someone shifting their weight in order to keep standing still.

It comes from the darkness just beyond the lantern's reach.

Trevor's heart slams against his ribs.

"We are not done," he says, surprising himself with the certainty in it. "You don't get to vanish after showing me that. You don't get to decide what I know about you and then… shut the door."

Another stretch of silence.

He feels ridiculous, talking to shadows.

And then, from the dark:

A whisper.

Not words.

Just the exhale of someone who has been holding their breath for a very long time.

The tiny flames along Trevor's spine ignite, racing upward.

He takes one step toward the dark. It feels like stepping off a ledge.

The lantern panics.

It flares, then shrinks, violet flame twisting, glass rattling in its metal frame. It tugs backward, the weight of it seeming to double in his hand as if something is trying to pull him away.

Trevor tightens his grip.

"I'm not leaving her," he tells it through clenched teeth.

The flame steadies, if not willingly, then begrudgingly.

He moves forward, the violet light crawling along the floor ahead of him. The shadows part reluctantly.

A bend in the corridor appears, sharp and sudden.

Trevor pauses, bracing one hand on the stone, listening hard.

Nothing.

Just his own breathing.
Too loud.
Too fast.

He swallows. "Rowan... I don't know what you think you're doing. But I am not afraid of you."

That's a lie.

He is terrified.

Of her.
Of himself.
Of what it means that he still wants to help her, even now.

The glove burns in his pocket like a brand.

He rounds the bend.

The tunnel beyond is narrower, almost claustrophobic, forcing the lantern light into a tighter cone. The ceiling dips more here. Trevor has to duck slightly. The press of stone above his head makes him feel like the earth itself is leaning closer to listen.

This section is quieter than the others. No distant drips. No shifting of rock. Even his footsteps sound small and cautious, like they're afraid to disturb something sleeping.

He is halfway down this throttled stretch of corridor when he sees something else on the floor.

He almost misses it.

Another small, familiar shape, half-tucked against the wall as though abandoned in a hurry.

Trevor's throat closes.

He crouches, the lantern's light concentrating around the object.

A second glove.

The pair to the one in his pocket.

He picks it up slowly.

This one is warmer.

It shouldn't be.

He turns it over in his hands. The fabric smells faintly of cold air and something like cedar. The cuff is worn in a way that speaks of years of use.

He can see Rowan's fingers in this. The way she curled them against the bridge railing. The way she tucked them under her arms when she told him she was always invisible.

The lantern hums, low and anxious, as he holds the glove there in the light.

"Rowan…" he whispers. "Why are you leaving pieces of yourself?"

The question hangs there, fragile.

He closes his fist around the glove, feeling his own pulse beating against it.

"You're not a monster," he says. It hurts to push the words out, but he does. "You made monstrous choices, but that's not all of you. It can't be. You don't kill them like someone who hates them. You…"

He stops, because finishing the thought feels obscene.

You kill them like someone who loves them.

He flinches from the truth of it.

"I need to understand," he says instead. "That's all. I need you to explain it to me before…"
Before I lose you completely.
Before I have to try to stop you.
Before I have to watch what the magic will do to you for this.

The lantern shivers in his hand, as if it understands all the unfinished sentences anyway.

He tucks the second glove into his other pocket, suddenly absurdly aware of how weighed-down his coat feels. Like he's walking around with Rowan's heartbeat split in two and stored against his sides.

"You said it was always for you," he murmurs.

The words from earlier replay in his mind, ticking like a clock.

This has always been for you. No. That's not right. It was always for me.

He takes another breath that doesn't quite make it all the way into his lungs and forces himself forward.

***

He doesn't hear her move.

He only feels it.

The prickle of being watched spikes sharply, sending a jolt up his spine. The breath of air on the back of his neck—warm compared to the corridor—makes every muscle in his body seize.

Trevor spins, lantern jerking.

The light smears across empty stone.

His heart hammers in his ears.

"Stop hiding," he says, but the words come out ragged. "Please. Stop hiding and talk to me."

The silence that follows feels deliberate.

Then—a sound.

Barely audible.

Like fabric shifting. A coat brushing a wall. Something—or someone—choosing a different vantage point.

She's not running.

He realizes it with a sudden, horrifying clarity.

She's repositioning.

The lantern feels like it weighs a ton now. His hand aches from holding it up, but the idea of lowering it makes his skin crawl.

Trevor backs up until he feels stone against his shoulder blades. He takes small breaths, slow and careful, trying not to hyperventilate.

"Rowan," he says, and this time, saying her name feels like stepping into a confessional. "I'm not your enemy."

A tiny, almost imperceptible sound drifts from somewhere ahead of him—a breath that could almost, almost be a laugh, if laughter had ever learned to be that quiet.

The corridor seems to darken by degrees, not because the lantern is dimming, but because the shadows are thickening on purpose. Familiar spaces become uncertain; the distance between him and the far bend feels elastic.

He licks his lips. "If you wanted to hurt me," he says slowly, "you would have done it already. So what are you doing?"

The answer comes not as a word, but as an absence.

She doesn't approach.
She doesn't retreat.

She waits.

For him.
To step forward.
To choose.

The lantern quivers again, glass chiming softly like a warning bell.

Trevor stares into the dark and feels the weight of the choice pressing down on his ribs.

He could turn around.
Backtrack.
Try to find another path.

But there is no other path now. Not really. Not for him.

He tightens his grip on the lantern, feels the two gloves resting against his sides like twin stones, and takes a step forward.

The darkness swallows him.

The magic protests, flickering violently.

He goes anyway.
By the time he realizes he has no idea how far he's walked, the corridor has widened again. The ceiling lifts, easing some of the physical pressure on his body, but mentally he feels no lighter.

The amethyst glow stretches a little farther here, licking at the edges of stacked stone crypts and carved alcoves. The air smells faintly of dust and something older, something that might've once been flowers.

His footsteps echo differently. The sound carries now, bouncing off distant walls before throwing itself back at him distorted.

He stops.

"Rowan," he says, voice ragged. "I don't know where you are. But you know where I am. You've always known. So if this is about me seeing you…" His throat tightens. "…then come out and be seen."

For several heartbeats, nothing.

Then, to his left, just at the edge of the lantern's reach, something shifts.

He trains the light there.

For a split second, he catches a hint of movement—a suggestion of a figure—then it's gone again, retreating just beyond the violet wash like it's playing with the border between light and shadow.

Trevor's stomach drops.

"You're watching me," he says quietly. "Please tell me that means you haven't given up on… being more than this."

He's not sure what "this" is. A murderer. A monster. A new kind of spirit waiting to be crowned.

The lantern seems to shudder in his hand, its flame thinning to a fragile thread.

The air carries another breath. Closer now. Behind him? Above? It's impossible to tell. The sound scrapes the inside of his skull.

He turns in a slow circle, lantern raised, heart pounding so loud he's sure she can hear it.

"Rowan," he says, and the word is equal parts plea and rebuke, "if you're going to run, then run. If you're going to kill me, then do it. But please, for the love of whatever's listening down here, do not haunt me from ten feet away."

The echo swallows his voice whole.

He waits. Muscles tense. Light twitching.

From somewhere down the corridor—faint, almost intangible— comes that same exhale.

And though there are no words, something in the shape of it feels like an answer.

I'm not running.

Trevor closes his eyes for half a second.

He opens them again, lifts the lantern higher, and takes another step toward the waiting dark.

Quiet Hunt

Trevor keeps walking because stopping would kill him faster.

The corridor rises and dips in gentle, uneven breaths, worn by years of unseen winters and forgotten bodies. The lantern feels heavier than it did an hour ago—like the magic inside it is fatigued, resisting the shape he forces it into. The violet glow is sickly now, limping across the cold stone in uneven pools.

He presses forward, breath shivering out of him in short, unsteady bursts. The weight in his pockets—the gloves, keys—knock softly against his hip with each step.

They're too warm against his hips.
Almost like living things.

"Rowan…" he whispers into the narrow dark, "please don't run from me."

But she isn't running.

He knows that now.
Knows it with the certainty that sinks into the bones, uninvited and undeniable.

She's choosing distance.
Choosing silence.

Choosing when and where he sees her.

His boots echo in thin, uneven patterns across the stone. The sound feels wrong somehow—too small, too swallowed, like the corridor is pressing in its own breath to listen.

The air grows colder the deeper he moves, and with it comes the soft, almost imperceptible textures of sound:

A fabric whispering against stone.
A shift of weight.
A faint click, like the edge of a heel turning.

Sounds that don't belong to him.

Trevor stops, heart pounding, lantern trembling in his grasp.

The silence swells thickly around him, heavy with the feeling of eyes.

He turns slowly, lifting the lantern so the violet glow splays out in unfocused arcs. His breath fogs faintly.

"I know you're there," he says. "Rowan—I know you can hear me."

A sound answers him, but only barely—a soft, controlled exhale somewhere too close to ignore and too faint to chase.

Trevor shivers.

"I won't hurt you," he tries, though the words hurt him to speak. "You know I won't. I would never."

The lantern stutters violently, jerking once in his grasp like it's flinching.

Trevor's jaw clenches.

"I still believe in you," he whispers.

His voice cracks so painfully that he closes his eyes for a moment, grounding himself against the cold stone wall. When he opens them again, the corridor ahead feels smaller somehow, like the space has tightened its ribs around him.

He walks.

***

The floor slopes downward for a stretch, forming a shallow tunnel of stone that feels older than the rest of the catacombs. The ceiling dips low enough that Trevor ducks instinctively. The lantern flashes bright for a heartbeat, then dim again, then bright—flickering like a heartbeat under siege.

He stops at the bottom of the slope.

A small object sits perfectly centered on the stone path.

Trevor's stomach lurches.

Not dropped.
Not scattered.

Placed.

The lantern trembles in his hand, its light outlining the object in a thin violet halo.

He crouches slowly.

It's a hair tie.

Black elastic, stretched on one side, a few strands of dark hair twisted through it. He knows it like he knows her gloves, like he knows the soft tremble of her voice when she said she'd always been invisible.

Trevor swallows the hard, cold knot forming in his throat.

She wore this earlier.
He saw it in the vision.
Saw her twist her hair up, hands gentle, careful.

He picks it up gingerly, fingers brushing across the loose strands clinging to it. It feels like touching a memory.

"You left this for me," he whispers.

He doesn't know if it's accusation or plea.

The lantern spits a spark that makes Trevor flinch, its flame warping to a needle-thin point before stabilizing again.

"Rowan… what are you trying to tell me?"

Silence, layered and patient.

He tucks the hair tie into his pocket with the gloves. The weight there tightens his chest—not guilt, not dread… something heavier.

He stands.

Keeps going.

And as he walks, something becomes horribly clear:

He didn't find that hair tie by chance.
He was supposed to find it.

Every step forward feels chosen, curated, designed for him.

"You're leading me," he murmurs.

The words echo down the stone corridor.

They do not return.

***

The corridor splits without warning—left and right, twin tunnels yawning like two diverging arteries. The lantern coughs light at both choices, unable or unwilling to point him in either direction.

Trevor licks his lips.

"This isn't funny," he whispers, voice trembling. "I'm not—this isn't a game, Rowan."

The lantern dims as if exhausted.

Trevor steps toward the left path—

—and freezes.

Because at the far end of the right-hand corridor, standing just inside the edge of shadow, is Rowan.

Not a hallucination.
Not the silhouette from before.
Not a smear of movement.

Rowan.

Her.

Full, real, unhidden.

Her hair falls loose around her shoulders, strands catching faint violet light. Her coat hangs open, the left sleeve slightly torn. Dust clings to her boots. Her face is quiet—eerily so. No fear. No panic. No apology.

Her hands hang loosely at her sides.
Her posture is relaxed.
Her breathing calm.

She watches him.

Trevor's legs lock. His breath collapses in on itself.

"Rowan…" he breathes.

She doesn't blink.

The tilt of her head comes slowly—graceful, controlled, almost compassionate. But the compassion isn't for him.

It's for what comes next.

His chest tightens painfully.

"Please," he whispers. "Please don't—don't disappear again."

For the briefest moment, her expression flickers—
not remorse, not hesitation, but recognition.

Of the fact he's still following.

Of the fact he hasn't run.

Then—
Rowan turns.

She pivots on one heel, her movement fluid and calm, and walks
away. No hurry. No sound. No fear.

She simply steps into the dark and is swallowed whole.

Trevor gasps and stumbles forward instinctively, lantern jerking
in his grip.

"Rowan!"

His voice cracks, raw and sharp.

Nothing answers.

Only the echo of his own cry fading into the stone.

He looks down the right-hand corridor, where Rowan vanished.

Then he looks down the left.

It's not a choice.
Not anymore.
Not even close.

He steps into the right-hand corridor.

The lantern flickers, almost tugged by invisible fingers, pulling him deeper.

He follows.
The deeper Trevor follows into the right-hand corridor, the more the space feels intentional.

The ceiling lowers.
The walls narrow.
Every footstep lands in a place that feels pre-measured, like he is walking through a funnel designed to thin out possibilities until only one remains.

The lantern's violet glow claws at the stone, its reach shrinking, shrinking, shrinking as if smothered by the weight of the air.

Trevor's breath grows harsher.

"Rowan…" he calls softly, afraid to disturb the quiet more than necessary. "Where are you going?"

The silence behaves strangely here. It doesn't swallow sound; it shapes it. The echo of his voice is wrong—thin, light, as though drifting through a long tunnel of cotton instead of stone.

Then—

A soft exhale behind him.

Warm.

Human.

Deliberate.

Trevor spins, lantern snapping upward like a drawn weapon. The purple light slices across the walls, the ceiling, the floor—nothing. No one. Only the faint ghost of warm air fading off his neck.

He stands frozen, heart galloping.

She was there.
Behind him.
Close enough to touch him.

And she chose not to.

His fingers tighten around the lantern's crooked handle. It flickers, then steadies—barely.

Trevor steps backward until his shoulders press lightly against the stone wall, grounding himself. His breath trembles with each inhale.

"You're not running," he says, much quieter now. "You're positioning."

He swallows.

"You're leading me."

Silence stretches long enough to answer him without words.

Trevor drags in a breath and keeps moving.

***

The tunnel slants downward and then cuts sharply right. Trevor has to duck instinctively, the uneven stone arch forcing him into a bow. The lantern throws short, jagged rays across the floor that flash against the outcroppings.

The smell changes too.

Not decay.
Not fresh blood.

Something metallic.
Cold.
Like the air just before a storm cracks open the sky.

Trevor freezes—not from fear, but from the recognition of atmosphere shifting around magic.

This wasn't here before.
This wasn't part of Rowan's world until the lantern changed color.

His throat tightens.

"The Present is coming…" he whispers.

Not fully.
Not yet.
But it's bleeding in—sharpening the edges of this reality.

Trevor quickens his steps.

He doesn't realize he's trembling until the lantern handle rattles lightly against his grip.

***

The corridor widens abruptly into a small alcove—no larger than a bedroom—roof fractured, stone pieces scattered across the ground like old bones.

And there she is.

Again.

Rowan stands on the far side, in the shadow of a half-collapsed archway. Her shoulders are slightly bowed, her head angled downward like she's examining something on the floor between them.

Trevor's breath collapses in his chest.

"Rowan."

She doesn't lift her head.

The lantern lowers instinctively as Trevor steps closer, hesitant, cautious.

"What are you looking at?"

His voice barely carries.

No response.

He steps closer still, the violet light stretching forward like a hand reaching toward her—
and then it hits the body.

Trevor stops so abruptly his breath hacks out of him.

A fourth body.

Laid out with awful, deliberate precision.

The upper torso is twisted, but not broken. The head faces the wall, hair matted. The throat—
Oh God.

Trevor slaps a hand to his mouth, gagging silently.

It isn't ripped open.
It isn't slashed.
It's crushed.

Finger-shaped dents bruise the skin in an almost perfect pattern, as if someone with inhuman strength squeezed down until bone splintered.

Trevor's knees wobble.

"No…" he whispers. "No, no, no—"

He drops to a crouch without meaning to, lantern quivering violently in his shaking hand.

He can't breathe.

He can't look away.

This isn't the work of a weapon.
This is intimate.
Personal.

Hands-on.

"Rowan," he says, voice breaking. "Who did this? Who—"

"Don't."

Trevor jerks upward at the sound of her voice.

Rowan has finally lifted her head.

Her eyes catch the violet light and glow faintly, like the gemstone mounted in the lantern itself. Her expression isn't empty—it's focused. Quiet. Measured.

"I didn't want you to see them like this," she says softly.

Trevor's stomach flips. His throat burns.

"Rowan... talk to me. Please. Don't shut me out."

But she steps backward into the darker fringe of the alcove, retreating—not like someone hiding, but like someone luring.

Trevor rises too quickly, nearly losing his balance.

"Rowan—wait—don't leave me with this—"

She lifts a hand, barely.

Not a wave.
Not a stop.
Just a gesture that chills him to the bone.

An invitation.

Then she turns and slips through the yawning black of the archway, vanishing soundlessly.

Trevor stares at the empty space where she stood, breath shaking so violently his teeth knock together.

The lantern flame leans toward the archway as though pulled.

Trevor wipes shaking fingers across his eyes and forces himself to follow.

Trevor steps through the broken archway, and something in the air shifts—so subtly he doesn't register it until he inhales.

The temperature drops another degree.
The silence tightens.
The space feels narrower, as if the stone itself is leaning in to listen.

The corridor beyond the archway is long, straight, and unfamiliar—not the looping, winding catacombs he and Rowan navigated earlier. This one feels... engineered. Like whatever part of this maze he's entered wasn't meant for the dead, but for something else entirely.

Trevor's hand is trembling so hard he has to grip the lantern handle with both hands just to steady it. The violet light jitters down the stone passage, stuttering with each breath he takes.

"Rowan?" he calls quietly.

No answer.

Only the faintest sound of soft steps far ahead—almost too soft to be real. A scrape, a whisper, the hush of cloth brushing against itself.

She's not running.

She's walking.

Measured.
Deliberate.
Patient.

Trevor's lungs constrict.

He follows.

***

The corridor stretches longer than it should—long enough that the lantern starts to dim from strain, flame thinning into a pale violet thread.

He moves faster.

"Rowan, please. Please—stop running from me."

His voice echoes in warped, delayed fragments, the acoustics bending and folding until the words sound hollow, stripped of breath.

His heartbeat thunders in his ears.

Then—
He sees something ahead.

Not Rowan.
Something smaller.

Trevor stops short, breath collapsing.

A ribbon.

Light blue.
Delicate.
Covered in dust.
Crushed gently at the center as if someone held it too tightly.

Trevor's hand trembles as he crouches and picks it up.

It doesn't belong here.
It doesn't belong in a catacomb.

It belongs in someone's hair.

He looks down at the ribbon, his throat clamping tight.

"Rowan..." he whispers. "Why are you leaving these behind?"

He turns the ribbon over slowly.

And then he notices something he didn't expect:

It's warm.

Not body-warm.
Not fresh-warm.

Warm like it was held.
Recently.
Long enough for the heat of a palm to soak into the fabric.

Trevor blinks back sudden tears.

"You're not warning me," he murmurs. "You're... marking the path."

The lantern flickers sharply, the flame spasming like a startled heartbeat.

Trevor stands, tucking the ribbon into his pocket with the gloves and the hair tie. The weight of her belongings drags at his coat, twists at his ribs.

He pushes forward.

He can't stop now—not when she's leaving a trail that feels so intentional.

***

The corridor widens again, this time into a low chamber with a ceiling that seems to pulse with moisture. Stone ribs arch overhead like the inside of an enormous throat.

Trevor steps inside carefully.

The air is different here—sharper, electric, like something is about to happen.

He lifts the lantern.

And freezes.

Because standing at the far end of the chamber, half-turned toward him, is Rowan.

Not vanishing into shadow.
Not slipping away.
Not hiding.

Standing still.

Waiting.

Her hair is tangled, loose around her face. Her shoulders are relaxed, arms hanging easily at her sides. Dust clings to her coat, glints faintly under the trembling violet light.

Trevor's mouth opens, but nothing comes out. His breath is a ragged, broken inhale.

"Rowan…"

She looks at him.

Really looks at him.

The expression on her face is impossible to read—neutral, but not cold; present, but not pleading. It's the expression of someone who knows exactly what she's doing.

Trevor steps toward her instinctively.

"You don't… you don't have to do this," he says, voice shaking. "You don't have to hide. You don't have to run. I'm not your enemy."

Something flickers across her face—too quick, too slight to name.

Not remorse.
Not fear.
Not guilt.

Recognition.

Of the fact he's still following her.
Of the fact he still believes in her.

She lifts her chin almost imperceptibly.

Trevor's breath catches.

"Rowan," he whispers, "please... talk to me."

She turns her head slightly, eyes sliding past him to the corridor behind him—as if checking whether the path is clear.

Trevor goes rigid.

She's not afraid of him.
She's not hiding from the truth.
She's checking that he's cut off.
That he's contained.

"Rowan...?" His voice cracks. "What are you doing?"

Rowan's gaze returns to him, and she takes one slow step backward. Just one.

An invitation.

Trevor's chest tightens in a violent twist of panic and ache.

"Don't... don't leave," he pleads. "Just don't—"

She tilts her head.

Not in pity.
Not in apology.

In acknowledgment.

Then she turns and walks into a tunnel on the far side of the chamber.

Trevor stumbles after her, lantern shaking wildly in his hands.

"Rowan!"

His voice ricochets off the walls in fragmented bursts.

He plunges through the narrow entrance after her—

And feels the temperature plummet.

The lantern dims to a trembling violet thread.

Trevor's breath catches.

She's close.
He can feel her pulse in the air.

He forces himself forward.
The tunnel Rowan chose is different from the others.

No winding.
No uneven dips.
No branching paths.

A single corridor, straight as a blade, leading down into a slice of darkness that swallows the lantern's purple glow before it can reach more than a few feet ahead.

Trevor's boots drag softly over the floor. The dust here is different—finer, lighter, rising in ghostly little puffs that swirl under the lantern's tremulous light, as though disturbed by more than just his steps.

Some of the dust trails spiral in strange ways, curling and twisting like strands of breath.

She walked this way moments ago.

He was getting.

His chest pulls tight.

The lantern shivers violently once, its flame shrinking into a tense, thin curl of amethyst.

Trevor pauses.

"Please," he whispers into the corridor, his voice raw, cracked down the middle. "You don't have to do this. Whatever this is— whatever you think has to happen—it doesn't. You're not alone. I see you."

A soft scrape answers him.

Not ahead.
Behind.

Trevor spins so fast he almost drops the lantern.

Nothing.

Just the empty corridor stretching behind him, the walls leaning in with quiet, predatory patience.

A bead of sweat runs down the back of his neck.

He forces himself to pivot back the other way—

And nearly stops breathing.

Because Rowan stands at the far end of the tunnel.

Not where she disappeared.
Not where she should be.

But here.
Waiting.
Directly in front of him.

Trevor gasps and staggers back a step, the lantern jerking up instinctively.

The violet light brushes across her form—her hair, her coat, the faint dust smudging her cheek—and she looks almost ethereal, like a figure pulled halfway out of a dream and caught between dimensions.

"Rowan…"

She doesn't move.

Her expression is calm—eerily so. Neither apologetic nor triumphant. Neither kind nor cruel.

Just… resolute.

The hair tie.
The gloves.
The ribbon.
The still-warm air on his neck.
Her silhouette after the reveal.
Her head tilt.
Her retreat into the dark.

204

None of it was random.

Everything that's happened has been Rowan choosing where he goes, how he sees, what he thinks he's chasing.

Trevor feels the truth rise like a tide in his chest:

She has been staging this.

Every corridor.
Every scrap she left behind.
Every appearance.
Every disappearance.

"Rowan," he chokes, "why? Why are you doing this?"

Her head tips, just slightly—
an acknowledgment of his seeing it
at last.

The lantern trembles violently in his hands.

Trevor takes a single step forward.

"Please talk to me," he whispers. "Please. Don't let this—don't let it be this."

Rowan's gaze softens.

Barely.
Fleeting.
Like a single snowflake melting on a warm palm.

It's enough to break him.

"Rowan—"

Before he can finish, she moves.

Not fast.
Not with violence.

Just a slow, fluid step backward into deeper shadow, her silhouette thinning, dissolving, slipping beyond the reach of the lantern.

Trevor lunges forward—

"Rowan!"

His voice cracks like a bone snapping.

The lantern jerks with him, flame leaping high—
and then slamming inward as though pulled by invisible force.

The amethyst glow tightens into a hard, focused needle of violet that points—not ahead, not behind—

Directly down at the floor.

Trevor freezes.

He lowers the lantern slowly.

There, carved into the stone floor beneath his boots, is a thin scratch—

a long, perfect line.

A dividing line.

A boundary.

Trevor sways.

Rowan didn't run.
Rowan didn't vanish.
Rowan didn't retreat.

She crossed the line, intentionally.

A threshold.

A marker.

A place where she wants him to follow.

A chill slams down his spine.

"You're choosing the ending," he whispers.

His throat burns.

"You're choosing where I die."

The lantern trembles violently, purple flame throbbing like a trapped heartbeat.

Trevor stands there in the narrow corridor, the line at his feet, the dark swallowing every inch ahead of him—

and the truth settles fully, finally, brutally:

Rowan isn't hunting him because she needs to.

She's hunting him because she planned to.
All along.

His breath shatters.

He steps over the line.

The lantern jumps, flame warping into a thin, sharp spike of
violet—

and the darkness ahead seems to exhale, welcoming him in.

The Present Unwrapped

The lantern convulses in his grip.

It doesn't flicker.

It fractures.

The flame splits into three slender shards of light—white, gold, blue—then slams inward and erupts into a single violent bloom of deep amethyst, bright enough to blind him for a heartbeat.

The corridor buckles.

The air shivers, thickening like gelatin around him. The walls tremble with a groan so low Trevor feels it before he hears it.

He staggers backward, shoulder slamming the stone.

"Wait—no—p-please—"

His voice sounds warped, as if dragged through water.

The lantern surges, a pulse of amethyst radiating outward. Stone ripples. Dust lifts off the ground in thin spirals. For a single impossible second, Trevor feels time stutter—like the corridor inhales sharply and then forgets how to exhale.

Trevor drops to one knee, gripping the lantern with both hands.

"Not yet," he begs. "Please—not yet—"

But the Present doesn't wait for anyone.
Not even him.

A wave of light crashes through the corridor, folding reality back
like a page being peeled open.

Trevor gasps—

And the next vision hits him like a fist.

***

He doesn't fall into it.
It falls into him.

The corridor blinks away.
A different corridor—still stone, still cold—floods into existence
in a violent wash of amethyst.

And Rowan stands in it.

Not Rowan tonight.
Not the Rowan who left him small artifacts like breadcrumbs.
Not the Rowan watching him from the shadows.

Rowan as she was in the act.

Her hair tied back.
Her expression calm.
Her hands steady.

A body lies at her feet.

212

Trevor's breath catches in a soft, wounded noise.

"No—"

Rowan kneels beside the body with the clinical ease of someone tying a shoelace. Her fingers check for a pulse she already knows isn't there. Her head tilts with detached precision. Her gaze is steady, unfazed.

She looks like she's completing a necessary task.

Not savoring.
Not regretting.

Just doing what she chose to do.

Trevor whispers her name like it might undo the moment:

"Rowan…"

The vision cracks apart, reality swallowing him whole as he collapses onto both hands, palms scraping against stone.

"No… Rowan, I don't understand—I—"

His voice breaks—not loud, not dramatic.
Just soft and devastated.

Heartbroken.

The lantern pulses once more.

Trevor barely has time to wipe his face before the next vision slams into existence.

213

***

This one is deeper.
Longer.
Heavier.

Rowan drags the second victim by the arms, boots scraping across the stone. Her breathing is steady. Her movements careful. She pauses every few steps to adjust her grip, realigning the bloodied weight so it won't fall awkwardly.

Trevor's whole body tenses.

"Stop—please—please don't show me more—"

But the Present doesn't ask permission.

Rowan pulls the corpse into a narrow corridor, arranging it with a strange sense of intent. Not artful. Not ritualistic. But deliberate. A positioning. A staging.

Trevor's throat closes.

The truth begins to take shape.
The trap wasn't an accident.
It wasn't coincidence.
It wasn't survival.

It was architecture.

She built this night.

Trevor presses his fist to his mouth, trying not to sob aloud.

"Rowan… oh God… what did you do…"

214

The vision blinks out.

Trevor sways, almost falling.

The lantern's glow dims for a moment—
quiet, apologetic—
before roaring violently back to life.

And the third vision detonates.

***

This one doesn't flash.

It unfolds.

Slow.
Unstoppable.

Trevor squeezes his eyes shut but the vision forces itself in anyway, blooming in the darkness behind his eyelids.

Rowan stands over the fourth victim.

Her hands close around the throat.

Not quick.
Not impulsive.
Not rage-filled.

A slow, certain crush.

The man's legs kick weakly. His fingers claw at her wrists. Rowan doesn't flinch. Her jaw sets. Her breath is calm.

And then—
softly, gently—
she hums.

A tune Trevor recognizes.

The same melody she hummed as a child near the Christmas tree.
The same warm, hopeful song that once saved her life.

Trevor's breath collapses with a shudder.

"No—no, Rowan—stop—please—stop—"

She doesn't stop.

He can't stop her.

When the vision finally tears away, Trevor stumbles back into the
real corridor, gasping as though he's drowning. Tears streak his face,
hot against the cold air.

And then he hears it.

A voice.

Soft.
Quiet.
Close.

"You weren't supposed to see it yet."

Trevor's head jerks up.

Rowan stands at the far end of the corridor, the lantern's amethyst glow catching her eyes and setting them aflame.

She isn't hiding now.

She's watching him break.

Trevor's first word is a whisper torn from the center of him:

"Rowan…"

She steps toward him.

Slow.
Calm.
Certain.

Trevor flinches.

"Rowan, please… don't… don't do this, don't—don't be this—"

His voice fractures on its own grief.

Her face softens.

Barely.

"You finally saw," she says.

Almost tender.
Almost proud.

Trevor's world cracks open.
Trevor presses himself against the wall as if the stone might somehow hold him together. His breath comes in short, trembling

217

pulls, the kind a person takes when the world they believed in has snapped underfoot.

Rowan moves another step closer.

Not hunting.
Not looming.

Approaching.

As though this is just the next natural part of the night.

The lantern's amethyst glow flares around her edges, outlining her in violet fire. Dust clings to her coat, her hair, her lashes. She looks almost ethereal like this—beautiful in a way Trevor hates himself for noticing.

"Don't be afraid," she murmurs.

Her voice is calm. Soft enough to be mistaken for kindness.

Trevor's breath shakes.

"I-I don't... I don't understand," he whispers. "You saved me... you helped me through the tunnels... you—you were trying to get us out—"

Rowan tilts her head slightly, the gesture gentle, almost affectionate.

"No, Trevor. You misunderstood."
A faint smile ghosts across her lips.
"I wasn't trying to escape."

His heart stutters painfully.

Rowan steps closer, closing half the distance between them. Trevor wants to back away, but the corridor is too narrow—there's nowhere to go, nowhere to breathe, nowhere to make this untrue.

Her voice lowers.

"I've been waiting for you."

Trevor's whole body goes cold.

The lantern flickers violently as if protesting the meaning behind those words.

Rowan continues, a quiet breath leading her into the truth:

"Those people… the ones you saw…"
She lifts her chin slightly.
"I didn't kill them for protection. Or survival. Or fear."

Trevor's throat constricts so sharply he can't speak.

"I killed them," Rowan says softly, "because they were lost."

He stares at her, unable to process.

"And lost souls," she continues, "draw you."

Her eyes flick briefly toward the lantern flame.

"You hear them. You smell them. You feel the break in them like a heartbeat."

Trevor's knees nearly buckle.

"Rowan… please… please don't say this—"

"You answered me," she says.
Very quietly.
Very simply.

Each word is a weight.

"I needed you. So I called you."

Trevor shakes his head, tears slipping down in slow tracks.

She steps closer.

"You came to me the night I almost jumped," Rowan says gently. "The night on the bridge. The night you saved me. You called it mercy." Her gaze sharpens. "But it wasn't mercy."

Trevor flinches as though struck.

"You gave me a taste of hope," she says. "And then you left. You left me in the same world that broke me. A world that never listens. Never sees. Never stops demanding we survive alone."

Trevor's breath breaks into a sob he tries to swallow down.

Rowan's voice doesn't rise.
It doesn't sharpen.
It doesn't tremble.

It grows quiet.

Honest.

"The world doesn't want to be saved, Trevor. It wants to be rescued."

A soft breath.

"And rescuing isn't mercy. It's slavery."

Trevor presses his hand to his mouth, trying to hold in the sound threatening to escape.

Rowan's gaze softens with something like pity.

"You help people," she says. "But you don't heal them. You give them new chains. You give them permission to keep hurting."

Trevor closes his eyes, tears falling freely now.

"Rowan… don't… please don't do this…"

Her voice sharpens—not with anger, but clarity.

"I refuse to be saved again."

A beat.

"I refuse to keep waiting for someone else to find me in the dark."

Trevor opens his eyes, trembling.

She steps close enough that he can feel her breath.

"Why shouldn't I decide who deserves hope?" she whispers.

The words drop like a blade between them.

Trevor's heart caves inward, a silent, brutal collapse of everything he's believed in.

"Rowan," he manages, voice barely there, "you murdered those people."

"Yes," she says.

No shame.
No boast.
Just truth.
Cold and certain.

"And I would do it again," she adds quietly, "if that's what it took to bring you to me."

Trevor feels something inside him crack.

Not loud.

Not dramatic.

Just a soft, breaking thing.

His voice comes out as a whisper made of pain:

"Why me?"

Rowan leans her head, almost tenderly.

"Because you're the only one who ever saw me," she says.
"And the only one who never should have."

Trevor's breath hitched sharply—
and that's when Rowan takes her final step forward.

Her voice is soft as snowfall:

"I didn't kill them for you, Trevor."

She lifts her eyes to his, unblinking.

"I killed them to summon you."

Trevor's world implodes.
Trevor can't breathe.

Not from fear.
Not from the cold.
Not even from the visions still burning behind his eyes.

He can't breathe because something inside him—
the part that believed Rowan could never be this—
has shattered so quietly he almost doesn't feel it,
he only feels the aftershock.

He presses his back to the stone wall, his fingers trembling so
hard the lantern rattles against its handle.

"You…"
His voice breaks.
"You're a murderer. Rowan—Rowan, you killed them."

"Yes."

The word lands softly.
Too softly.
As though it should bring him comfort.

Trevor shakes his head, swallowing a sob that still slips out
around the edges.

"No... no, you—Rowan, you're good, you're so good—" His voice cracks into something thin and aching. "You saved me that night on the bridge... you talked to me like I mattered... you told me I wasn't alone—"

Rowan's expression flickers—just briefly—into something too complicated to name.

"I meant every word," she says quietly.

Trevor's breath fractures.
"Then why—why would you do this?"

"Because hope," Rowan whispers, "is a beautiful lie."

He recoils.

"No—no, Rowan, please—"

Rowan steps closer, slow and steady, like someone approaching a frightened animal.

"You think hope saves people," she says.
"You think mercy is a gift."

Her voice doesn't rise.
It tightens.
Not sharp—precise.

"But mercy is a leash."
A breath.
"And hope... hope is a knife you hand to the world so it can cut you again."

Trevor squeezes his eyes shut, tears slipping free.

"Stop… please stop…"

"You didn't save me," Rowan murmurs. "You stalled me."

Trevor's eyes snap open, wounded.

She continues before he can speak.

"That night on the bridge, I was ready to let go. Ready to fall. But you appeared and told me things could change."
She laughs—just once, a quiet exhale with no humor.
"And for a moment… I believed you."

Trevor's voice is a breathless whisper.
"I wasn't lying."

"I know you weren't." Rowan's expression softens, almost fond.
"And that's the problem."

Trevor looks like he's been struck.

Rowan steps closer still. She is only a few feet away now, the lantern's violet glow painting her face in cruel, soft lines.

"I lived because you told me to," she says.
"Not because I chose to."

Trevor's knees weaken.

"Rowan…"

"And I won't do that again."
She tilts her head gently, as though explaining something difficult to a child.

"I won't let anyone—any person, any magic, any ghost—tell me how to live or who to save."

Trevor feels the truth sliding into place like a blade slipping between ribs.

"You killed them…"
He swallows painfully.
"You killed them so I'd come find you."

Rowan's voice is quiet.
Affectionate, almost.
"I needed your light."

Trevor shakes his head violently.
"No—no, Rowan, this isn't you, this isn't who you—"

"It's exactly who I am."

Her tone is gentle.
Dangerously gentle.

He stares at her with red, trembling eyes.

"But you—"
His voice wavers.
"You said you were invisible. You said no one ever saw you."

"You saw me," Rowan says simply.
"And I saw you."

A faint smile touches her lips.
"In some ways, Trevor… we've been walking toward this night since that first Christmas Eve."

Trevor's whole body trembles.

He doesn't know when he started crying again, but the tears slide down silently, hot against his cold skin.

"You didn't summon me," he whispers, wounded.
"You manipulated me."

"No," Rowan says softly.
"I aligned us."

His heart breaks.

Quietly.
Completely.

He takes one step back.

Rowan notices.

Her eyes soften into something like recognition—

—right before Trevor turns and runs.

He bolts down the corridor, breath tearing out of him in ragged bursts, boots hammering against the stone as the lantern's amethyst glow whips wild arcs across the walls.

Behind him:

A single, calm step.
Then another.
Then another.

Rowan doesn't chase.

She follows.

Measured.
Patient.
Exactly as much distance as she intends.

Her voice drifts into the narrowing corridor, warm and terrible:

"Run, Trevor.
You'll only get as far as I need you to."
Trevor doesn't think.
He just runs.

Every instinct in him screams for escape, for air, for space—
anything but the tightening sensation that Rowan is behind him,
walking with the serenity of someone who already knows the
outcome.

The corridor he sprints down bends sharply, stone scraping his
shoulder as he stumbles through the tight turn. The lantern jerks
violently with each panicked step, throwing frantic spasms of amethyst
light across the walls.

His breath is fast, shallow, torn.

"Please," he sobs into the dark. "God, please—"

He doesn't know if he's begging the universe
or the catacombs
or Rowan
or himself.

The path widens suddenly, opening into a crooked chamber with
cracked stone columns and a floor uneven with ancient debris.

Trevor's ankle rolls, and he nearly goes down, catching himself on a broken pillar. His palm stings—blood smears the stone.

He turns, trembling.

Rowan is not there.

The chamber is empty.

Trevor lets out a shuddering breath—half relief, half terror.

"Okay," he gasps. "Okay, okay… think—think—"

He takes a shaky step backward.

"Maybe she—maybe she took the other path—maybe—"

A whisper of air moves behind him.

Trevor whirls—

Nothing.

But the cold in the air thickens.
And the stone at his back feels warmer.
As if someone stood there a moment ago.
As if someone is very close.

He slowly raises the lantern.

"Rowan…?"

His voice breaks in the middle—like a snapped violin string.

Silence answers him.

229

But the silence is wrong.
Weighted.
Expectant.

Trevor swallows hard, backing slowly toward the next corridor.

"You don't... you don't have to do this," he whispers to the empty chamber. "You can still choose something else. You're not trapped yet—you're not—"

His shoulder brushes stone.

Not the wall.

Something hanging from it.

He turns the lantern—

And sees a fresh gouge in the stone.
A long, singular scrape.
New.

Made by something sharp.
Deliberate.
Purposeful.

A mark.

Trevor chokes on a breath.

"No... no, no, no—Rowan, please—"

A footstep.

Soft.
Barely there.

He spins to the left—nothing.

To the right—nothing.

Above—nothing.

But behind him—

He feels her.

Not touching.
Not speaking.
Just there.

The sensation of being observed, studied, understood so deeply it hollows him out.

Trevor squeezes the lantern tighter, tears blurring the amethyst glow.

"Rowan—please—I don't want to be afraid of you—"

"You're not."

Her voice is so close he flinches violently, nearly dropping the lantern.

He spins—

But she isn't in front of him.

The corridor behind him is empty.

Her voice drifts from somewhere deeper, softer:

"You're afraid of what comes next."

Trevor's heart pounds against his ribs.

He stumbles backward into a narrower tunnel, breath shaking, boots scraping across uneven stone.

He lifts the lantern—

And sees her.

Down the corridor.

Standing in the amethyst light as though it belongs to her.

Trevor's breath collapses into silence.

Rowan doesn't move.
Doesn't blink.
Doesn't chase.

She only lifts her head slightly, eyes glinting in the violet.

The air between them feels living.

Charged.

Certain.

Trevor whispers, barely audible:

"…why are you doing this…?"

Rowan's lips part.

Her answer is a single, quiet truth:

"Because this is the only way you'll understand me."

Trevor takes one stumbling step back—

And Rowan takes one calm step forward.

A predator's echo.
A ritual.
A beginning.

Trevor turns and runs again, panic flooding every nerve.

Behind him, Rowan walks.

Softly.
Steadily.
Unhurried.

The lantern shudders violently as Trevor plunges deeper into the maze, the Present visions flickering in his periphery like aftershocks.

At the edge of the darkness, Rowan's voice follows him like a heartbeat:

"Run as far as you can.
I'll be right behind you."

Trevor sobs, breathless.

False Sanctuary

Trevor didn't remember how long he'd been running. Only the sharp ache in his ribs told him he was still alive. The catacombs twisted beneath him like an endless esophagus of stone and shadow, swallowing his breath, each turn a blind gamble. Rowan's last words clung to his mind like frost.

"Hope is a leash."

He didn't believe her.
He didn't want to.

His foot slipped on a slick patch of stone and he caught himself on the wall, gasping. The lantern swung wildly in his hand, throwing feverish flares of amethyst across the corridor. For a moment he thought he saw blood on the wall—no, a crack in the stone—no, nothing at all. His mind kept pulling shapes where there were only shadows.

Then the corridor widened.

Trevor stumbled into it before he even realized what he was seeing: a chamber with a vaulted ceiling, carved with old arches that had long ago crumbled into dust. The air here felt different—cooler, cleaner, almost like the hint of a winter breeze crossing through a cracked window.

He froze, panting, then sank to his knees.

This room felt... gentler.

Neutral.

Like the catacombs hadn't quite decided what to do with it yet.

He let the lantern rest beside him. Its glow softened against the stone, less frantic, less alive. Trevor pressed the heels of his hands to his eyes, fighting the sting there, the tears he could no longer pretend were from the cold.

"Rowan," he whispered, the name breaking inside him. "Please don't let this be real..."

His voice echoed back to him in a soft, pitiful loop.

Rowan. Rowan. Rowan.

He folded forward, shoulders shaking. He didn't want to think of the lantern turning amethyst. He didn't want to think of the fourth body. He didn't want to think of Rowan's face when she'd said hope is a cage.

His hands trembled uncontrollably.

The lantern flickered—as if responding to him. Not magically, not with intention—but like a candle reacting to the tremor of breath.

Trevor drew a shuddering inhale.

Maybe this was safety.

A pause.

A breath he desperately needed.

He didn't believe it.

But he needed to.

He wiped his eyes with trembling fingers and forced himself upright, leaning against the wall. "I'm not giving up on her," he whispered to the empty room. "She's hurting. She's confused. She's scared. She—she must be scared."

The silence that answered him wasn't comforting.

It felt like listening to a room hold its breath.

He stood on unsteady legs and moved deeper into the chamber. There was a collapsed pillar near one wall, its base broken into jagged chunks. Behind it, he spotted a narrow recess—barely wide enough for him to press into.

A hiding place.

It was pathetic.
Cowardly.
Necessary.

Trevor wedged himself behind the pillar, pressing his back into the cold stone. Dust settled onto his coat and hair. He clasped the lantern tightly, shielding its glow beneath his coat to keep it from casting too much light.

His breath stuttered.
He forced himself to breathe through his nose, slow and careful.

The footsteps came almost immediately.

Not loud.
Not purposeful.
Just... present.

Soft pads of boots against stone.

Measured.
Unhurried.

Rowan wasn't calling his name.
Wasn't taunting him.
Wasn't pretending to search.

She walked like someone who didn't need to chase.

Trevor clutched the hair tie in his pocket with his free hand, his eyes squeezed shut. He didn't know why he'd grabbed it—maybe a part of him thought tokens mattered. Maybe a part of him still needed to believe Rowan was that person on the bridge.

The footsteps drew closer.
Closer.
Then—

Silence.

Trevor pressed a hand over his mouth.
He didn't dare breathe.

He waited.
And waited.

The minutes stretched into something unbearable. His lungs burned. His legs ached. His pulse thudded so loud he worried she'd hear it.

Then—

A single, soft footstep.
Not moving away.
Just shifting weight.

She was still here.

Listening.

Trevor's eyes filled with tears.

She's waiting… she's waiting for me to move first.
The realization was a cold blade between his ribs.

His breath quivered behind his hand.
He stayed frozen.

But Rowan didn't move either.

She wasn't hunting him.
She was giving him the chance to panic.
To reveal himself.

He squeezed his eyes shut harder, willing himself to become
smaller, quieter, nothing.

The silence thickened.
Like the room exhaled around him.
Like something unseen held its hand over the lantern's light.

Trevor shivered.

He couldn't stay here.
He couldn't stay still.
He couldn't—

A faint shift of dust near the entrance told him Rowan had
repositioned, but not left.

He had to run.

He had no choice.

Trevor waited until the silence felt stretched thin, like an over-pulled string ready to snap.

He couldn't tell how long Rowan had stood there, immobile, just beyond the veil of shadow. The possibility that she wasn't even breathing made his skin crawl.

He needed to move.

He needed to change something.

He couldn't be found crouched behind a rock like a terrified animal—not when Rowan was becoming something he didn't know how to understand.

With agonizing slowness, Trevor slid sideways and began to crawl out from behind the collapsed pillar. His knees and palms dragged noiselessly across the dust. The lantern remained tucked to his chest, his coat muffling its glow.

Please don't see me.

Please don't hear me.

Please let there be enough of you left, Rowan...

The chamber had two exits: the one Rowan guarded... and one opposite her, a slanted incline carved into the stone. Treacherous but passable.

Trevor moved toward the incline on hands and knees, too afraid to stand upright.

When he reached the base of the slope, he dared a small breath.

It felt like his first breath in years.

He clutched the lantern, rose to his feet, and climbed.

Dust cascaded under his boots. His fingers scraped rock as he pulled himself upward.

Halfway up the incline, the lantern flickered violently as if recoiling from something unseen. Trevor froze.

A shadow at the top of the slope shifted.

He lifted the lantern just enough to illuminate the figure standing at the crest.

Rowan.

Silent.
Still.
Watching.

Her face was unreadable—neither angry nor pleased. Her long hair hung around her shoulders like a curtain of shadow, the amethyst glow catching subtle glints in her eyes. She wasn't out of breath. She wasn't flushed from exertion.

She had simply waited for him to try this path.

"No," Trevor breathed, the word breaking apart like wet paper. His legs buckled. "No… please."

The lantern sputtered, dimming. Not from magic—because his hands were trembling too violently to hold it steady.

Rowan didn't move toward him.
Didn't raise a hand.
Didn't threaten.

241

She only tilted her head slightly.

Not curious.
Not mocking.

Patient.

Trevor's breath rattled from his chest. He stumbled backward, tripping over his own feet as he slid down the slope uncontrollably. He hit the chamber floor sideways, the lantern clattering beside him.

Pain shot through his shoulder. He gasped, scrambling away from the incline.

Rowan didn't descend after him.

But she leaned forward a fraction, one hand lifting—not beckoning, not reaching, but opening, palm up.

The gesture collapsed what little sanity Trevor was holding by threads.

It wasn't a threat.
It wasn't even a trap.

It was an invitation.

"Rowan…" he whispered, his voice hoarse with terror. "Don't do this. You're scaring me. You're scaring me so badly…"

Her voice drifted down to him, soft and steady:

"You're not scared of me, Trevor.
You're scared of what you were too kind to see."

He shook his head so hard it made his vision blur.
"Don't... please don't talk like that..."

Rowan stepped down one slow step.
Stone dust whispered beneath her heel.

Trevor backed away on his hands, dragging himself until his spine
hit the chamber wall. He curled one knee upward as if it could shield
him.

His breath was high, thin, desperate.

"I tried to help you," he pleaded. "I—I saved you once. I tried—
"

"And I'm grateful," Rowan said quietly.

She meant it.
Her tone was gentle.
It was infinitely worse than if she'd screamed.

"You helped me survive long enough to become myself."

Trevor's heart broke open.

He didn't know what she meant.
He didn't want to.

"Rowan... please... I didn't want this. I never wanted this."

"I know," she whispered.
Her eyes softened—an expression he recognized painfully.
"There's nothing cruel about you. That's why it worked."

His breath stalled.

What worked?

Rowan descended another step, slow and controlled. Trevor felt the shift in pressure around him, like the entire chamber was acknowledging her movement.

"You thought hope was a gift you offered me," she said. "But hope was the chain you wrapped around yourself."

Trevor's eyes widened, tears spilling over.

Rowan continued:

"People like you cling to mercy as if it's sacred. As if sparing others is something noble. But it only binds you. Makes you blind to the truth."

"What truth?" Trevor choked out.

"That mercy is just another way to control someone."
She reached the bottom of the slope and stood still again.
"And hope is the worst leash of all."

Trevor covered his face, shaking his head.

"I didn't control you—"

"You tried not to," Rowan said softly.
"That's the only reason it held."

Held.

The word landed like a stone in his stomach.

Rowan took one step toward him.
Trevor flinched violently.

She didn't touch him.
Didn't reach.

Just spoke.

"You saved me on that bridge. You offered hope to a ghost of a girl you didn't truly see. But you put something else in motion that night."

Trevor's hands dropped from his face.
He stared at her, terrified.

Rowan smiled faintly.

"You called me into being."

"No…" Trevor whispered. "No. No, that's not… that makes no sense—"

"It doesn't have to," Rowan murmured.
"It only had to work."

Trevor's breath hitched, and for a moment the only sound in the room was the trembling rattle of his inhale.

Then—

The lantern beside him sputtered again.
Not purple.
Not amethyst.

A thin black thread curled through the glow like ink in water.

Trevor's terror sharpened into something primal.

The Future was bleeding in.

Rowan didn't look surprised.

He did.

Trevor pressed himself harder against the cold wall behind him, as if the stone could absorb him, protect him, save him. His eyes locked onto the lantern in front of him—the amethyst flame pulsing, then thinning, then splitting with that dark thread stirring through it.

The onyx filament shimmered faintly before fading again.

But Trevor had seen it.

He'd felt it.

The Future was coming.

"No…" he whispered. "Not now. Not yet. Rowan, please, this isn't right. This isn't how things work."

Rowan watched him with unreadable calm. No gloating. No hunger. No malice.
Something worse: certainty.

"Trevor," Rowan said softly, "why do you think you were here tonight? Why do you think you found me? Why do you think the catacombs closed?"

Trevor clutched the hair tie in his hand again, desperate for some fragment of the girl he thought she was—the girl he'd met on that bridge. The one who'd cried with him, who'd been saved by him, who'd whispered that she didn't know how to keep going.

He couldn't reconcile that Rowan with the one standing before him now—silent, confident, almost luminous in the amethyst glow.

"You needed me," he said. "That's why. Because you were hurting. Because you were in trouble. Because you needed someone to—"

"To what?" Rowan asked gently.
"Rescue me? Redeem me? Give me hope?"

Trevor's lips parted.
He didn't know how to answer.

Rowan stepped forward—one quiet, graceful step. She didn't reach for him. Her hands remained at her sides. But the presence of her approach made Trevor's bones tremble.

"You didn't save me," Rowan said softly.
"You delayed me."

Trevor's chest constricted.
He felt like he couldn't breathe.

Rowan crouched down, not close enough to touch him, but close enough that the lantern's glow shadowed across half her face.

"You don't understand yet," she said, "and that's why it hurts. But you will."

Trevor shook his head violently.

247

"No. No, Rowan, please, I don't want to understand this. I don't want to see you this way—"

"You already do," Rowan whispered.
"You saw me from the moment you stepped into these catacombs. You just didn't know what you were looking at."

Trevor's voice cracked.
"Rowan, I don't want to lose you…"

Rowan exhaled slowly, a warm, steady breath that ghosted over Trevor's cheek.

"You already have."

The lantern pulsed.

Once.
Twice.

Trevor's gaze darted to it, horror rising in his throat.

A second black thread formed.
Then a third.
Each one thin as hair.
Each one shimmering into the purple glow like ink sinking into water.

"No," Trevor breathed.
"No no no no no—"

Rowan didn't flinch.
Didn't look away.
Didn't seem alarmed.

"Trevor," she murmured, "you can't stop what's coming."

He shook his head, tears falling freely now.

"This isn't how it's supposed to go," he whispered.
"You're supposed to help people. You're supposed to guide them. You're supposed to be—be—"

"A servant?" Rowan asked quietly.
"A shepherd?
A symbol?"

Trevor's sob was small, broken, helpless.

Rowan rose to her feet slowly, like someone finishing a prayer.

"I'm not a ghost anymore," she said.
"I'm not a lost soul."
She turned away from him, her gaze drifting up the incline she'd blocked.
"I'm something new."

Trevor's terrified whisper dragged itself out of his throat:
"Rowan... what are you?"

Rowan didn't answer.

Instead, she turned her head slightly over her shoulder, just enough for the lantern's mixed light to graze her features.

And in the purple glow, the dark threads shimmering through the flame reflected in her eyes—thin, black, web-like veins of something inevitable.

She spoke quietly:

"What you made me."

Trevor cried openly now, chest shaking, palms flat against the stone floor. His world was collapsing inward—his purpose, his role, his understanding of magic, of hope, of mercy. Everything he believed about himself turned brittle.

The lantern pulsed again, a flicker of black on amethyst.

Rowan stepped into the corridor.

She didn't look back.

Her voice drifted into the air behind her like a whisper of frost:

"Follow when you're ready."

Trevor didn't want to follow.
Didn't want to move.
Didn't want to breathe.

But the catacombs felt smaller without her.
Colder.
Hungrier.

And the lantern, traitor that it was, brightened—waiting for him.

Trevor sobbed, wiped his eyes with shaking hands, and dragged himself to his feet.

"Rowan…" he whispered, as if the name itself could warm him.

The lantern flickered.

The onyx threads deepened.

Trevor stepped after her.

And the Future followed.

Last Plan

Trevor forced himself to breathe through the shake in his chest, but every inhale felt thin, like the air had to be coaxed into his lungs instead of arriving naturally. The walls—always too close—felt tighter now, as though the stone was holding its breath along with him and waiting to see what he'd do next. He wiped his palms on his trousers, but the sweat only smeared the dust across his skin.

He needed to think.

Not feel, not panic, not break—think.

He closed his eyes, leaning one hand against the wall, and forced himself back through every step of the last two hours in the catacombs. He replayed them with a precision he didn't know he still possessed. The tunnels he and Rowan crossed. The tight turns. The cramped choke-points. The chamber where the second body lay. The stairwell that spiraled downward too long. The narrow crawl passage that scraped his elbows raw.

Trevor pictured all of it in his mind's eye like a map he'd drawn on tissue paper—wrinkled and imperfect, yet still usable if he handled it gently.

Rowan's traps were precise.

But Rowan was not omniscient.

She was methodical, yes. Calculated, yes. Terrifyingly intelligent, yes. But she was not all-seeing. The labyrinth was too sprawling, too ancient, too unruly for even her to have total foresight.

There had to be a path she didn't anticipate.
A corridor she didn't account for.
A seam in the stone she hadn't considered.

Trevor wiped his face again, pushing away tears he hadn't realized were falling.

He dragged himself upright, bracing his weight as he took three slow steps forward. The lantern swung from his hand, casting amethyst light that jittered across the walls in nervous patterns. The shadows didn't fall naturally—they stretched in ways that made the geometry of the stone look slightly wrong, as though depth itself were misbehaving.

"Come on," Trevor whispered to himself. "Come on, Trevor, think."

He retraced the exact turn where Rowan had guided him to the second staircase. He remembered how she'd paused at the landing, her gaze flicking toward the left corridor—not with hesitation but with confirmation, like she was verifying something she'd already set in place.

Which meant left had mattered to her.
Which meant maybe right mattered to him.

He swallowed hard.

He took the right corridor.

It felt immediately different—not safer, not wider, but less scripted. As if the air here hadn't been breathed recently. The walls hadn't seen recent footsteps. Rowan hadn't bothered shaping this path.

Trevor's heart began pounding—not with fear this time, but a fragile bloom of hope.

The lantern brightened slightly, the amethyst gaining a warm edge. For a moment he let himself pretend it was responding to his bravery, not his desperation.

He moved faster, feeling the cavern floor slope gently downward beneath his boots.

He whispered, "Okay… okay… this can work."

The stone corridor opened into a wider chamber, its ceiling much higher than any he'd seen so far. Ancient archways loomed overhead, carved with unreadable markings half-eaten by time. Dust fell from some whenever his steps got too close.

Trevor paused in the center, turning slowly.

There were five possible exits.

Five.

Five paths Rowan hadn't funneled him toward.

Five options, which meant five chances she hadn't predicted.

Trevor let out a trembling laugh—small, shaky, but real.

He approached the nearest archway. A cold draft pushed against his face, subtle but unmistakable. Air meant space. Air meant a way out—maybe not to the surface, but to a place Rowan hadn't shaped to her purposes.

His hands shook with adrenaline.
He pushed forward.

He imagined bursting into a chamber Rowan didn't expect.
Imagined finding a ladder or a maintenance shaft.
Imagined stumbling into a relief crawlspace and clawing through to daylight.

Imagined Rowan's face when he emerged from the catacombs alive.

Imagined telling her he forgave her, even now.

That he meant it.

Trevor squeezed the lantern tighter.

He stepped through the archway.

And kept going.

Every footstep was a promise he made to himself—this will work, this has to work, it can't all be predetermined.

The corridor here sloped noticeably, the walls growing slicker with condensation. A bead of water ran down the side of the stone and dripped onto the floor beside his boot. The sound echoed strangely, like the chamber's acoustics had forgotten how noise was supposed to work.

He pressed forward, breath catching when he saw what lay ahead: a narrow incline leading upward. Not steep like the previous shafts he'd climbed—this one was almost manageable. Less treacherous. Less engineered.

A path Rowan wouldn't have chosen to seal.

Trevor felt his heart leap.

"This is it," he breathed. "Oh God… this is it."

He started to climb—slow at first, then faster, fingers scrambling for purchase along the uneven stone. Dust caked beneath his nails. Tiny pebbles skittered under his boots. His breath grew ragged, but he didn't stop.

He would reach the top.
He would.
He had to.
There was still time to reach her. To reach the real Rowan. To make her remember who she was before all of this—

The lantern pulsed violently in his grip.

A harsh amethyst flicker sliced through the air.
A thin black filament spiraled upward through the glow like smoke rising in backwards motion.

Trevor froze.

"No," he whispered hoarsely.
"No, please—"

He lifted the lantern toward the top of the incline.

A figure stood there.

Rowan.

Already there.
Already waiting.
Already inevitable.

His fingers went slack, and the lantern hung crooked in his grip, light casting trembling shards of amethyst across the walls.

Trevor slid back down the incline, boots skidding, palms scraping until he hit the base hard and collapsed to his knees.

Rowan descended a single step.

Calm.
Quiet.
Certain.
Trevor stumbled backward from the incline, breath hitched in his throat, the pulse in his neck pounding so hard he thought it might burst. Rowan didn't move further down the slope. She didn't need to. Her presence was enough to crush the illusion of progress he'd built in the last half hour.

He pushed himself to his feet, legs trembling, but Rowan didn't come closer. She simply watched him from the slope—calm, steady, patient. As if she knew that even without advancing, he would turn and flee.

And she was right.

Trevor spun and bolted down the opposite corridor, the lantern swinging wildly in his grip. The light jittered, throwing frantic shapes across the walls. Dust billowed up from the floor as he ran, choking him, making it feel like the air itself was resisting him.

He sprinted until his lungs screamed, until his ribs ached with each breath.

But when he finally slowed—

The corridor was wrong.

He blinked hard, trying to make sense of it, but the architecture didn't match the tunnel he'd just taken. The ceiling arched differently. The walls were smoother. The air was colder.

"How—" Trevor whispered, voice barely audible.

He hadn't changed directions.
He hadn't taken a fork.
He hadn't turned at all.

The corridor had changed under him.

He backed up two steps, then three, eyes darting along the walls for any sign of a junction.

Nothing.

Only smooth, unbroken stone.

Trevor pressed a hand to the wall, fingers trembling, trying to feel a seam or natural break. Instead, the stone felt warm beneath his palm—like it had been touched recently. Like it remembered Rowan.

His pulse spiked.

"No… no, no, that's not possible—"

He turned sharply and hurried forward again. Not running this time—too afraid to disturb whatever was shifting the maze. He tried to breathe slowly, quietly, as if the tunnels might respond to volume.

The lantern dimmed, then flared, responding to his fear in inconsistent, unsettling bursts.

Trevor entered another chamber—not the same one as before, but similar enough to be uncanny. High ceiling. Thick dust. Archways leading outward like the petals of a stone flower.

Except something was different here.

The shadows didn't fall where they should.

Trevor held the lantern higher. The shadows of the archways stretched outward—but not away from the lantern. They stretched sideways, bending at unnatural angles, as if the light had to bend around an unseen shape.

His breath hitched.

The Future bled.

The lantern pulsed again, this time with three distinct throbs of amethyst and ink-black.

Trevor stumbled back from the archways, heart hammering. He felt the subtle shift in air currents—something drifting behind him. He spun reflexively, lantern up.

Nothing.

Just the corridor.

Empty.

But the air still moved, like someone had just brushed past.

"Rowan—?" he whispered.

Not a shout.
A plea.

The echo came back wrong—flattened, delayed, as if the acoustics had been pulled through molasses.

Trevor remembered her footsteps from earlier.
Not hurried.
Not aggressive.
Just… there.
Always there.

He remembered something else, too:

She'd never once sounded out of breath.

He swallowed hard and turned back toward the archways, choosing the one to his immediate left. He didn't know why—instinct, maybe. Or fear. Or defiance. Or the childish hope that choosing something slightly different than what Rowan anticipated might break the invisible script.

He entered the corridor.

Left.
Left was safer.
Left had to be safe.

He walked quickly but quietly, trying not to disturb whatever might be shifting the catacombs. The lantern flickered in his grip again, its light stuttering like it wanted to warn him of something but didn't know how to speak.

The corridor narrowed, forcing him sideways. Dampness coated the walls, making them slick. He brushed against something soft and fibrous—moss or something like it. But when he brought the lantern close, the texture twisted away from the light, contracting like muscle.

Trevor jerked back with a choked gasp.

"No—no, don't—don't do that—"

He pressed on, breathing raggedly. He rounded a tight bend—

And froze.

He was back in the narrow corridor with the shallow, sloping floor.

The exact one he'd just fled.

Trevor staggered backward, shaking his head.

"No. No. I didn't— I couldn't have—"

The walls glistened faintly now as if they were wet. A slow drip echoed from somewhere unseen, timed irregularly, like a clock wound improperly. The rhythm made Trevor's stomach twist.

He turned to flee again—

A soft echo drifted toward him.

A footstep.

Then another.

Measured. Light. Almost tender.

Trevor's pulse stopped for a second—just a single suspended beat.

He pivoted, heart in his throat.

The corridor was empty.

But the footsteps weren't coming from behind him.

They were coming from somewhere within the stone itself.

As if Rowan wasn't following him.

She was everywhere he was going to be.

"Stop," Trevor whispered, voice breaking. "Please stop—please—"

The footsteps ceased.

Trevor didn't know if that was better or worse.

He pressed forward once more, slower now, every muscle trembling. The corridor opened into another chamber, this one smaller—more intimate. Bones lined the walls. Skulls, stacked with precision, formed patterns that might once have meant something to someone. Their empty sockets cast hollow reflections in the lantern's glow.

Trevor swallowed hard and stepped into the chamber.

For a moment, nothing moved.

Then, very softly, the lantern changed.

Amethyst.
Black.
Amethyst.
Black.

Trevor's breath caught.

This wasn't Rowan closing in.
This wasn't Rowan chasing.

This was Rowan anticipating.

Guiding.

Shaping.

Not through magic.
Not through supernatural power.

Through inevitability.

Through design.

Through the truth Trevor had refused to admit from the moment he saw the first body:

He had never been ahead of her.
He had only been following the path she wanted him to take.

His throat tightened painfully.

"I can still reach you," he whispered to the empty chamber. "I can still—"

His voice cracked.

"You're still in there. You have to be."

Somewhere deep in the catacombs, a soft echo answered:

Not words.
Not footsteps.

Just a shift.

A turning.

A decision.

Trevor's eyes stung.
He tightened his grip on the lantern.
He stepped toward the next corridor.

And the catacombs, obedient to Rowan's will or Rowan's inevitability, reshaped themselves to let him through.

Because she wasn't following him.

She was leading him.

And Trevor, despite everything, still followed.
Trevor didn't know how long he walked before he realized the tunnels were sloping upward.

It was subtle at first, so gradual he might have missed it if his legs weren't so tired. Each step burned a little more than the last. His breath came shorter. The lantern's weight seemed to increase with every meter.

Upward.

His heart stuttered with something dangerously close to hope.

Upward meant thinner air.
Upward meant proximity to the surface.
Upward meant... maybe, just maybe... daylight.

He tried to tamp that thought down as soon as it formed, the way you'd clamp a lid over boiling water. Hope was dangerous now—that much of Rowan's philosophy had already wormed into him. But it was too late. The idea had slipped under his ribs and lodged there, pulsing, stubborn.

Upward.

The corridor narrowed as it climbed, the walls curving inwards like two hands cupping him. Scratches lined the stone—some man-made, some natural. Trevor trailed his fingers over them as he walked, feeling gouges worn into the rock.

Boot marks.
Drag marks.
Finger grooves.

People had been here before.

He wasn't the first lost soul to try this path.

The thought chilled him, but it didn't stop him. If anything, it made him move faster. He wasn't those people. He had a lantern. He had Rowan. He had—

His throat tightened.

Did he still have Rowan?

He pushed the thought away and focused on the incline ahead. The corridor opened into a taller shaft, the ceiling rising and the floor tilting into a jagged ramp. Above, somewhere in the gloom, he saw it—a faint, hazy pallor different from the lantern's glow.

Not quite light.
Not quite darkness.

Something between.

Trevor's breath caught.

"Oh God," he whispered. "Please. Please…"

He adjusted his grip on the lantern, tightening his fingers until they ached, and stepped onto the incline.

The stone was loose beneath his boots, dust and grit sliding along with him as he climbed. He had to lean forward, using his free hand to brace himself against the rough wall. Pebbles skittered away from his feet, ricocheting downward with sharp clacks that echoed too loudly.

Halfway up, his legs started to shake.

"You've got this," he muttered to himself, the words more breath than sound. "Just—just a little further. One more push. One more."

The pale haze above seemed to recede with every step, always just out of reach.

Trevor dug his fingers into a crack in the wall, using it as a hold, hauling himself higher. Stone scraped skin from his knuckles. Warm wetness smeared over the rock—blood. He didn't stop.

His shoulders burned.
His lungs burned.
His hope burned hardest of all.

"Rowan," he whispered. "Please let this mean something. Please let—"

The lantern spasmed in his grip.

The amethyst light ruptured, flaring bright and harsh, before thinning around a sudden dark core. A filament of black twisted upward through the glow like some invasive root system threading through the heart of it.

Trevor froze, chest seizing.

"No," he choked. "Not now. Please not now…"

The black brightened, then dimmed, then flared again, like it was trying to pulse in time with his own heartbeat.

He forced himself to lift his head.

And saw a silhouette at the top of the slope.

Someone standing between him and that not-light, not-dark.

Not tall. Not looming. Just… there.

As the lantern stabilized, the amethyst glow washed up the incline and found her.

Rowan.

Trevor's fingers spasmed and nearly lost their hold.

She stood at the lip of the shaft, just where the stone flattened out into whatever lay beyond. The hazy pallor behind her turned her into a cutout—dark figure framed in pale glow, edges soft, impossible to miss.

She wasn't breathing hard.
She wasn't flushed.

She might as well have been waiting for him at the top of a staircase in a quiet house.

Trevor's world dropped out from under him.

He didn't remember letting go, but suddenly his knees were sliding. His boots lost purchase on the gritty stone, and he slipped. His body lurched, balance gone, and he tumbled backward down the incline.

The fall wasn't catastrophic—more a series of bruising, clumsy slides—but every impact jolted fear deeper into his bones. His elbow cracked against the wall. His shoulder struck a jagged protrusion. The lantern clattered from his hand and tumbled with him, wild, spinning arcs of light smearing across the walls.

He hit the base hard enough to knock the breath from his lungs.

For a few seconds, all he could do was lie there, staring up at the shaft while his chest spasmed, trying to remember how to inhale. The lantern rocked to a stop beside him, its light fluttering with agitated flickers.

The silhouette at the top of the incline hadn't moved.

Trevor forced a breath in. Tears blurred his vision, turning Rowan's shape into a wavering smear. He coughed, rolled onto his side, and pushed himself upright on unsteady arms.

His legs trembled as he staggered back, crab-like, until his spine hit the opposite wall. He stared up, throat making small, useless sounds.

Rowan stepped down one careful pace.

The amethyst light caught her face now, carving out details from the silhouette. Her expression wasn't cruel. It wasn't amused. It wasn't even cold.

It was... weary.
And certain.

"Rowan..." Trevor rasped.

She descended another step, slow and measured, boots whispering against the grit. She held no weapon. She wore no crown of bone or ice. She didn't radiate supernatural fury.

She just was.
Unavoidable.
Unshakable.
Exactly where he had always been headed.

"Rowan, please," he said, voice cracking. "I'm trying. I'm trying so hard to— I— I thought if I just got somewhere you didn't plan, if I just—"

His words scattered.

He dragged a hand through his hair, fingers trembling so badly he had to stop. His chest hitched. A sob escaped before he could swallow it.

Rowan stopped halfway down the incline and tilted her head slightly, studying him. Lantern light flickered in her eyes, catching strange glints there—a hint of amethyst, a hint of something darker threaded through it.

"Trevor," she said softly, "you're exhausting yourself."

There was no scold in it.
No sarcasm.
No mockery.

Just observation.

Her gentleness carved him open.

He let out a sound that might have been a laugh if it hadn't broken in the middle.

"What am I supposed to do?" he whispered. "Just—just stand still and let this happen? Just watch you—watch you become this and… and not even try?"

Rowan's gaze softened, a tiny shift in the muscles around her eyes.

"You're still pretending you have a different choice," she said, almost tenderly. "That's what's tiring you out."

Trevor squeezed his eyes shut. Tears spilled over, hot against chilled skin.

He wanted to shout.
He wanted to curse.
He wanted to say something that would snap her out of it.
Something that would jolt the real Rowan free.

Instead, all that came out was a shaking whisper:

"I don't know how to stop loving you."

The words startled him the instant they left his mouth.
Not romantic love. Not that.
But something broader, messier, deeper:

The love you feel for someone whose pain you've seen up close.
The love you feel for someone you've stood beside on a bridge while they broke apart.
The love bound up with responsibility and memory and belief.

He heard the silence after the confession like a physical pressure.

Rowan's face didn't change dramatically, but something in her posture shifted—shoulders easing, chin tipping down fractionally, as if the weight of the moment settled on her too.

Her voice, when it came, was so soft it nearly blended into the cold air.

"I know," she said.

Not mocking.
Not rejecting.

Just accepting it as fact.

And somehow that hurt more than anything else.

Trevor's body sagged against the wall. His fingers slipped off his knees. He looked small there, hunched and shaking, as if the tunnels had finally carved him down to his simplest shape: a man who cried quietly for someone already lost.

Rowan stepped off the incline, boots touching the flat stone floor.

She didn't cross the last few feet between them.

She didn't need to.

The distance between them wasn't measured in steps anymore.
Trevor drew his knees to his chest, arms wrapped tight around them, as if he could fold himself into a shape too small to be noticed by fate. His breath trembled out of him in uneven bursts. He didn't bother wiping his face anymore. The tears came too frequently, too quietly.

Rowan didn't approach him.
She stopped a respectful distance away, as if closing the last few feet would be an unkindness.

The lantern between them pulsed with a fractured rhythm now—amethyst light splintered by black rooting through its center. Every beat sent thin veins of shadow up the walls like skeletal fingers stretching toward the ceiling.

Trevor noticed.

He stared.

And something inside him cracked.

"...Rowan," he whispered, barely audible. "Please don't let it do that."

Rowan followed his gaze to the lantern. The black filaments pulsed again, spreading like cracks under ice.

"That isn't the lantern," she said softly. "That's me."

Trevor flinched as if struck.

She didn't soften the blow. She didn't apologize for it. She only tilted her head with calm curiosity, as though she were observing her own reflection for the first time.

"This is what happens when you stop pretending," Rowan said. "When you see things as they actually are."

Trevor shook his head, but there was no strength in it. "This isn't you. You were never like this. You—you wanted connection. You wanted someone to hear you. You wanted—"

Rowan's expression gentled.

"That's what you wanted."

Trevor blinked hard, tears catching in his lashes.

Rowan crouched slowly, matching his height without getting closer. She rested her elbows on her knees, fingers laced.

"I know what you're doing," she said. "You're trying to talk to the version of me you remember. The one you saw on the bridge. The one who still believed someone else could save her."

Trevor swallowed painfully. "That was you."

Rowan gave a small, almost fond exhale.
"It was a shell. A temporary thing. A moment of weakness I mistook for clarity."

Trevor recoiled. "No. No, Rowan, you were hurting. Anyone would have. You were—"

"Invisible?" she supplied gently.

The word sliced through him.

His breath faltered.

Rowan continued quietly, almost conversationally.
"You think invisibility made me fragile. That my loneliness was a wound someone else needed to treat. You want me to be afraid of it, or angry about it, or broken by it."

She shook her head.

"I wasn't broken. I was observing."

Trevor dragged his sleeve across his face. "That's not—no one chooses to be unseen."

"I did," Rowan said simply.

Trevor stared at her, eyes wide, disbelieving.

Rowan met his gaze with utmost sincerity.

"People reveal their truest selves when they don't think they're being watched. When they believe you're background. When they treat you like a ghost."
She paused.
"I learned more that way than I ever did when people pretended to care."

Trevor's voice cracked. "So you let the world disappear you? You let—"

Rowan's tone sharpened by a single degree—not anger, but conviction.

"I let the world tell me the truth."

She rose gracefully to her feet.

"And the truth is simple, Trevor. Hope keeps people waiting for something that never comes. Mercy keeps them tethered to pain. And your work—your existence—"

She gestured toward him gently with an open hand.

"—was keeping me chained to someone I wasn't anymore."

Trevor pressed a shaking hand to his chest as if trying to hold himself together. "I never chained you. I never tried to contain you. I tried to help you."

"And you did," she said warmly.

That warmth hurt more than cruelty.

"But help has an expiration date," Rowan continued. "A point where it stops being a lifeline and becomes a cage." She motioned around them—at the tunnels, at the shadows warping, at the lantern dimming. "This is me becoming what I was meant to be."

Trevor's voice scraped raw.
"Rowan... what is that?"

She didn't hesitate.

"Someone who decides."

The word echoed—thick, heavy, final.

The shadows along the walls rippled. The temperature dropped. A cold that didn't feel like winter seeped into the air, a thin veil that stole sensation from Trevor's fingers as he clutched his arms.

"Decides what?" he whispered.

"Who deserves hope."
She took a step toward the next corridor.
"Who deserves mercy."
Another step, confident.
"And who deserves neither."

Trevor's breath shattered in his throat. "Rowan, please—"

She paused at the threshold.

Not turning fully, just enough for the lantern's flickering light to outline her profile.

"You keep begging me," she said softly. "And I don't know if you understand the most important part."

Trevor blinked through tears. "What part?"

Rowan looked at him with a tenderness that made the moment knife-sharp:

"I'm not doing this because I want to hurt you."
A heartbeat.
"I'm doing this because you gave me the courage to stop hurting myself."

Trevor's heart fractured.
His breath hitched in a sob he couldn't swallow.

Rowan held his eyes for a lingering moment—
A goodbye in everything but name—
Then turned toward the tunnel ahead.

"Come," she said quietly. "There's more you need to see before the end."

Trevor stared at her back, tears blurring her into a silhouette, as the lantern's black filaments pulsed harder—thicker—spreading around the edges of the amethyst like an eclipse shadow consuming light.

For a moment, Trevor didn't move.

His fingers dug into the stone at his sides.

His chest heaved.

His entire body trembled with the weight of refusing to accept the truth—

And then he rose.

Slowly.
Fragile.
Broken and still trying.

He stepped into Rowan's shadow.

Because he didn't know how not to.

Decision

The corridor had been narrowing for some time, though Trevor only really noticed when his shoulder brushed stone.

It wasn't that the walls had suddenly pressed in; it was that he'd finally stopped shaking long enough to feel where his body was in space again. The echo of his earlier collapse still lived in his muscles, in the raw burn of his throat, but beneath that, something quieter had taken root.

He wasn't numb. He wasn't calm. His heart still hurt in a way that felt bruised and swollen. But the wild, frantic edge of fear had burned away, leaving behind a strange, clean focus.

Ahead of him, Rowan walked without looking back.

Her lantern swung in a controlled arc, the amethyst light sweeping over the stone in regular pulses. The black veins threading through it had thickened, feeding on whatever current was moving between the catacombs and the future, but her grip on the handle was steady. She walked like someone who had accepted the ending and was simply moving toward it.

Trevor's footsteps no longer dragged.

He matched her pace—not quite beside her, but not as far behind as he had been. The cold air seeping through the stone brushed his cheeks, but he kept his gaze trained on Rowan's back, taking in the set of her shoulders, the stiff line of her spine.

He knew what people looked like when they'd given up. He'd watched it happen to more souls than he could count—watched the moment they stopped fighting and simply let the night carry them.

Rowan didn't look like that.

She looked like someone carrying a decision that hurt to hold.

"Rowan," he said quietly.

Her stride hitched. It was small, hardly more than a stutter in her gait, but he caught it. The lantern jerked in her hand, its light faltering for a beat before recovering.

He kept his voice low, careful, steady.

"I'm still here."

The words settled into the stone around them. Dust shook loose from a fissure above, drifting down in pale flecks that sparkled briefly in the lantern light before vanishing in the dark.

Rowan didn't turn, but he saw her hand tighten around the metal handle. The tendons in her wrist stood out sharp in the purple wash.

"You shouldn't be," she muttered.

"I am," Trevor said. "And I'm not done with you."

That, more than anything, seemed to land.

Her shoulders lifted, then dropped on a shaky exhale. For a moment, she slowed—not enough to admit it openly, but enough that the distance between them shrank. Trevor stepped forward, closing the gap by another foot.

He let the quiet stretch.

The catacombs pressed in around them, the ceiling dipping lower, the air growing colder in a way that felt deliberate. The lantern's glow skimmed over ridges in the stone, catching on faint scratch marks—nicks, grooves, the ghosts of hands that had passed this way long before. The world down here had been full of people once. Now it held just the two of them, walking toward the same end for different reasons.

"You can keep going," Trevor said, after a time. "But you heard me."

Rowan's jaw flexed. The lantern trembled once—barely—and the black thread pulsing through it thickened before settling.

"Don't start," she whispered.

He wasn't sure if she meant the conversation or the hope.

Trevor eased out another breath and followed as she turned a corner.

The corridor spat them into a cramped junction, three passage mouths yawning ahead. Rowan didn't hesitate; she headed for the middle, angling the lantern so the light cut into the darkness. The air in that direction smelled faintly different—older, somehow, with a mineral tang like old pennies and wet stone.

A few more turns and the passage widened, the ceiling arching up to form a dome of rough-hewn rock. An opening gaped on the left, a hollow in the wall where the darkness was thicker.

Rowan lifted the lantern and angled toward it.

Trevor felt the pull of that darkness before they reached it, like a gravity well. His chest tightened with a dread he recognized now as the echo of the last three bodies they'd found.

"Wait," he said.

Rowan didn't.

Trevor stepped ahead of her.

He didn't rush; he simply lengthened his stride and moved into the archway first, letting the lantern light spill past his shoulder as he crossed the threshold.

The room beyond was small, its walls curving gently like the inside of a cupped hand. The air was colder here, leached of warmth in a way that raised goosebumps along his arms. His breath fogged faintly.

The fourth body rested against the wall, half-sitting, half-slumped.

This one hadn't been left where it fell. Knees bent, back propped carefully, hands folded over the chest as if someone had taken time to arrange them. There was a carefulness to it that the others had not been granted, a tidying up after the violence.

Trevor's stomach tightened. He forced himself forward.

The man couldn't have been more than fifty. Lines bracketed his mouth, the kind etched by worry rather than laughter. His hair was graying unevenly at the temples, his jaw covered in the faint shadow of stubble. His eyes were half-lidded, and the peaceful expression on his face was a dreadful lie; a faint dark ring around his throat and bruises on his wrists told a different story.

Trevor crouched next to him, knees popping softly. The stone was icy beneath his palms as he leaned on one hand for balance.

It wasn't the brutality that hit him hardest. It was the detail.

A button fastened neatly on the man's shirt. A fold smoothed along his sleeve. A lock of hair brushed out of his eyes and tucked aside.

Someone had done this. Someone who cared how he looked after he died.

"You stayed," Trevor murmured.

Behind him, Rowan stepped into the room. The lantern light expanded, catching the planes of her face, carving out hollows beneath her eyes.

"What?" Her voice sounded rough, unused.

Trevor kept his gaze on the dead man.

"The others," he said quietly. "You left them where they fell. But here…"

He gestured with a small lift of his hand.

"You stayed with him longer. You put him together again."

Rowan's silence thickened the air.

Trevor drew in a breath that hurt on the way down.

"This isn't who you are," he whispered. "Not really."

The words weren't a plea. They sat somewhere between observation and hope.

Behind him, the lantern's glow flickered.

"It's exactly who I am," Rowan said.

Her voice had lost its iron. It sounded stretched thin, tugged tight over something that wanted to tear.

Trevor rose slowly to his feet and turned to face her.

"If you truly believed that," he said, "you wouldn't have brought me here."

Rowan blinked too quickly. The lantern trembled.

"I needed you to see," she said. "So you'd understand."

"If you were certain," Trevor replied, "you wouldn't need me to understand. You wouldn't need anyone to agree."

Her eyes flashed in the purple light.

"That's not what this is."

"Then what is it?" He took a step toward her. "Because from where I'm standing, it looks like you wanted someone to tell you there's still another choice."

She shook her head, but the motion was small and frayed at the edges.

"It's not—"

"You brought me because some part of you wants someone to stop you." His voice stayed soft, but the certainty in it made the stone itself feel more solid. "You brought me because you didn't want to be alone when you did this."

Her fingers tightened around the lantern's handle until the metal creaked. For a moment, her face looked younger, stripped of the hard angles her decisions had carved into it. She looked like someone who'd been standing on a ledge for a very long time and finally turned to see who'd joined her.

"Trevor…" she said, and his name sounded like it hurt her to say it.

He stepped close enough that the lantern light broke around them both.

"You don't have to finish this," he said. "You don't have to let this be the end of who you are."

She stared at him, eyes bright, throat working.

"Who I am," she whispered, "is why we're here."

He shook his head. "Who you are is why I'm still here."

The lantern's amethyst deepened, the black thread roiling through it like smoke caught in glass. For a heartbeat, it seemed to pulse in time with the frantic rhythm of her breath.

"What if I can't stop?" she asked.

"You can," he said. "You're just afraid of what it means if you do."

Her jaw clenched.

"If I stop now, then everything I've done—everything I've decided—"

"—was a mistake," Trevor finished softly.

The word hung between them.

Rowan flinched as if struck.

He didn't move.

"Mistakes can end," he said. "They don't have to define the rest of you."

She let out a sound that might have been a laugh if it hadn't broken halfway through.

"You always make it sound simple," she said.

"Sometimes," Trevor replied, "it is."

They stood facing each other, the dead man at their backs, the walls curving around them like a closed fist. Something in Rowan's expression shifted, a crack running through stone.

She looked down first.

Her gaze fell to the lantern, Trevor's fingers curled hard around the handle. The light spilling from it painted her knuckles in bruised violet.

"You should have stayed on the bridge," she murmured.

Trevor's heartbeat stumbled.

The image rose unbidden in his mind: snow thick in the air, the rail cold beneath his palms, Rowan's face turned toward the river that looked more like a void than water. He'd thought, back then, that the choice had been simple. Step forward or step back. Live or die.

He saw now that she'd been standing on a different edge entirely.

"If I'd stayed," he said quietly, "we wouldn't be here. But you would still be alone."

Her eyes snapped up to his. There it was again—that flash of something soft and terrified, something that had nothing to do with hatred or hunger.

He felt it as clearly as if he'd touched it.

"You don't have to be," he said.

Rowan swallowed, and the muscles in her neck jumped.

"You don't know what that costs me," she whispered.

"I know what it's costing you now."

She didn't answer. Her silence was more revealing than any argument.

The lantern throbbed once, light swelling until the chamber walls briefly drowned in purple. When it dimmed, the black inside it had grown thicker, curling through the amethyst like roots or veins.

Rowan tore her gaze away from him and stepped toward the doorway.

Trevor followed.

The corridor outside felt even narrower after the tight, curved room. The air was dense with the chill they'd carried out with them. The world smelled of stone, old dust, and the faint metallic tang of the future pressing against the present.

Rowan walked faster, her movements sharpened by some renewed urgency. Trevor kept pace, not letting her swallow the distance between them again.

"You can't fix me," she said without looking back.

"I'm not trying to fix you," he replied. "I'm trying to keep you."

That slowed her.

For three steps, the only sound was their boots against stone.

"Don't say things like that," she muttered.

"Why not? They're true."

She laughed, but it was a ragged thing.

"Truth is the last thing I want from you."

"What do you want from me, then?" he asked.

290

She didn't answer.

They walked on.

The corridor twisted, turned, dipped briefly, then rose. The ceiling lowered until Trevor could touch it with his fingertips if he stretched. He didn't. He felt superstitious about disturbing anything he didn't have to.

At last, the passage narrowed into something more like a tunnel. The stone drew close around them, the walls chalky and damp. Ahead, the darkness thickened, the lantern's reach seeming to shrink as if swallowed by the rock.

The passage ended in a constriction barely wide enough for one person.

It looked like a throat.

Rowan stopped.

The lantern's light spilled over the tight opening and met a deeper dark beyond, the kind that wasn't just absence of light but the suggestion of something waiting in it.

Trevor could feel the temperature drop another notch. The hairs along his arms and neck lifted.

"Is that it?" he asked quietly.

Rowan didn't respond. She stared at the pinch of stone, the set of her shoulders taut, as though tension were the only thing keeping her upright.

Trevor stepped around her.

She didn't try to stop him this time.

He moved until he stood between her and the narrowing passage, the lantern now casting his shadow back over her.

"No farther," he said.

Rowan's eyes flicked to his, startled.

"Move," she said. The word lacked its usual blade.

"No."

He let the refusal sit there, solid as the walls around them.

"If you want to go through there," he said, "you're going to have to look at me first."

Her jaw worked.

"This isn't about you," she said. It sounded like she was trying to convince herself.

"I know," he replied. "That's why it matters what you're about to do."

She stared at him, pupils wide in the lantern glow.

"Rowan," he said more softly, "look at me."

It took her longer than it should have.

Slowly, like someone turning toward a sound they know will hurt to hear, she lifted her head until her gaze met his.

Everything else in the world fell away.

He saw exhaustion there, etched in fine lines around her mouth. He saw defiance, the stubborn set of someone who'd built a worldview like a fortress and lived inside it for years. But under that, swimming up unbidden, he saw grief.

She looked like someone who had been waiting at a door for a very long time and had just realized that stepping through meant she couldn't come back.

"If there's anything left in you that doesn't want this," he said, "anything at all—don't take another step."

Her lips parted.

The lantern's light painted a faint sheen over her eyes. A single breath shuddered out of her, visible in the cold as a fogged exhale.

"You think it's that easy," she said.

"I know it isn't," he replied. "But it's still possible."

Her gaze flicked to the passage behind him, then back to his face.

"If I stop now," she whispered, "if I just… walk away… what does that make everything I've done?"

"Wrong," he said. The word came out gentle, not cruel. "It makes it wrong. It makes it something you chose once and can choose against now."

A tiny line appeared between her brows.

"You want me to admit I've been wrong my entire life."

"I want you to choose yourself over your ideas," Trevor said. "Just once."

Her eyes shone wetter now. She turned her face slightly, as if trying to escape the full force of his gaze and failing.

"You don't understand," she said. "They—the people I've seen, the ones I've watched—"

"I know what you've seen," he cut in softly. "Lonely people. Cruel people. People who hurt and keep hurting. But that's not the only truth."

"It's the one that doesn't lie," she said. "Hope keeps them waiting for something they don't deserve. Mercy keeps them chained to their own weakness. You think I'm doing this because I hate them, but I don't. I'm doing it because I see them."

"And I see you," he said.

The words landed with a weight that made the stone feel suddenly heavier.

"You brought me here," he went on, "because I was the last person you ever let give you hope. You said it yourself. That's what I was to you."

Her eyes closed for a moment, lashes damp.

"Trevor..." she breathed.

"If you really believed what you're saying," he said, "if you believed hope only breaks, you wouldn't be standing here listening to me. You wouldn't be letting me talk."

"I'm letting you talk," she said, opening her eyes again, "because once this is over, there won't be anything left to say."

"Then let it be over differently," he replied.

She gave a frayed laugh.

"You think I can just… turn around and go back?"

"Yes."

"And then what?" she asked. "I go home? I go back to the cemetery? I pretend I didn't lure you into a tomb and kill four people in order to do it?"

His chest ached. "I don't know what it looks like," he said. "I don't have a map for that. But I know the difference between someone who has no choice and someone who still does."

He took a breath that felt like it scraped his insides raw.

"Rowan, you still do."

Silence filled the space between them, thick and fragile.

Her eyes searched his like she might find a way out of herself there, some escape route he could give her. He didn't have one. All he had was the presence he kept offering, the hand he hadn't dropped even when she bloodied it.

For a heartbeat, the tension drained from her face.

Her shoulders lowered by a fraction. Her grip on the lantern loosened. Her mouth quivered as though on the verge of forming a different word—yes, maybe, or please.

Trevor's breath caught.

This was it.

He could feel it, the knife-edge of it, the precarious wobble of everything they'd been walking toward. If she stepped back, if she took his hand—

She stepped forward instead.

Not into the passage. Into him.

She closed the small distance until he could feel the cold radiating from her, until the fabric of her coat brushed his chest. Lanternlight swung between them, casting fractured glows over their faces.

Up close, she looked desperately young.

"I can't undo what's already been done," she whispered.

"There's still what comes after," he said.

Her gaze dropped to his mouth, then back up to his eyes. Something like longing flickered there, raw and exposed.

"You should have stayed on the bridge," she said.

It didn't sound like accusation.

It sounded like apology.

Before he could answer, she stepped to the side, slipping past him with a suddenness that left him reaching for her a second too late. The cold rush of her movement brushed his arm as she angled herself into the narrow throat of the stone.

The lantern's glow folded into the darkness ahead of her, struck the tight walls, and came back warped. The black veins in the glass pulsed faster, thicker, overtaking more of the amethyst with each beat.

"Rowan—" he started.

She didn't look back.

The sound in the tunnels changed. A low hum rose in the stone, the vibration so faint he felt it before he heard it. It ran up through his boots, into his legs, into his ribs. The future, pressing closer. The boundary between what had been and what would be thinning to a membrane.

Trevor stood there, heart pounding, watching the small of her back as she moved deeper into the constriction. She looked impossibly alone in that moment, swallowed by the earth.

She had made her decision.

His, when it came, did not feel like a choice at all.

He could stay here. He could let her go. He could turn and walk a different direction and let this become her story alone.

He stepped after her.

The stone closed around him as soon as he entered the tight passage. His shoulders brushed both walls. The lantern's hum filled the space, the light strobing faintly, painting Rowan's figure in broken flashes of violet and shadow as she moved ahead of him.

Whatever waited beyond this narrow throat, he wouldn't let her face it alone.

He'd been her last hope once. That would mean something, even if it killed him.

Behind them, the wider tunnel exhaled one last time and fell still.

They walked forward into the dark.

The One Who Saw Too Much

The narrow throat of the passage spat them out into a small, rounded chamber—no larger than a maintenance cell and shaped like the inside of a ribcage. The stone walls curved inward, slick with condensation that glistened under the lantern's glow. The ceiling pressed low enough that Trevor instinctively ducked when he stepped inside.

The air was colder here. Not the natural cold of underground stone, but the kind that felt claimed by something. A temperature chosen, not inherited.

Rowan crossed the threshold behind him, and the entire room shifted.

Not physically—Trevor would have felt that—but in atmosphere. In intention. The way a room changes when someone walks in who knows exactly why they're there.

Rowan exhaled a slow, controlled breath.

Her posture straightened, shoulders settling into a line of unsettling calm. Her breathing evened. Her jaw unclenched. The tremor that had haunted her fingers in the corridor was gone. She moved with a grace that was too smooth to be comforting, too controlled to be natural.

Trevor had seen her uncertain.
He had seen her afraid.
He had seen her almost break.

But this—

this was the woman who had arranged four bodies with deliberate hands.

The woman who had built a labyrinth inside her own loneliness.

The woman who had waited for him all night like a hunter waits for a final hinge in the dark.

She lifted the lantern slightly, and its amethyst light deepened, the black veins swirling inside it like ink dropped into water. The pulse of the magic inside no longer felt reactive—it felt timed. Harmonized. As though it had been waiting for this room, this air, this moment.

Trevor swallowed.

The cold hit the back of his throat like a warning.

"Rowan," he said softly—because saying nothing was worse. "Talk to me."

She didn't turn.

She didn't tense.

She simply raised one hand—

a quiet, precise motion—

and Trevor stopped speaking.

Not because she'd silenced him,

but because he recognized the gesture.

He'd seen it before on people who'd made catastrophic decisions.

It wasn't a command.

It was closure.

Rowan lowered her hand slowly, her eyes still fixed on the far wall as though reading something written there that only she could see.

When she finally turned toward him, the expression on her face made Trevor's breath go thin.

Calm.
Cold.
Perfectly aligned.

There was no trace of the quivering breaths from the corridor.
No hesitation.
No grief.
No girl from the bridge.
No trembling woman beside the fourth body.

This time with steel.

Trevor's chest tightened. It wasn't fear—he recognized fear after centuries of witnessing it—but a slow, sinking understanding.

The Rowan who had looked at him with watery eyes a few moments before, wasn't a person returning.

She had been a memory surfacing.

What stood in front of him now was a version of Rowan arriving anew.

.

Her true one.

Rowan lifted the lantern.

The black veins inside spidered outward, pressing against the glass like they wanted to break free.

Trevor felt the Future bleed humming in his ribs, vibrating through bone, buzzing down his fingers.

Something in him whispered:

You've reached the end of what words can do.

Rowan stepped farther into the chamber, her eyes never leaving his.

"You followed me," she said.
Her voice was soft. Too soft.
"Even after everything you saw."

Trevor tried to find the right words, but she shook her head once—slowly, deliberately.

"No more," she said.
Not angry.
Not triumphant.
Just absolute.

Her stillness was terrifying.
Not because it was monstrous—
but because it was certain.

Trevor felt the temperature drop again.

And for the first time, he truly understood:
Rowan Mercer wasn't fighting with herself anymore.

She had decided.

Rowan moved to the center of the chamber, placing the lantern on a raised slab of stone that looked like an altar never meant for worship. The amethyst glow stained her hands violet. Her shadow stretched long behind her, splitting into two silhouettes as if the lantern's fractured magic refused to settle on one version of her.

Trevor stayed near the entrance of the chamber—far enough to give her room, close enough to intervene. His pulse beat like a warning drum in his ears.

Rowan lifted her chin slightly.
"Do you know," she began softly, "what the world does with people like me?"

Trevor opened his mouth, but she continued—
not interrupting him,
but simply speaking louder than his breath.

"They don't see us," she said. "Not really. They look past us. Through us. They assume someone else will notice. Someone else will care. Someone else will offer something—mercy, hope, kindness." She let out a quiet laugh, empty of amusement. "But that someone else never comes."

She stepped around the slab, her hand brushing it as she passed, the cold stone startlingly gentle against her fingertips.

"I grew up believing invisibility was a curse," Rowan said. "I thought if I just spoke louder, moved differently, stood in the right place at the right time… someone would look up. Someone would say my name like it mattered."

Her eyes flicked to Trevor.
"That never happened."

Trevor felt that line like a blade under his ribs.

But Rowan didn't stop.

"I learned something," she continued. "Something quiet. Something truthful. The world doesn't want the invisible to be seen. We make them uncomfortable. A reminder of how easily they could become forgotten too."

She walked in a slow half-circle, the lantern's glow splitting her face into warm gold on one side and cold violet on the other. Her shadow rippled across the curved wall like a second Rowan pacing beside her.

"So I adapted," she said. "I became what they already believed I was. A ghost in their peripheries. A soft voice no one remembered. A presence no one questioned."

Her tone didn't rise, but it sharpened.

"And in that stillness... I watched. I saw the world for what it truly is. Not a place broken by cruelty." She shook her head. "But by hope."

Trevor blinked.
"What?"

Rowan smiled—and it was not unkind, which somehow made it far worse.

"Hope convinces the world that everyone is worth saving," she said. "That broken people can be mended. That lost souls can be carried home. That someone like me can be redeemed if only someone tries hard enough."

The lantern flared—
not brighter, but deeper, as if a depth inside it had cracked open.

"Hope is the lie that kept me still," Rowan whispered. "Waiting. Believing. Begging the universe to offer me something it never intended to give."

Her breath trembled slightly—not with vulnerability, but with force held tightly inside her ribs.

"You," she said to Trevor. "You were the only exception."

Trevor froze.

"You saw me," Rowan said quietly. "Not because I was worthy. Not because I asked. But because that's what you do. You give mercy to the forgotten. Hope to the hopeless. You step into the shadows because you can't bear the thought of a soul being left alone."

She took a step toward him.
Then another.

"And that is why you have to die."

Ice crawled through Trevor's chest.

Rowan stopped an arm's length away from him—close enough that he could see the tiny reflections of the lantern's shattered light spinning in her pupils.

"I was the last hope you were ever meant to give," she said, voice low. "Now you are the offer I must take."

Trevor's breath caught.
He didn't move.

307

He couldn't.

Rowan continued, softer still.

"I will not live my life begging for someone to save me. I will not let the world decide my worth. And I will not allow hope—yours or anyone else's—to demand I sit quietly in the dark waiting to be chosen."

The chamber felt smaller.
The walls closer.
The air tighter.

Rowan lifted her hand and placed it gently on Trevor's cheek—not tender, not cruel.
Just final.

"Tonight is mine," she whispered.
"My choice. My becoming."

The lantern flared like a heartbeat.

Trevor felt something inside him break
—not from her touch,
but from the quiet truth in her voice.

Rowan stepped back, lowering her hand as if setting down the last piece of a puzzle she'd spent years assembling.

"When you die," she said, "I decide who deserves mercy. I decide who receives hope. I decide who is worth saving."

Her voice didn't rise in triumph.
It didn't tremble in fear.
It simply was.

308

Pure.
Absolute.
Terrifying in its clarity.

Trevor realized then that Rowan Mercer wasn't killing him out of rage, hurt, revenge, or madness.

She was killing him
because she believed
deep in her bones
that she was right.

And that made her unstoppable.
For a long moment after Rowan stepped away, Trevor couldn't move.

Not because of fear.
Not because of shock.
But because something inside him had gone startlingly still.

Her words hit him harder than any physical blow could've managed.
Not the threats—he'd heard a lifetime of threats from the dying, the desperate, the lost.

No.
It was the conviction.
The quiet assurance.
The absolute belief that she had won before the fight had even begun.

Rowan Mercer looked at him with the certainty of someone who had already buried him.

Trevor inhaled slowly.
And something in that breath clicked.

A line snapped taut in his chest.
Not anger—
resolve.

He straightened.
It wasn't much—just the set of his shoulders, the lift of his chin—but in the cramped chamber, it was a shift large enough to change the air.

Rowan noticed.
Her eyes narrowed an almost imperceptible fraction.

Trevor spoke quietly.
"You think hope is a lie."

Rowan didn't react.
Her face remained composed, almost serene.

Trevor took a step toward her.

"But hope is the only thing that ever found you."

Her expression flickered—so faintly someone else would have missed it.
Not him.

Trevor had watched centuries of people crumble, harden, heal, break again.
He knew micro-expressions the way surgeons knew anatomy.

"You weren't invisible because the world wanted you gone," he said. "You were invisible because you hid. Because you stopped

310

believing anyone would ever look. Because you stopped letting
yourself be seen."

Rowan's jaw tightened—one muscle feathering beneath her skin.

Trevor pressed on.

"And yet I saw you anyway."

The lantern trembled.
A single, sharp pulse.

Rowan's eyes snapped toward it instinctively.

Trevor wasn't sure whether the magic had reacted to his voice…
or she had.

He stepped closer.

"You think killing me gives you control," he said. "You think it
lets you choose who gets mercy. But that's not how it works." He
pointed to the lantern. "If I die, that doesn't become yours. It turns
you into it."

Rowan's breath hitched.
Barely—but enough.

Trevor softened his tone.

"You know it. Somewhere deep inside, you know it."

Her eyes flicked toward him again, searching his face as if
cataloging every line, every flaw, every truth she wanted to reject.

Trevor let the silence build, then broke it.

"You want to stop being unseen? Then fight for it. Fight for yourself. Fight for your life. But don't pretend taking mine makes you free."

The lantern pulsed again—
harder this time, a ripple of amethyst cracking the shadows on the wall.

Rowan's composure thinned.

Trevor stepped forward until there was only a foot of space between them.

"You don't get to decide hope dies," he whispered. "Not while I'm still breathing."

Something cold, sharp, and electric swept across Rowan's expression.

And Trevor realized—

She had never expected him to fight back.
Not like this.
Not with truth.
Not with conviction.

Not with her own loneliness turned gently, devastatingly against her.

"You won't win," she said quietly.
No threat.
Just certainty.

Trevor exhaled.

"Maybe not," he said. "But I'm sure as hell going to try."

He didn't look heroic when he said it.
He didn't puff his chest or square his stance.
He simply said the words the way Rowan said hers—

with absolute, unshakeable belief.

For the first time since this night began, Rowan stepped back.

It wasn't fear.
It wasn't doubt.

It was recognition.

Trevor wasn't prey anymore.

He was an obstacle.

A real one.

The lantern's amethyst core deepened, swirling faster, its black veins writhing like something alive.

The chamber felt charged—
a breath before lightning,
a lull before collapse.

Trevor lowered his voice one last time.

"You said you watched the world," he whispered. "Then you should know—hope doesn't die easily."

He tilted his head just slightly.

"And neither do I."
For a heartbeat, neither of them spoke.

The air vibrated with a tension so sharp it was almost a sound. Trevor's declaration still hung there—thin, fragile, glowing at the edges like something made of light instead of breath.

Rowan didn't move.
Didn't blink.

Then, very slowly, she inhaled.

The change was subtle at first—a shift of her shoulders, a softening of her jaw—but then it widened, rippling outward like a drop in still water. She lifted her head as though the ceiling itself were lowering over her, and her eyes darkened in a way that was not emotional but elemental.

"Trying," she murmured, "isn't enough."

The lantern pulsed behind her—
a deep amethyst throb
that made the shadows shiver violently along the walls.

Trevor's heartbeat quickened.
But he stood his ground.

Rowan's gaze roamed his face, lingering a second too long near his mouth, his eyes, the place on his cheek where her hand had rested earlier. There was a strange, almost wistful silence in her expression— as if she were committing something to memory.

Then it vanished.

A smile touched the corner of her lips. Not cruel.
Not mocking.
Something worse.

A smile of understanding.

"You really meant that," she said quietly.
"That you'd fight."

Trevor swallowed hard. "Yes."

"Good."

The way she said it sent a cold line down his spine.

Rowan stepped back toward the lantern—just one pace, but
enough that Trevor felt the shift in power. She slid her fingers beneath
the handle, and when she lifted it, the amethyst light surged upward in
a violent column, scattering fractured violet across her face.

Her shadow grew long behind her.
Too long.
Too sharp.

"You think you saw me tonight," she said.
"You didn't."

She angled the lantern slightly, and the veins of black inside
writhed, pushing toward the glass as if starving for release. The light
bled across her features, sculpting her into something almost
ceremonial.

Trevor's breath caught.

Rowan tilted her head.

"Then again," she whispered, "you were the one who taught me how to see."

She stepped past him—slow, soundless—until her shoulder nearly brushed his. For an instant he thought she would stop, maybe even falter, but she kept moving, her voice drifting back like a ghost.

"You wanted to fight, Trevor."
A pause.
"So, fight me."

He turned, but she was already halfway through the chamber's exit, her silhouette melting into the curved tunnel beyond. The amethyst glow stretched with her, hugging the walls, reshaping the darkness into a path that felt ordained.

Trevor stumbled after her, the cold thickening around him.
"Rowan—"

"Don't follow blindly," she said without looking back.
"Not anymore."

She disappeared into the catacombs, and the lantern's bruised light swallowed the space she'd occupied.

Trevor felt something he hadn't felt all night—
a horrifying flicker of exhilaration.

She wanted him to chase her.
She wanted him to struggle.
She wanted him to resist.

Not because she doubted the outcome—
but because she wanted to earn it.

Trevor steadied himself.

The future bleed thrummed through his ribs again, a quiet trembling that felt like a countdown.

He stepped into the corridor.

The air felt different now—
charged, reactive, as if the catacombs themselves were listening.

Rowan's voice floated from somewhere deeper in the labyrinth, soft and echoing.

"Come find me."

His pulse hammered.
He started forward.

Because there was no way to stop what was coming
—
but there might still be a way
to change
how it ended.

And the worst part?

As he pushed into the darkness after her,
the hope he'd felt earlier didn't die.

It grew.

The Sound Heard

The tunnel swallowed Rowan whole.

Trevor stepped after her, pulse stuttering, lungs dragging in the cold. The moment he crossed the threshold, the temperature shifted—not sharply, not violently, but like an idea settling over skin. The air felt dense, as if it wasn't just filling the space but paying attention to it.

He froze.

This wasn't the same quiet that had haunted the earlier catacombs.
This was a quiet with intention.
A quiet that listened.

Trevor let his eyes adjust to the faint amethyst haze ahead. The walls glistened with condensation, thin as sweat on glass. His breath came out in pale, ghostly ribbons.

Rowan's footsteps echoed distantly—not fast, not fleeing, but measured. Each tap of her boots was deliberate, as if she walked to a metronome only she could hear.

She wasn't running.
She was choosing the rhythm.
Choosing how he followed.

Trevor willed his body forward because standing still felt worse. The tunnel narrowed around him, the walls drawing in with the patient confidence of a beast that knew exactly what it cornered.

He didn't dare call her name.
He knew better.

Rowan wasn't someone you called after.
Tonight proved that too clearly.

He placed each step carefully, testing his footing, listening for the slightest change in acoustics. The floor dipped once, then again, then curved, and Trevor marked each shift in his mind. If he had any chance—any—of keeping ahead of her, it would come from knowing these passages better than she expected.

The lantern pulse flared behind her shape—dim, steady, slow. A resting heartbeat. Trevor's own pulse tried to match it but only managed a jittering imitation.

He followed.

The corridor forked twice before straightening into a narrow throat flanked by walls carved unevenly from the earth. Trevor traced his fingertips along one, feeling its texture—powdery limestone here, sharper shale a few feet down. He wasn't sure why he noted it. Maybe survival made people catalog strange details.

Or maybe Rowan's speech had struck deeper than he realized.

Her voice still echoed in his skull.

Hope keeps you waiting.

Trevor swallowed hard and kept moving.

If she believed that, he needed to prove the opposite.

The footsteps ahead suddenly stopped.

Trevor held still, breath frozen in his throat. The silence thickened, swelling until it felt alive.

He waited.

Then—

A single, soft crunch of gravel behind him.

Trevor spun.

Rowan stood at the mouth of the tunnel he'd just come from, lantern low, her silhouette a long shadow carved out of violet light. She didn't smile. Didn't tilt her head. Didn't speak.

She simply looked at him.

Measuring him.

Trevor ran.

He darted into the left-hand passage—narrower than the others, ceiling sloping low enough to brush the top of his hair. Rowan's footsteps followed, unhurried, precise.

She wasn't giving chase.
She was tracking.

At the end of the corridor, a collapsed archway waited—a mess of rubble and beams and rusted metal braces. Trevor threw himself to his knees and crawled sideways into a gap barely wide enough for a ribcage. Stone scraped across his cheek. Dust filled his lungs. He squeezed into the space until the tunnel's glow disappeared and only thin fractures of light cut through the debris.

Rowan reached the archway seconds later.

Trevor could sense her kneeling even before he saw her shadow cross the cracks between stones. Her hand entered his view first— steady, clean, fingers trailing gently along the rubble as if she were reading a secret message written on stone.

She didn't reach into the gap.

Didn't try to pull him out.

Instead, she exhaled softly.

"Good," she murmured, just loud enough for the stone to carry it.
"You're learning."

Her footsteps faded.

Trevor stayed pressed into the rubble for several long seconds after she disappeared, lungs shaking against his ribs. He crawled out only when the corridor's pulse steadied, checking each shadow twice.

He had escaped.

But she'd let him.

The realization crawled up his spine like ice.

***

Trevor moved quickly, keeping low, taking turns at random until he reached a junction where four tunnels met. He paused, listening for her.

Nothing.

The silence was thicker now, pressing against his ears like cotton.

He chose the third tunnel on instinct.

Halfway down, he stepped into a larger chamber—one Rowan had passed earlier without stopping. The light was thin here, the amethyst glow catching on scattered objects across the floor.

At first, Trevor thought the debris was random.

Then he saw the rope fibers.
The faint bloodstains.
The carved grooves in the wall where someone had struggled.

His breath knotted.

Rowan's traps weren't improvisations.
They were iterations.
Refinements.

She had been perfecting the act for longer than he'd wanted to believe.

A soft scrape pulled his gaze up.

At the far end of an adjoining corridor, Rowan stood framed by its throat, lantern held just high enough to illuminate her eyes. The light carved her shadow across the floor, long as a spear.

She still didn't rush.

She walked—slow, unbroken steps, each one echoing evenly like ritual.

Trevor fled through a side tunnel. His boots slapped stone, heartbeat rising into his throat. Behind him, Rowan's footsteps remained a steady metronome.

Not hunting.
Pacing.

Her voice reached him after the second turn, floated through the tunnels like a breeze navigating a maze.

"I want you to run, Trevor. Try! Do something."
A pause.
"I want to see how far hope can run."

Trevor pushed faster, lungs burning.

He refused to let her be right about him.

***

He stumbled into a half-forgotten utility room—walls lined with abandoned tools, broken crypt panels leaning like toppled gravestones. A rusted security gate hung crooked on one hinge.

Trevor scanned the room—fast, desperate, assessing.

Not a place to fight.
A place to delay.

He grabbed the sagging gate and dragged it across the entrance. Metal shrieked. His arms shook under its weight. He jammed rubble and a fallen beam against its base, creating a barricade—not strong, but enough to steal seconds.

Footsteps approached.

The lantern glow spilled across the floor like liquid.

Rowan stopped on the other side of the gate.

Trevor froze.

Her fingers curled around one of the bars, knuckles pale in the violet light. The gate trembled with the pressure of her grip. She could break it. Snap it. Tear it open.

Instead, she leaned her forehead lightly against the metal, breath whispering through the gaps.

"Trevor…"
Her voice softened to something quiet, intimate.
"You're better at this than I thought."

The words struck him harder than if she'd threatened him.

Trevor backed toward the far wall, scanning for another way out—and found it. A half-obscured passage, narrow and low, hidden behind a leaning coffin lid. Rowan hadn't looked this way earlier. She hadn't needed to.

Her fingers tightened on the bars.

Trevor eased into the narrow passage.
Stone scraped his back.

He moved deeper.

Rowan sensed it.

Her breath hitched—sharp, precise.

She lifted the lantern, its amethyst veins swirling violently.

And then she whispered:

"Run."

Trevor ran.

For the first time all night—
he wasn't just surviving.

He had bought real time.
The narrow passage Trevor slipped into contracted around him, compressing the air from every angle. The ceiling dropped low enough he had to hunch forward, palms sliding along damp stone to keep balance. His breath rasped loud in the tight space. Too loud. He forced himself to slow it, quell it, bury it beneath the pulse in his ears.

Behind him, the faintest sound—
not footsteps,
not a voice,
but the shifting weight of someone choosing when the floor should creak beneath them.

Rowan wasn't following yet.
She was listening.

The realization made him move faster.

The tunnel curved downward into a steeper slope, the floor slick and uneven. Trevor stumbled once, catching himself against the wall. His fingers brushed faint scratches carved at shoulder height—a cluster of lines, almost frantic, etched by someone else on another night.

His stomach twisted.

He didn't have long.

He kept going.

The tunnel widened suddenly into a cavern where the ceiling opened thirty feet overhead, supported by a grid of ancient stone pillars. Each one was carved with faded symbols—religious? Ritualistic? He couldn't tell. The lantern's glow wasn't here yet, but its faint aura still breathed in the distance, as though it remembered the shape of Rowan's hand.

Trevor stepped lightly, listening to his own footsteps echo. The sound ricocheted off the pillars, making it impossible to tell which direction Rowan might come from.

He circled around a collapsed column to regain his bearings, letting the silence settle again.

Then—
a single sound.

A boot tapping gently against stone.

Trevor spun, chest tightening.
The echo swallowed direction; it could've come from anywhere.

Anywhere.

He edged behind the pillar, lowering himself into the darkest shadow available. Cold seeped through his clothes, biting at his skin. Every instinct screamed this was the wrong place to stop.

He forced those instincts quiet.

Wait.
Listen.
Breathe.

Two breaths.
Three.
Four.

A soft hum drifted through the cavern—barely more than breath, a melody without words. Rowan's voice carried it, weaving between the pillars like she was walking her fingers along the room's bones.

Trevor clenched his jaw, the sound scraping something raw inside him. She wasn't humming because she was calm. She was humming because she wanted him to hear her calm.

A psychological blade.
A performance of composure.

He pressed his back against the stone.

Rowan's voice drifted again, echoing differently this time. She had moved.
But from where to where?

Trevor scanned quickly, eyes sharp, searching for anything he could use—loose stones, broken beams, an incline, a hiding place.

Then he saw it: a ventilation shaft half-collapsed near the floor, its grate bent upward just enough for a person to slip under.

A small person.
A desperate one.

Trevor hurried across the cavern floor, keeping low, boots making almost no sound. He reached the shaft and knelt, fingers hooking the bent grate. It groaned softly—a small, metallic whine.

He froze.

The humming stopped.

Only silence—
thick, charged, listening—
filled the cavern again.

Trevor eased the grate up another inch.
Another.
Another.

The lantern glow swelled faintly at the far end of the cavern, angling around a pillar as Rowan moved.

Trevor sucked in a breath, held it, then slid himself under the grate and into the narrow shaft. Dust coated his palms and filled his throat. He dragged the grate down behind him as quietly as possible.

Rowan's footsteps reached the cavern floor.

He held still.
Absolutely still.

Rowan paused near the center of the cavern, lantern held at chest height, its amethyst core swirling slowly. She turned her head, scanning the pillars, listening as though she could hear him through the stone.

Trevor pressed deeper into the shaft, barely daring to breathe.

Then Rowan spoke—so softly he wasn't sure if it was meant for him or for the catacombs themselves.

"You're getting clever."

He nearly flinched.
The tone wasn't mocking.
It wasn't even impressed.

It was… curious.
Like she wanted to understand him now.

She stepped around the broken column, light spilling along the cavern floor like violet fog.

"I wondered," she murmured, "how long it would take you to stop running like prey."

The lantern pulsed.

Trevor bit the inside of his cheek to keep from reacting.

Rowan tilted her head, listening to the echoes she created.

"Good," she murmured finally.
"You're making me work."

She moved off again—slow, sure, the lantern's glow trailing behind her like a ribbon dragged through water.

Trevor waited until her steps faded past the left corridor before inching forward in the shaft. The metal scraped faintly beneath his weight, but the sound was swallowed by the passage.

The shaft turned sharply and sloped upward toward a narrower section. Trevor dragged himself forward, muscles shaking from the angle, lungs tight from the dust.

Halfway through, the floor vibrated softly—
a subtle tremor, not enough to shift debris,
but enough to remind him that he wasn't moving through solid ground
so much as through the veins of something ancient.

He clawed forward until the shaft opened into a small alcove carved into a side tunnel. He pulled himself free and collapsed against the wall, chest heaving.

Time.
He had bought time.

Not much.
But more than he'd had all night.

He forced himself upright.
He couldn't rest.
Not now.

Trevor pressed deeper into the tunnel.

The air cooled again—sharp, needle-like.

The moisture on the walls crystallized in thin patterns like spiderweb frost.

The lantern's glow returned, faint, just barely bleeding onto a distant corner.

Rowan had turned around.
She was coming this way now.

Trevor ducked behind a jut of stone, heart hammering.

Her footsteps were closer this time.
Measured.
Steady.
Her breathing audible—calm, even, almost meditative.

Trevor realized once more what made her terrifying:

She wasn't angry.
She wasn't frantic.
She wasn't reveling.

She was becoming.

He braced himself, watching the faint shimmer grow brighter.

Rowan's silhouette appeared around the bend—slow, gliding, an almost regal shape cast in fractured violet.

Trevor's mouth went dry.

She paused, turning her head slightly as if scenting the air.

Then—
as if she could feel the direction of Trevor's heartbeat—

332

she began walking toward him.

He forced himself into the narrowest break in the stone wall, flattening himself against the cold rock, trying to become part of it.

Rowan's footsteps drew nearer.
Her lantern glow spilled brighter.
She stopped directly in front of the jut of stone hiding him.

Trevor's breath caught high in his throat.

Her fingers brushed the edge of the rock.
Slow.
Thoughtful.

"Where will you go now?" she whispered.

Trevor's pulse spiked.

She leaned closer—
close enough that Trevor felt the warmth of the lantern grazing the side of his face even through the stone.

"Where does hope hide," she breathed,
"when it knows it's running out of time?"

Trevor lunged sideways, breaking from his cover.

Rowan straightened sharply, not startled—simply adjusting trajectory. He sprinted past her, ducking under the sweep of her arm, slipping into a smaller tunnel on her left.

Rowan turned after him, footsteps picking up pace, her voice chasing like a blade thrown through the dark.

"Yes—run."

Trevor's lungs burned as he pushed into the next corridor, deeper than he'd ever gone.

He could almost feel her breath behind him, close enough to be heat on the back of his neck.

Then—

He found it.

A narrow gap in the stone wall, barely visible through grime, just wide enough for a shoulder.

He shoved himself inside and slid down into darkness.

Trevor hit the sloped floor hard, sliding down a short incline until he collided with a shallow depression carved into the ground. Dust exploded beneath him in a muted cloud. The impact knocked air from his lungs, leaving him gasping.

He didn't move at first.
Couldn't.

He lay there, ribs throbbing, while the world narrowed to the sound of his own heartbeat thudding against the stone.

Above him, Rowan's footsteps approached—slow, steady, unhurried.

She wasn't chasing.
She was following inevitability.

Trevor forced himself onto his elbows, searching the darkened hollow. The ceiling was low, arching downward like the curve of a rib. The walls were smooth stone dyed with centuries of damp. No exits. No branching tunnels.

Just a single break he'd slid through and—

His eyes locked on a small, rusted door frame half-embedded in the right-hand wall. The door long gone, only a warped metal edge remained. A maintenance alcove.

Trevor crawled toward it, teeth gritted against the pain in his side. He squeezed himself into the alcove just as Rowan's lantern glow spilled across the upper lip of the depression.

He pressed himself flat against the far wall, body aligning with the shadows.

Rowan reached the top of the slope.

She didn't descend.
She stood at the edge, lantern dangling from her hand, its amethyst veins swirling with a lethargic hunger.

Trevor willed himself invisible.
Silent.
Stone.

Rowan's breath slipped between her teeth, steady and controlled—almost serene. She lowered herself into a crouch, lantern casting a soft violet halo over the incline.

Trevor's pulse thundered.

Rowan tilted her head.
Listening.

For a moment, he thought she'd come down.
Thought she'd sweep the lantern across the hollow and find him with the ease of a predator following heat.

Instead, she smiled.

Softly.
Almost tenderly.

"You're close."

Trevor's skin prickled.

Her head turned slowly toward the right—directly above the alcove.

Not seeing him.
Sensing him.

She stood, straightening with a fluid grace that stripped the moment of all humanity.

She didn't descend.

She stepped backward from the slope and vanished from view.

Trevor kept still, counting seconds in the dark.
Five.
Ten.
Twenty.

Nothing.

When his breathing finally steadied, Trevor risked moving again. He slid out of the alcove, muscles aching, and climbed the incline cautiously, testing each foothold.

He could feel Rowan's presence through the air—faint, diffused, like heat radiating through stone.

At the top of the slope, he hesitated.

Then he heard it—

A faint scraping sound.
Deliberate.
Metal sliding against stone.

Trevor pressed against the wall and peered around the corner.

Rowan stood halfway down the connected corridor, her back to him. Her hand traced idle shapes across the stone, her fingers leaving faint streaks where she dragged the lantern's heat.

She wasn't searching.

She was waiting.

Trevor's breath hitched.

Her posture was wrong—not tense, not alert, but relaxed, as though she had already calculated every possible path he could take and decided which ones she wanted to let him find.

He stepped back silently.

She spoke without turning.

"You bought time," Rowan said quietly. "Use it."

Trevor froze.

Her voice wasn't taunting.
It wasn't mocking.
It was almost… approving.

"You're adapting," she said. "Changing. Becoming something more than a soul hoping to be saved."

She finally turned, lantern hanging at her side, the amethyst veins beating like the pulse of something alive inside the glass.

Trevor's breath locked in his chest.

"You're becoming interesting."

She took one slow step forward.

Trevor retreated, instinctively. His heel brushed the edge of the slope—his body a second from tumbling.

Rowan stopped.

She lifted the lantern slightly.

Its light fractured.
Then dimmed.
Then surged again—hard enough to cast her silhouette in violent cuts across the walls.

Trevor jerked back, sliding into the tunnel on the right, using the momentary flare to vanish from her line of sight.

He sprinted deeper, the air thinning around him, each breath slicing cold into his throat.

Behind him, Rowan didn't give chase.

Her voice followed instead—

"Run, Trevor. Run because you can."

He pushed harder.

"Run because you should."

The tunnel twisted sharply around an abrupt corner.

"And run," she whispered, voice echoing like a promise he
couldn't outrun,
"because I want to see how far hope goes before it breaks."

The words chased him long after her footsteps faded.

Trevor didn't slow until he reached a break in the stone where
darkness pooled like ink. He pressed himself into it, hands gripping
the wall to steady the tremble in his limbs.

He was alive.
Not because she'd spared him.
Not because he'd tricked her.

But because—
for the first time—
he was genuinely outpacing her.

Even if only by seconds.

Those seconds mattered.

Trevor closed his eyes, chest heaving, sweat cold under his
clothes.

For the first time all night, he felt something
dangerous,
vital,
terrifyingly alive
ignite in him:

hope turned into action.

He pushed off the wall, swallowing the pain in his ribs, and
moved deeper into the catacombs.

He wasn't running blindly anymore.
He wasn't following her pace.

He was setting his own.

And somewhere behind him, Rowan—
lantern glowing like a bruised heart,
steps measured,
breath steady—
smiled again.

Because the hunt had finally become
exactly
what she wanted.

The Lantern Turns

Trevor pressed his back to the curved wall as he slipped into a narrow alcove, the catacomb air thinning around him. It was colder than before—not the normal kind of cold, not the moist burial chill—but something sharper, metallic, humming just beneath the skin. Frost was forming in strange patterns across the stone: branching veins that crawled outward, as if reaching for him.

He knew she was close before he heard anything.
There was a shift in pressure, a tremor too low to be sound.

Trevor swallowed hard and stepped farther into the chamber. The ceiling dipped here, dense with honeycombed recesses where old bones rested behind rusted bars. It felt like sheltered ribs of something long dead.

Then Rowan's silhouette appeared at the far end.

She didn't lunge or storm or hurry. She walked with the unhurried calm of someone arriving at a place she'd always intended to go. Each step punctuated the quiet like a signature, her boots brushing through the dust in a steady, almost ceremonial rhythm.

The lantern in her hand dimmed suddenly.

Trevor blinked. The chamber plunged into darkness for a heartbeat. In that heartbeat he felt his spine turn to ice.

Then the lantern flared back to life—

but wrong.

The amethyst center had gone too dark.
Not dim, not violet—
black.
A perfect void, circled by a thin, bruised halo of violet light that throbbed like a pulse.

Rowan lifted the lantern slightly, as if weighing it. She didn't react to the transformation.

Trevor did.

The shadows around her didn't behave. The light fractured around her shoulders, splitting in ways that made no physical sense. For a single flickering second, her outline doubled—one Rowan standing where she always had, and a taller, thinner echo rising half a step behind her. That echo glowed faintly, as though light were trapped beneath the skin trying to burn outward.

Trevor's breath snagged. He pressed back into the wall.

Rowan looked at him with calm eyes.
"Trevor."

But he didn't just hear her voice.
There was a second voice underneath—soft, merciful, unbearably warm.
The kind of voice that belonged to someone who saved strangers on Christmas Eve.

Rowan didn't notice.
She waited for him to respond.

Trevor couldn't. His throat was too tight. Something in the air tasted like copper and winter and endings.

Trevor slid sideways, edging into a different alcove, a roundish chamber with walls lined in old ribs and skulls arranged in patterns meant to honor, not frighten. The onyx lantern's glow crawled after Rowan like a living shadow, fracturing the geometry as she stepped forward.

Her face appeared in the glow, then disappeared, then reappeared, illuminated from too many angles and not enough.

Trevor blinked, but the distortion worsened.

Rowan existed twice.
No—she existed now and later, layered on top of each other like a double exposure.

Present Rowan:
Human. Determined. Cold fire behind her eyes, not supernatural, just relentless.

Future Rowan:
Backlit from beneath her skin.
Edges burning faintly like smoldering paper.
Hair lifting slightly as if stirred by a breeze Trevor couldn't feel.
Eyes deep and lightless, not dead but endless.

Her footsteps echoed twice—
the real sound first, then the same sound a fraction of a second later, hollow and too close.

The breath she exhaled fogged the air in two separate shapes.

Trevor's chest tightened as understanding crept over him with the certainty of frost.

This wasn't what she became if she killed him.
This wasn't what she became because of malice or grief or anger.

This was what she became because she must.

Because this was the shape Christmas hope carved into those who bore it.
Because the magic that saved the lost did not choose the willing.

It chose the inevitable.

Trevor felt horror rise in him—
but then something else glimmered beneath it.

Future Rowan wasn't void.
There was warmth there, twisted and painful, but unmistakable.
Something like mercy, but strangled by the weight of responsibility.

If she carried mercy in her future,
then mercy still existed inside her now.

Trevor inhaled sharply, the icy air cutting his lungs.

Maybe—
just maybe—
he could reach that part of her.
The part that wasn't lost.
The part that was still Rowan, still human, still reachable.

Hope swelled in him like a dangerous flame.

Rowan, in the present, tilted her head slightly, as if sensing something shift—not in the tunnel, but in him.

And then she kept walking.

The corridor narrowed ahead, a slender stone throat barely wide enough for two bodies to pass without brushing. A choke point. A place where, if Trevor kept running, she'd catch him anyway.

So he didn't run.

He stepped forward into the narrowing corridor and stopped.

Rowan did the same.

The lantern jerked in her hand, the onyx center pulsing violently. Light tore sideways, striking the bones and scattering fractured shadows.

The "bleed" surged.

Future Rowan snapped into place over Present Rowan like a second skin. Her silhouette towered a fraction taller, her hands illuminated by internal fire. For a moment, her shadow stuck to the ceiling instead of the floor.

Trevor swallowed his fear.

"Rowan."
His voice shook, but he didn't back down.

Her eyes softened with something almost respectful.

He took a breath he didn't feel himself take.
"I can see you."

A tiny crease formed between her brows. "You always could."

"No."

Trevor stepped closer, trembling.

"I see what you become."

Rowan's expression didn't flicker, but the lantern did.

Its pulse spasmed, black swallowing violet for a heartbeat.

Trevor forced himself to keep going.

"You're not freeing yourself by killing me. You're binding yourself. You're walking straight into the thing you hate most."

Rowan blinked once.

Very slowly.

A human gesture, yes—but something hollowed it.

"You think you're escaping hope," Trevor whispered.

"But you'll become it."

A soft, strangled exhale slipped from her.

Trevor couldn't tell if it was humor or grief.

The future-voice layered beneath her present voice whispered something he couldn't understand, something too warm, too gentle.

The lantern stuttered so violently it washed the walls in seizure-light.

Trevor took his moment.

He slammed his shoulder into a support beam, knocking loose a lattice of old stones. They avalanched down into the narrow corridor, spilling between them in a choking cloud of dust.

Rowan stepped back, caught off-guard for the first time since the chase began.

Trevor shoved a rusted metal grate between them, its hinges screaming as it slammed shut. The latch—miraculously—held.

He stumbled backward into the next chamber, lungs burning, eyes stinging.

Across the barrier, Rowan stared at him.
Calm.
Collected.
More resolved than before.

As the dust cleared, the Future Bleed passed over her again, slow as a tide. Trevor saw her future silhouette overlapping her real form— still human, still Rowan, but brightening at the edges with the weight of what she would carry.

"Inevitable," Rowan murmured.
Her real voice said it.
Her future voice whispered it.

Trevor didn't wait to hear more.
He turned and ran.
Trevor burst into a larger chamber at the top of a slight incline, lungs burning. The air was different here—colder, fresher, touched by a thin thread of winter. There was a seam in the stone where wind crawled inward, a faint suggestion of a stairwell or an old maintenance shaft leading upward.

A way out.
A real one.

Trevor staggered toward it—

—just as the Future Bleed surged like a wave.

Future Rowan stood already at the top of the steps.

Not moving.
Not reaching.
Just watching, illuminated from within, the faintest halo of inverted light spilling behind her.

Trevor froze in place.

Present Rowan stepped into view seconds later, emerging from a side corridor. She hadn't caught up physically—but the Bleed made it look like she had always been here waiting.

Her two selves overlapped, out of sync.

Trevor's breath shook.

Future Rowan whispered, her voice impossibly layered:
"They always think it's this easy."

Present Rowan tilted her head.
"What?"

Trevor didn't answer.

Because behind her, the future version took one step forward—but present Rowan's body didn't move.

The afterimage stepped through light that wasn't there, casting impossible shadows that pulled toward Trevor like reaching hands.

Trevor's hope shifted shape.
He no longer hoped to escape physically.

He hoped to change the shape of what Rowan would become.

348

To interrupt the path, even for a moment.
To scratch some mark into the future she would inherit.

Rowan took a slow, even breath.
Her eyes softened—not with mercy, but with inevitability.

Trevor backed into the far wall, chest heaving, staring at the place where future Rowan occupied the exact spot Trevor sensed his own ending.

Present Rowan stepped—not aggressively, not hungrily, just surely—toward that same spot.

Her silhouette and her future silhouette converged.

Trevor braced himself.

Not for survival.
But for meaning.

The onyx lantern pulsed once, twice, then stabilized into a dark, steady glow.

Rowan whispered,
"Trevor."

But the future voice beneath her whispered something softer, merciful enough to break him.

And Trevor understood:

He would not live through the next chapter.
But he could decide what she carried into the one after.

Inevitable

Trevor knew it was a dead end before he saw the wall.

The floor rose under his feet in a subtle incline that wasn't quite natural, a slow, insistent push that nudged him forward whether he wanted it or not. The tunnel opened into a rounded chamber where the ceiling sagged low and the walls folded inward, smooth with age and damp. There were no branching corridors here, no side doors, no cracks big enough to pretend might lead anywhere else.

The room felt like a held breath.

He stopped in the center of it, one hand braced on the wall to steady his shaking legs. The stone was cold, but not the same chill he'd felt all night. This was deeper. Quieter. The kind of cold that implied nothing would warm it again.

Behind him, somewhere down the tangled corridors, the onyx lantern pulsed.

He couldn't see the light yet, but he felt it. It beat against the stone like a slow, dark heart, each throb sending a faint vibration under his boots. The air around him seemed to contract and release in time with it, as if the catacombs themselves were syncing to that rhythm.

The Future Bleed tugged at him in little glitches.

351

If he turned his head too fast, there was a half-second where his own outline didn't keep up, a faint echo of his body lagging, then snapping back into place. When he blinked, shadows seemed a fraction misaligned before they corrected themselves.

It was weaker now. Thinner.

Like someone fast-forwarding through the last seconds of a recording.

Trevor closed his eyes and listened.

For the first time since this started, the instinct to run didn't surge up automatically. There was nowhere useful to run to. He could bolt back into the maze, find another vent, another gap, another narrow pocket of stone—but at best that would buy him a handful of minutes. At worst, it would just make his last moments smaller and more pathetic.

He opened his eyes.

The rounded chamber was almost featureless. A few low niches cut into the walls held old bones stacked neatly, anonymous and undisturbed. The ceiling bellied low enough that if he reached up, he could probably touch it.

This was where the path ended.

Trevor took a breath and heard how steady it sounded. His hands were still shaking; his heart hadn't gotten the memo. But beneath all of that, another feeling settled in—something like clarity. Or surrender. Or both.

He could not choose whether he died tonight.
He could only choose what he did with the seconds he had left.

Maybe that was all "hope" ever really had been anyway.

He turned to face the tunnel mouth and waited for Rowan.

He heard her before the light reached him.

Her footsteps moved with the same measured pace they'd kept the entire hunt, never rushing, never stumbling. The stone carried them cleanly, a metronome ticking down to an inevitable end. With each step, the pressure in the air increased, tightening around his chest.

Then the glow seeped in—slow at first, like spilled ink.

The onyx lantern's light crawled along the floor, then up the curved walls, warping the shadows into stretched, uncertain shapes. The core of the flame was still a depthless black ringed by thin, bruised violet, but there was a faint, colorless halo around it now. A ghost of something softer trying to push through.

Rowan stepped into the chamber.

The Future Bleed stuttered to life as she crossed the threshold. For a heartbeat, Trevor saw two of her: the Rowan of now, solid and human and terrible, and another layered an inch behind her, a taller, thinner outline lit from within. The second silhouette's edges fuzzed like paper beginning to smolder, flickers of pale light licking along her shoulders and hair.

Then the echo-image wavered and thinned, dissolving faster than it had before.

Time, or whatever this was, was running out.

Rowan's gaze lifted and found his. She didn't smile. She didn't bare her teeth or widen her eyes or relish the moment. She simply looked at him, and he had the ugly impression she'd been seeing this room inside her head all night.

"Trevor," she said quietly.

Her voice came as a single sound now. The strange double-layering he'd heard before was almost gone. Almost. There was a faint ghost of a second tone beneath it, there and gone so quickly he couldn't be sure he hadn't imagined it.

He swallowed, then shook his head.

"I'm done running," he said.

The words surprised him by how blunt they sounded. No trembling drama, no heroic flourish. Just a simple statement that recognized the shape of the moment.

Rowan's expression tightened by a degree. "Are you?"

"I'm tired," he admitted. "And I'm not stupid. Even if I found another opening, another gap in the wall… it wouldn't matter. This doesn't end with me walking away."

Her eyes searched his face for a moment. If she found anything there, she didn't show it.

"So you're just going to stand there?" she asked. "And… what? Let it happen?"

Trevor shook his head again. "No. I'm going to look at you. And you're going to look at me. And you're not going to pretend this is just… another body in a long line of them."

354

Rowan's jaw flexed.

The lantern's onyx center gave a hard, irregular pulse. The Future Bleed surged, trying to bloom again. For a second, the future outline snapped over her more sharply: hair lifting slightly as if caught in unseen wind, eyes sinking into dark wells that reflected nothing.

Trevor forced himself not to flinch.

"You saw it," she said softly. It wasn't a question.

"Pieces," he said. "Enough."

She stepped farther into the room. With every pace, the Future Bleed tried to assert itself, flickering a faint second image over her, then shuddering out before it could fully form. It reminded Trevor of someone trying to push a reflection through a mirror and failing.

Trevor took a breath that burned on the way in. "You think this frees you," he said. "From hope. From mercy. From... that job." He nodded faintly toward the lantern. "You think killing me breaks the chain."

Her mouth tightened. "It's not about freeing myself. It's about ending a lie."

He shook his head. "No. It isn't."

Something inside him—the same reckless streak that had made him follow strangers into dark places on faith alone—pushed the words forward.

"I saw you," he said. "Not just now. Later. What you become." His voice caught and pushed through anyway. "You're not empty,

Rowan. You're not just... void. There's mercy in it. Horrible, twisted mercy, but it's there. You're carrying it whether you want to or not."

Rowan's fingers tightened on the lantern's handle. The onyx center stuttered, violet ringing it in a jagged halo.

"I saw you," Trevor repeated, softer. "You still care. You still hurt. You still... see people. It's just buried under all that weight. Under all of them."

Rowan's gaze flickered, a tiny, involuntary movement.

"And you think," she said slowly, "telling me that will stop this."

"I think telling you that might change how it lives inside you," he said. "Later. When I'm gone. When you're standing where I was standing. When someone else is in this room and you're the one holding the lantern."

The Future Bleed made one last desperate attempt at full clarity. For a moment, the future silhouette slid into place directly over her— perfectly aligned. Trevor saw a Rowan who glowed faintly along the bones, whose eyes held an impossible depth, whose presence filled the space with a constant, humming pressure.

It lasted less than a heartbeat.

Then it snapped back, as if the future had exhausted the last of its strength trying to warn him.

Rowan looked—just for that one sliver of time—unsettled.

Not broken. Not convinced. But no longer untouchable.

"And if I don't want that mercy," she asked quietly. "If I would rather let it all burn?"

Trevor huffed a humorless breath. "Then you shouldn't have come when I called that night on the bridge," he said. "You shouldn't have been the one who found the kid who didn't jump. You shouldn't have given me anything to see the real you. I guided you then."

Her eyes flickered, remembering. "I didn't—"

"You did," he cut in. "And even if you don't remember it the way I do, it happened. You stood there. You talked. You stayed long enough for me to go home. That part of you is still there. I saw her. In the future."

He swallowed.

"I just wanted you to know that before you kill me."

Silence settled between them.

The chamber didn't echo like other rooms; the curved walls swallowed sound, pressing it close. Trevor could hear his own pulse, hear the faint hiss of his breath, hear the soft rasp of Rowan's fingers adjusting on the lantern's grip.

She took another step closer. The room contracted.

The Future Bleed, exhausted from fighting the inevitable, barely flickered now. His vision wanted to split, but couldn't quite manage it. The world was condensing down into a single version, a single moment, a single track.

Rowan exhaled through her nose, a slow, steady breath. "Last chance to run," she said. "If you're lying to yourself."

Trevor lifted his chin. His legs felt like water, but they held. "I'm not," he said. "And even if I was, you'd catch me before the lie finished."

For the first time all night, something like sorrow crossed her face. It flashed quickly, an instinctive wince, then vanished under the colder shape of resolve.

She stepped close enough that he could see the small lines at the corners of her eyes. Close enough to smell stone dust on her skin. Close enough that if he reached out, he could have touched the sleeve of her coat.

He didn't move.

"Last chance," he murmured. "For you."

Rowan's eyes met his fully—no flinch, no dodge. If there was anything left in her that wanted to turn away, it drowned in the magnet pull of what stood behind this moment.

"No," she said, almost gently. "It isn't."

She let go of the lantern with her right hand.

Trevor saw the hand come up before he felt anything. The motion was deliberate, almost slow, as though she were placing a key in a lock. Her fingers curled around something he hadn't seen her pick up—a shard of metal, rusted at the edges, points dulled by time and sharpened again by use.

He didn't look at it.
He looked at her.

"Thank you," he whispered.

He wasn't sure which part he meant. For the night on the bridge. For the lantern. For the fact she'd stayed human long enough to talk.

Rowan's mouth trembled. Just once. Once, and then it held.

She drove the shard into his chest.

It wasn't a cinematic blow, no gasping thunderclap of pain. It was a pressure, a hard, wrong intrusion that turned the world white for a second. Sound dropped away to a distant ringing.

His body tried to recoil; the wall behind him kept him upright.

The onyx lantern shuddered, then steadied. The pulsing he'd felt all night smoothed into one continuous hum so low he could barely hear it. The room seemed to lean around the point where her hand met his chest.

Trevor's breath caught and then hitched around something wet. Heat spread under his sternum, blooming outward in a slow, sick flower.

He blinked. The Future Bleed, which had been sputtering at the edges of his vision, finally fell away completely. No more double-shadows. No more ghostly outlines. No more glimpse of what she'd be.

The world dropped to one layer: Rowan's face, close to his, dark eyes wide and too bright.

He saw resignation there.
He saw a flash of fear.
He saw something like apology.

His thoughts scattered. He gathered them around the only thing that mattered.

Maybe this will change you, he thought. The words barely formed. Maybe, when some other lost soul stands where I'm standing, you'll remember this. You'll hesitate. You'll hold the lantern differently. You'll… soften, even if you don't know why.

His knees buckled. The wall slid away behind him; the floor rose up. He wasn't sure if Rowan caught him as he fell or if gravity simply did its job and she let it. There was a moment of pressure against his shoulder, then stone, cold and hard, met the back of his skull.

The room dimmed at the edges like a photograph burning in from the corners.

Trevor held onto her face as long as he could with what remained of his focus. Her features blurred, sharp again, then blurred once more. His own breath rasped shallow, each inhale a thread.

"I saw you," he tried to say. He didn't know if the words made it out or stayed trapped in his head.

Her lips parted as if to answer.

The dark rolled in.

It wasn't sudden. It was a slow, inevitable fade, like the tide pulling back from a beach it had visited every day of his life. There was no tunnel, no light, no choir. Just a narrowing circle—Rowan's eyes, the lantern's faint ember, the curve of the room—shrinking down and down and down until everything met in the center and—

nothing.

Silence dropped into the chamber like a stone.

She saw the light fading in his eyes. She knew, even as he fell, that he would never forgive the heart he tried to save. Rowan leaned close, her lips brushing the cold of his cheek.

"In another life," she whispered, "you will understand the pain this took."

Rowan knelt where she'd landed when he fell, one hand still hovering over his chest as if she weren't sure whether she'd let go yet. The shard was gone. Or maybe it was still there and she simply couldn't see it. The details blurred at the edge of a mind that no longer trusted what it understood about space.

The lantern dangled from her other hand, its weight dragging against her fingers.

The onyx core no longer pulsed. The black remained, but something had changed inside it; a faint, colorless light flickered beneath the darkness, like a hidden coal that refused to go out.

Rowan's breath rattled once, a half-formed exhale that never fully left her lungs.

The air pressed in.

It wasn't a gust. It wasn't wind. It was pressure, building from every direction at once, converging on the space she occupied. Her ears popped as if she were standing at the bottom of deep water. The tiny hairs along her arms lifted, sensing static that had nothing to do with electricity.

Her shadow on the curved wall behind her shuddered.

It stretched upward in a fast, unnatural jerk, like someone had hooked it from above and yanked. Her arms stayed at her sides, but the shadow's arms lengthened, trailing dark fingers up the wall. Its head narrowed, then elongated, then snapped back into rough human proportions.

Rowan tried to breathe and felt nothing happen.

Her chest expanded, but no air entered. No sound left her. The pressure built in her ribs and throat instead, an internal vice tightening.

Something warm moved up from her chest toward her mouth.

It wasn't blood. It wasn't breath. It was… words. A familiar arrangement of them, pressing against the backs of her teeth, insisting on being spoken. A soft greeting, a line she had heard once on a bridge and countless times since in the dark edges of her mind.

She realized, with a small spike of terror, that she could not stop them.

Her lips parted.

A light—not from the lantern, not from the room—flared in front of her eyes, leaping straight from the center of her vision outward. It wasn't bright in the way sunlight was bright. It was flat, depthless white that wiped detail out in an instant, erasing stone and bone and Trevor's still body in the same stroke.

Her feet left the floor.

There was no graceful float, no angelic ascension. It felt like a hook had sunk into the center of her sternum and yanked. Her spine arched; her head snapped back. Her fingers spasmed open, the lantern slipping from her grip.

For one impossible second, every part of her wanted to fight it.

She wanted to claw at the air, grab onto the stone, wrap both hands around the rusty bars of the bone niches and anchor herself down. She wanted to stay in this horrible room with this dead man and the mess she'd made rather than be dragged into whatever waited.

But there was nothing to hold.

The pressure inside her throat broke.

A single, half-formed syllable escaped—
the beginning of a welcome, gentle and doomed.

And then the world inverted.

The chamber vanished. The light collapsed inward like an eye closing. Rowan's body snapped out of existence in absolute, surgical silence—no pop, no bang, no flash that left scorch marks, just a sudden absence where something had been.

The lantern dropped.

It didn't clatter the way it should have. It hit the stone floor with a muted, respectful thud, as if the air cushioned it at the last second. The glass didn't crack. The handle didn't bend.

Inside, the faint ember winked once more, then went dark.

Trevor's body lay alone in the chamber.
No footsteps.
No breath.

No light.

The catacombs, which had listened all night, sank back into their old, indifferent silence.

The moment that had always been coming had passed.

Somewhere else-
Elsewhen - a new one waited to begin.

The Binding Ties

The scream came first.

It tore out of Rowan's throat in the exact pitch, the exact shape, the exact animal panic of the moment she'd been taken—raw sound ripped from somewhere behind her ribs.

Then it cut off as if someone had slammed a door on it.

Air rushed in after, cold and sharp and full of snow.

Rowan staggered forward, boots skidding on ice-slick stone. Her hand shot out on reflex and hit metal—iron bars damp with frost. It took a beat for her legs to remember balance, another for her lungs to remember how to breathe.

She dragged in a shuddering inhale and, only then, realized she was outside.

A wrought-iron fence bristled in front of her, its spikes crowned in white. Beyond it, the cemetery stretched in rows and clusters, stones hunched under winter, angels iced over and staring skyward with blind, salt-stained eyes. The sky above was low and colorless, clouds heavy with more snow they hadn't decided to drop yet.

Behind her, the mausoleum doors stood closed.

Not the catacomb doors from that night—the labyrinth she knew by feel—but a different mausoleum entirely. The stone was older, the carvings worn shallow. A small plaque near the door handle bore a family name she didn't recognize.

Rowan grabbed the edge of the plaque anyway, fingers digging into the cold metal as the rest of her caught up to the fact that she was still standing.

A laugh bubbled up, sharp and humorless. It fizzled out before it reached her tongue.

She remembered stone.
She remembered Trevor's eyes, too wide and too bright.
She remembered the pressure in her chest, the hook under her sternum, the way the world had gone white, not from light but from absence.

And then—this.

Her chest heaved. Her pulse raced. The night pressed against her skin, thinner and hotter than it should have been in this kind of cold. She felt like someone had dragged her through glass and spat her out on the other side of... what?

The wind shifted. Bells rang faintly in the distance—high, chiming notes floating from somewhere beyond the cemetery walls. It took her a second to place them.

Church bells.
Carols.
Midnight service.

Christmas Eve.

Of course.

Rowan squeezed the plaque once before letting go. Her fingers left a faint imprint in the thin crust of frost, an almost-hand print that faded as quickly as the warmth sank into the metal.

Something prickled at the edge of her awareness.

Not sound. Not sight. A presence. Several, actually—soft and diffuse and wrong in the way Trevor had once been wrong when he came where he didn't belong.

She went still.

At first she thought it was the grief of the place itself. Old stones, old names, the weight of everyone who'd ever stood here and loved someone under the ground. But the sensation resolved into something narrower, more focused.

Not here, she realized.
Not under.
Above.

Her gaze lifted.

They stood among the graves.

Not solid. Not glowing, either. They were impressions, cut-out silhouettes against the snow-muted dark. Some were only shoulders and heads, the suggestion of a coat or a dress. Others were clearer—faces blurred around the edges, eyes wide and hollow with the shock of still being here when they shouldn't be.

They weren't looking at her. They were looking at nothing and everything—their last fear, their last want, their last unfinished thought stretched out in front of them like a rope they couldn't follow.

369

Lost souls.

Rowan's first instinct was the same as it had been in the catacombs: catalog, calculate, decide. She wanted to look at each face and tally sins, dismiss pleas, assign worth. She had a new clarity about what people did with the hope they were given, how they twisted mercy into expectation. The sight of them stirred something sour and electric in her.

Her tongue curled around words that tasted like ice.

You don't deserve saving.
You had your chances.
You were seen and you squandered it.

She opened her mouth to say it.

What came out was:

"Hey."

The word wasn't hers.

It rode up her throat in a voice that didn't match the shape of her mouth, catching on the back of her teeth before sliding free. It was soft. Gentle. The kind of soft that could move someone back from an edge.

A few of the silhouettes turned.

They didn't turn to the sky. They didn't look toward the church or the gate or the distant road. They turned toward her.

Rowan's pulse spiked.

She tried again, forcing the muscle of her jaw to obey.

She meant to say, No. Don't look at me. You will not take this from me too.

What emerged instead, warm and unbearably familiar, was:

"I see you."

The words came out like breath on glass.

The nearest lost soul—a woman with hair that hung in indistinct strands and a cardigan that blurred at the edges—flinched as if struck. Her outline brightened for a moment, holding more shape, more density.

Rowan's fingers dug into her own palms hard enough she should have felt pain. She didn't.

She recognized that line. Not just the phrase, but the cadence, the way the vowels sat, the slight lift at the end of the last word.

Trevor.

This was Trevor's voice.

Not exactly. The echo was layered under hers, threaded through it, braided so tightly she couldn't separate where one ended and the other began. But the warmth, the steady certainty—those weren't hers. She had never sounded like that for anyone.

More silhouettes turned.

They saw her.

371

It took her a second to understand that part. Rowan had spent a lifetime feeling unseen, but she'd also spent a lifetime being able to disappear when she wanted. Now, as the lost souls turned their faces toward the mausoleum steps, toward her, the focus in their hollow eyes sharpened.

They weren't looking past her. They weren't looking at some comforting abstraction behind her shoulder.

Their gazes locked on her like she was a lantern in the dark.

Rowan staggered back a step.

"No," she said—or tried to.

The word warped on her tongue. Her mouth shaped it; her throat did not comply. What spilled out instead was:

"You're not alone."

Her voice broke on the last syllable. Not with emotion—she refused to claim that—but with whatever force was pushing those words through her against her will.

The nearest souls flared brighter, edges sharpening. They seemed to tether to the sound, like paper lanterns catching light.

Rowan's heart slammed against her ribs. She felt like she was watching someone else use her mouth, her lungs, her breath.

Images flickered at the edges of her memory—
a bridge,
a younger version of herself,
a man she'd thought was just a man until he wasn't.

372

Trevor, leaning on a rail, talking like the world wasn't ending around her, offering warmth she did not ask for and did not deserve.

He had sounded like this.

A weight settled on her head.

It wasn't a hand. It wasn't a blow. It was pressure that came from nowhere, compressing the crown of her skull and working downward. Something cold touched her scalp, pricking lightly at first, then anchoring.

She gasped and reached up.

Her fingers struck ice.

Not the stray crust of snow that had landed on her hair, but something solid and set in a circle, resting just where a crown would sit. It was cold enough that her fingertips burned from the contact, but it did not melt under her touch.

Rowan grabbed at it, meaning to rip it off.

The structure held.

She traced its shape instead, because she couldn't not. A ring, smooth where it met her hair, sharper at the front where three arched prongs rose and curved backward like frozen antlers. They felt like ice but didn't give under her fingers. Thorns of something rougher— wood, or what felt like it—threaded through the icy frame, barbs catching against her skin when she pressed too hard.

Between the icy circling band and the twisted wooden barbs, she felt the delicate bumps of small leaves and berries—mistletoe, woven through like decoration, like an afterthought that changed everything.

And set along the centerline of the three forward prongs were stones she knew without seeing:
one that pulsed with a quiet, milky depth—opal,
one that hummed with a buried ache—amethyst,
and one that did not shine so much as swallow—onyx.

Past. Present. Future.

Her trap, she realized with a cold, sinking clarity, had never just been hers.

It had been waiting for someone to wear it.

Rowan squeezed the crown until her fingertips went numb.

"Take it off," she hissed.

What came out was:

"It's okay. I've got you."

Her voice—not her voice—carried over the graveyard, and every lost soul that had turned toward her took an involuntary step closer. Their faces, though still smudged and indistinct, softened around the eyes. The hard edges of panic blurred.

Rowan's stomach lurched.

She tried again to damn them. You're weak. You're the reason the world rots. You could have saved yourselves.

Her throat refused.

"You're not broken beyond fixing," she heard herself say. "You're not a mistake."

Each line was a new cut.

The woman in the cardigan put her hands to her face and sobbed—soundless, but visible. A man in a suit whose tie hung wrong at his neck straightened, shoulders loosening. A teenager near the fence, hood up, outline jittering, froze and stared at Rowan like he'd just been grabbed from behind and steadied.

Rowan trembled.

Every instinct screamed at her: twist the words, choke them, turn them into knives. She tried to change the shape of what she said, to poison the mercy mid-sentence.

"I hate you," she breathed.

What the souls heard was:

"I won't leave you."

Tears stung her eyes, sharp and sudden in the cold. She blinked them back with a violent shake of her head, angry at the pure reflex of it. The cemetery spun for a second before righting itself.

The crown on her head grew heavier.

Snow began to fall, slow at first, big flakes drifting down to land on stone and iron and shoulders that didn't quite exist. It collected on the graves, on the fence, on the mausoleum steps—and slid cleanly off her, unable to cling to the icy band circling her skull.

Rowan looked out over the field of the dead and almost-dead.

The Lost.

The ones Trevor had spent his second life finding, guiding, refusing to abandon.

This was her world now.

Not choice. Not power. Not revenge.

A service.

A sentence.

Somewhere inside her, buried so deep she wanted to claw it out, a part of her knew that this was exactly what she'd wanted to kill: the idea that anyone could show up for people like this. For her. For who she had been.

Now she was the one who would show up.

She tried one last time to stay silent, to clamp her jaw shut and turn her back, walk away into the dark and let these vague, flickering shapes fade without her.

Her body did not obey.

She stepped down off the mausoleum stoop, boots not quite crunching in the snow. The souls parted for her, not out of fear, but the way people parted around an emergency worker, an usher, someone whose presence promised a terrible kind of help.

They saw her.

Rowan recoiled at the realization. She had railed against invisibility her whole life, even when she'd wrapped herself in it for safety. The universe had answered by making her the most visible thing in every room that needed her—and only to the people she most wanted to judge.

She walked to the woman in the cardigan first.

The woman's outline flickered around the edges, as if a wind only she could feel tugged at her, fraying her away from herself.

Rowan stopped an arm's length from her and fought down the snarl in her throat.

"I don't—" she started.

What came out, warm and steady, was:

"You're allowed to be tired."

The woman's shoulders shook. Her figure brightened, the blur smoothing just enough to suggest a face Rowan might have recognized in a coffee shop and forgotten by the afternoon.

"That doesn't mean you don't matter," Rowan heard herself add, and each word felt like dragging glass through her own skin.

Somewhere beyond the cemetery walls, a car drove by, tires whispering on slush. A dog barked, muffled by distance. In here, in the snow, the only sounds were the far-off bells and her own unwilling benedictions.

Rowan turned her head, seeking any edge, any break in this invisible perimeter.

The Lost Souls watched her with a mixture of dread and desperate hope.

She had been the last hope she meant for him to ever offer. That's what she'd told him.

Now he was gone.
And she was here.
And the offer hadn't ended. It had multiplied.

There would be other bridges.
Other tombs.
Other Christmas Eves.
Other nights and mornings and hours where people stood at the edge of their own endings and waited for the world to notice.

The crown on her head pulsed once, a cold, echoing ring that vibrated down her spine. She felt, dimly, the tug of places in the distance—hospital corridors, silent bedrooms, parking lots where someone sat behind the wheel too long.

She would go to them.

Not because she chose to.
Because choice had been removed from the equation.

Rowan clenched her fists until her nails bit into her palms. She wanted to scream until the snow melted, until the graves cracked, until the crown shattered under the force of it.

She opened her mouth.

What came out, soft and terrible and undeniably hers now, was:

"I'm here."

The Lost Souls closest to her steadied.

Something inside her howled, a sound no one else could hear.

Rowan walked deeper into the cemetery, toward the next flickering outline, the next pair of hollow eyes.

The crown sat cold and perfect on her head, thorns woven with evergreen, ice and wood and stone binding her to a duty she had tried to murder.

No one passing on the road would see her.
No one leaving midnight mass would know she was there.

To the living, she would be what she'd always feared:
unseen, unthanked, unnamed.

To the lost, she would be inescapable.

A prisoner of hope.
A prisoner of mercy.

Forever walking, forever welcoming, forever screaming where only she could hear it.

And above the graveyard, as snow fell and bells rang and Christmas crept quietly into another year, Mercy's Crown gleamed faintly in the dark—
a circlet of ice and thorn and time, resting on the head of a woman who would never, ever again be truly alone.

She had been falling for a long time. Tonight she simply arrived – into her own catacomb, and the cold that would keep her.

Above her, Christmas morning broke. She didn't look up.

Acknowledgement

Writing Mercy's Crown was a journey I wasn't expecting to take. A journey into the cold place-some imagined, some all too real. I'm grateful to the people who kept a light on for me along the way.

To my family and friends, thank you for your patience, your encouragement, and for believing in me even when the pages felt impossibly dark. To the early readers who offered your time and your honesty, your feedback shaped this story more than you know.

And to every bookseller, librarian, and reader who chooses to spend their time with my work-thank you. You're the reason these stories matter.

Most of all, thank you for walking with Rowan into the dark and not turning back.

-Matt

About the Author

Matt Walker is an American horror author whose work blends emptional depth, atmospheric tension, and quiet dread. He is the creator of The Noise, an eight-story horror collection known for its unsettling intimacy and lingering aftershocks.

When he isn't writing about haunted places, cold memories, or people on the edge of becoming something else, Matt works in Human Resources, building real-world stories one conversation at a time.

He lives in the United States, where he is always working on his next story to capture your breath and heart.

Also By Matt Walker

The Noise – A collection of eight unsettling horror stories.

Coming Soon
Crossfall : A Rock and a Hard Place
Kindred
Beyond the Noise
Checkmate

Follow for More
TikTok/Instagram - @mattwalkerauthor

www.ingramcontent.com/pod-product-compliance
Lightning Source LLC
Chambersburg PA
CBHW010522100726
47903CB00011B/2861